TIME FOR
REDEMPTION

TIME FOR REDEMPTION

SUSAN C. MULLER

Published in the United States of America by
Stanford Publishing Company

Cover design by
Najla Qamber Designs
http://www.najlaqamberdesigns.com

Editing by
Carla Rossi Editing
Alyssa Willard

Interior Design and Formatting by:
E. M. Tippetts Book Designs

For Bobby

CHAPTER ONE

Kara

A solid string of red brake lights filled the freeway as far as Kara Grimes could see.

She pounded on the steering wheel until her hand hurt. What was wrong with these idiots? This was Houston. Nobody drove the speed limit. Even the slow lane was fast.

Yet here she was, poking along at thirty-five—when she moved at all.

She'd never make it home in time.

Fifteen minutes. If she'd left work fifteen minutes earlier, she'd have missed the worst of the traffic.

But Doc Collier asked her to stay and help him with his last patient because April had to pick up her kids at day care before they charged her a late fee and Kara didn't have any kids. She'd turned him down too many times already. She couldn't tell him the real reason. And the patient just kept talking and talking and wouldn't leave.

And now she was late.

If this tie-up cleared, she could make it home before Devin, but she could never have supper ready.

She flipped on the radio, searching for a traffic report. If there were some type of accident or road work ahead maybe she could use that as an excuse. Instead she caught the weather.

A cold front from Canada had blown farther south than expected, bringing the predicted temperature for tonight down to an unseasonable low in the forties. Unusual for this early in September.

She glanced through the windshield at the gray, drizzly afternoon and shivered.

That was it! The cold weather. She'd make pancakes and bacon. Yes, sure, she'd promised him smothered pork chops, but hadn't he told a story about his mother always making breakfast for supper when the weather turned bad?

Did she have all the ingredients? She had milk and eggs, but what about bacon? There was a package in the freezer. Thawing it in time would be tricky but she could do it.

She hit the horn. If these sluggards would get out of her way she could pull this off.

THE AROMA OF sizzling bacon filled the house. The pancake

batter was ready and the table set. Kara even had time to change into casual clothes, fluff her hair, and slap on a swipe of lipstick.

She'd waited to flip on the heat until moments before Devin was due home. That way the house still had a slight chill, but was not cold.

The back door slammed. Devin dropped his bags in the laundry room and wandered into the kitchen. "Why is it so cold in here?"

"I don't know. The heater's running but it seems to be taking a while."

She'd cut it too close.

Devin sniffed the air. "Is that bacon I smell?"

She plastered on her biggest smile. "Yes. With pancakes and the real maple syrup you brought home from Vermont."

"What happened to the pork chops I asked for?"

He hadn't asked for them. He'd asked what was for supper then mentioned he'd be home by six when she answered.

"I got cold driving home from work and I remembered that story you told about how your mother always made you pancakes when the weather turned nasty."

This was it. Now or never. Would her explanation work?

"Yeah, because she was too lazy to cook a real meal."

Damn. Using his mother was always risky. Sometimes she was an angel who could do no wrong. Other times she was the bitch from hell.

"I'm sorry. I thought I was fixing a nice surprise for you.

I could still cook the pork chops if you prefer." She pulled the sleeve of her blouse down over her latest bruise and waited, holding her breath.

"Nah. That would take too long. I'm starving and that bacon smells too good. Did you make a couple of eggs to go with it?"

Her mind whirled, picturing the nearly empty carton. Two left, but one was cracked. "Of course. I know what you like."

Devin settled into his recliner and put his feet up. "It's still cold in here. Why don't you get me a cup of hot chocolate while I wait for you to get the food on the table, and Kara, we *will* have the pork chops tomorrow night, right?"

The chill in his voice sent her heart skittering around in her chest. "Absolutely."

CHAPTER TWO

Tom

The clank of the steel door opening reverberated through the cement-block room. The vibration traveled up through the soles of Tom Meyers's wingtips and straight to that little nerve behind his eyes.

He glanced up from his notes and there she was, Kara Grimes.

She looked smaller than on TV. Her brown hair hung limp and lifeless past her shoulders. Her eyes sunk into deep hollows. The only word he could think of to describe her skin was *pasty*.

Three weeks in jail was hard on anyone, but a middle-class, suburban housewife with a decent job, monthly hair appointments, and a bathroom full of beauty products had farther to fall than most.

She sank into the only chair as if the weight of the chains connecting her waist to her wrists and ankles was more that she could carry.

After studying him with dead eyes, she shook her head. "No thanks. I can't afford you."

Not the words he was expecting. "Why do you say that?"

"Suit worth more than everything in my closet put together, hand-painted silk tie, fifty-dollar haircut. I'll bet even your shoes are expensive."

They were but that wasn't the point. "You can't afford *not* to hire me. Not since that useless public defender screwed up your case. We can worry about my fee later. After I get you off."

If he got her off. No, make that *when* he got her off. This wasn't the time for self-doubt. A lengthy murder trial could cost upwards of $200,000.

He had money, but not that much to throw away.

While he'd never been a gambler, and a *sure thing* didn't exist in the legal profession, he was willing to bet on this one. The investigation had been so sloppy there was a better than even chance he could avoid a trial altogether.

The local media lived for a good mystery to liven up their daily list of street crimes and sports stories. Take a slow news day, add an innocent husband, murdered in his own bed by his gold-digging wife and you had a case-du-jour sensational enough that with it in his win column the money could be recouped down the line. New clients would flood in and he'd never have to pay for advertising again.

Kara lifted her head. The first spark of life he'd seen. "I didn't do it."

Why did they always insist they were innocent when they so seldom were?

"I'm more interested in why the police think you did. Take your time. Start at the beginning. Tell me exactly what you told them and nothing more. After today, never talk to them again without me present."

You'd think with all the crime dramas on TV people would learn to keep their mouths closed. But they never did. Thus, the need for lawyers.

She shrugged as if she'd told the story so many times she might as well be reciting the multiplication table. "The weather was nasty that night, cold and raining. By the time I got home from work, my feet were wet and I was shivering. The house was cold because the heat wasn't on. Devin used to tell me how his mother always made breakfast for supper when a storm blew in and that sounded great to me."

"Okay, stop there for a moment. Remember, I only want what you told the police. Don't add or explain. Anything you say to me has to be the absolute truth. Do you understand?"

"I do."

Kara glared at him and he couldn't decide what her expression meant. Was she angry because she thought he had accused her of lying or because she was lying? "Go on. So, you cooked eggs and bacon?"

"And pancakes. He'd brought real maple syrup home from

his last trip to Vermont and he wanted to try it. He was still experimenting with his insulin dosage. He always told me his numbers were good so I didn't worry."

"What did you say happened after supper?"

Again with the angry look. Too bad. If she lied, and he knew it, he couldn't put her on the stand

"I cleaned the kitchen. We watched the ball game and went to bed. Nothing unusual. My back was hurting so I took an ibuprofen. Devin was out by the time I turned the lights off. I didn't know anything was wrong until the alarm went off the next morning."

"What happened then?" This was the test. He knew what she told the police. Would she tell him the same thing or would her story change?

"I called out it was time to get up. Then I went to the bathroom. When I got back, he hadn't moved. I went around to his side of the bed to shake him, but something was off. There was a hum from his C-PAP machine but his face was... wrong."

So far, she was sticking to the same story. That didn't make it true—or false.

Kara shuddered and closed her eyes. "I took off his mask and just knew. I shook him anyway, because, well, you have to try. I may have stood there for a minute, but certainly no more than that. As soon as I could breathe, I grabbed the phone and called 911."

"What did you do while you waited for the ambulance?"

"Ran to the front door, unlocked it and left it open."

Tom glanced down at his notes as if he didn't have every word memorized. "The police report says you were dressed."

Her shoulders slumped as if carrying the weight of the last few weeks had exhausted her. "I rushed back to the bedroom and saw the clothes I had set out for work lying across the dresser. I threw them on because I knew the house would be swarming with people any minute and I only had on my robe."

His head snapped up. Was this a new detail? "You weren't wearing a gown or pajamas?" He made a note to search for any sleepwear hidden away and check it for trace evidence.

"Never when Tom was home. He always said sleeping skin-to-skin was best."

Her slight blush stood out like a neon sign on her pale skin. How long since he'd seen a woman blush? Faking tears was easy and he'd seen plenty of clients do that—both male and female—but was it even possible to fake a blush?

Tom lifted his head and lowered his shoulders, stretching out his neck and back.

Someone, sometime in the not-so-distant past, had urinated in the corner of the tiny interview room. Couple that with the odor of prison food and unwashed bodies, the clang of steel doors and prisoners shuffling down stone corridors and the straight-backed chair with no padding, and he'd developed a backache to go along with his killer headache.

Jail interviews were the worst part of his job. He much preferred sitting in his own office, leaning back in his leather chair, sipping a cup of the best coffee, and taking notes of the facts he could use.

He rubbed his temples and willed his headache to back off. There had to be a way to get this woman out on bail.

He held up one hand in a stop motion. "Kara, when I said start at the beginning, I meant the actual beginning. How you met Devin? What made you fall in love with him—which I'm sure you did before you married him?" Surely she wouldn't be dumb enough to say she never loved the guy.

If so, she'd kept that hidden along with all the other things she wasn't telling him.

"Devin was seven years older than you. Was that a problem?"

"No. That might be what attracted me to him in the first place, although I didn't realize it at the time. He seemed mature, settled, maybe a psychiatrist would even say a father figure since I never had one of those. My life had been chaotic with an invalid mother to care for from an early age."

Tom checked his notes. "Your mother had ALS, that's Lou Gehrig's disease, right? What was that like?"

"She never caught a break her whole life. She had to drop out of high school when she got pregnant with me. Apparently, my father was a football player and the whole team backed him up saying she was a slut who slept with half the school. Her parents threw her out at sixteen so the jobs she got weren't great. I was six when she married my stepfather. When I was in middle school, she started dropping things, losing her balance, slurring her speech, missing work for strange, undiagnosed pains. She got fired from a couple of jobs for being drunk although she wasn't. That's when my stepfather left. If she hadn't gotten the house in her divorce, we'd have been homeless."

"And you took care of her." It was a statement, not a question, but he needed to get a feel for Kara as a person.

"At first it was just cooking, washing up. Later I helped her bathe and dress. I'd settle her on the sofa with her lunch and a glass of water on the table beside her before I left for school. Eventually I dropped out to care for her full time. Family history repeating itself."

"But you're not expected to inherit the disease?" How could you go through life, watching your mother waste away while knowing the same fate awaited you?

"No. She had the sporadic form not the familial type. I'm no more likely to have it than you or anyone else in this hell hole."

The little man with the big hammer inside Tom's skull pounded away. Time to wrap things up. "That's enough for today. If you decide you want to hire me, we need to make it official."

"My public defender really did screw things up, didn't he?"

Big time. "Those attorneys are overworked and underpaid. Yours was unprepared. He should have fought to keep certain things off the record. I won't make that mistake."

She rubbed her face, and the chains attached to her wrists

rattled like Scrooge's ghostly visitor in *A Christmas Carol*. "The thing is, I don't have any money. I had a credit card for buying groceries and such, but I had to check with Devin before using it. He paid the bills and balanced the bank statement. My paycheck was deposited automatically. I thought his was too, but apparently not."

"But you own the house and have your own separate bank account." How would she react to him knowing that little detail?

A spark of light flashed across her eyes. A sign of embarrassment? Anger? "A house I inherited along with a mortgage I can't pay if I don't work. As for that bank account, it's only two thousand dollars. Not enough to cover the taxes."

Later he'd need a better explanation. Juries didn't like secret bank accounts. "My office will make arrangements with your mortgage company to accept interest-only payments for the time being which we can cover. When I get you off, we'll go after your husband's assets and you can repay me."

Claiming a share of Devin's assets would be tricky but she didn't need to hear all the difficulties involved. "For now, I need you to sign these papers appointing me as your attorney of record."

He reached into his $800 briefcase and slid a stack of documents across the table then handed her a plastic gimme pen he'd picked up from some hotel. He'd learned the hard way not to bring his Montblanc to the jail. "Tomorrow, we'll go into detail about the first time you met Devin and your abbreviated courtship. Until then, don't talk to *anyone* in this place, guards or inmates. There's not a soul in this building who wouldn't sell your story for a pack of cigarettes or a reduced sentence."

HOT WATER POUNDED against the back of Tom's neck as he sank lower in the hot tub. The setting sun streaked the sky with shades of pink and purple.

Steam rolled off the water, and with it, the tension in his body.

He'd stopped by his office only long enough to drop off the signed papers from Kara Grimes and issue a string of instructions to his secretary. This put him home before dark. A rare feat any time except the longest days of mid-summer.

He sometimes felt like a mole rat. Never seeing the sun. Toiling away, long after dark, under florescent lights.

There was a time when he'd used a sun lamp to offset his pale skin. Now he didn't bother. He was what he was—a forty-five-year-old, five-nine, bulldog with a spectral complexion, hair that had turned completely white six years ago, and what some called startlingly blue eyes.

Make that a pit bull, because while he could be your best friend, once he got his teeth into something he never let go.

And he'd gotten his teeth into the Kara Grimes case.

The woman was a puzzle. Obviously intelligent, she'd gotten her GED while caring for her invalid mother. She supported them both by doing medical transcriptions at home, and learned accounting and office procedures from online videos. And made herself invaluable to a busy doctor.

Yet she had no idea what her husband was up to.

Hard to believe since women were supposed to have a sixth sense about things like that.

Not that he'd ever totally understood women.

His mother had seen to that—first cold then hot, loving then distant, demanding then ignoring, demonstrative then reserved, generous then miserly. Well, she'd never been exactly loving or demonstrative or generous.

Guess that left cold, demanding, and miserly. Sounded about right to him.

And she was the good parent. His father had simply been a crook. A wealthy influential one, but a crook nonetheless.

He'd heard it said—usually behind his back, but not always—work was his mistress. And he was satisfied with that. What woman would want him anyway? He was a picky, demanding, workaholic with emotional baggage.

The timer went off and the air jets stopped. His headache had all but disappeared.

He rose from the water and wrapped himself in an oversized towel before padding into his condo. A quick call to Uber Eats and an order of Samosa Chaat from the nearest Indian restaurant was headed his way.

He had work to do and no time to cook if he had any hope of getting Kara out on bail.

The legal research was easy, he could handle that, but he didn't have the time or the talent for the investigative leg work.

He needed to learn everything he could about Kara and Devin Grimes. There were holes in her story not even her own mother would have believed.

Luckily, he knew someone whose specialty was filling holes.

CHAPTER THREE

Kara

Kara lay in her bunk after lights out. Of course, the lights weren't totally out. The guards had to be able to see because bad things happened in the dark.

So it was never completely black . . .or quiet.

She turned onto her side and pulled the scratchy blanket up to her ears, blocking out as much light as possible. She had already learned to block out the noise.

Funny, the things she was proud of. The ability to adjust was one of them. It was amazing what a human could become accustomed to as if they were normal.

She mentally marked off another day. A day that held a surprise, making it different from the last twenty-two.

Having a prison guard lead her out of the cell block was

an adventure in itself—worth being chained like a mad dog so she could barely shuffle down endless corridors.

Discovering a strange man waiting for her was something of a shock. Not completely strange. She'd seen him on TV discussing legal issues on some Sunday morning news program—but why would an expensive lawyer take an interest in her case? Surely not out of the goodness of his heart. Her bullshit antenna had quivered immediately.

A door clanged somewhere and the sound echoed through the cell block, breaking her concentration. The thin mattress offered little cushion for the cement slab bed, and after only a few minutes her hip screamed in protest.

She punched her pillow into shape and shifted onto her back.

So, her new lawyer wanted to know how she met Devin. How she married him. How she came to be in such a mess.

She wondered that herself.

She couldn't tell him everything. Wouldn't tell him everything.

How could he possibly understand, with his perfect hair, and perfect teeth, and perfect life?

How much was it safe to say to someone she needed but didn't trust?

She stared at the ceiling and let it play out like a movie, highlighting every stupid decision she'd made along the way.

Doctor Collier's office was busy for a Friday afternoon. Kara didn't have time to deal with the rep pushing some new medication for eczema, even if he was good looking.

No, not good looking. Not in the traditional sense. More dignified, self-assured. The exact qualities she lacked.

The rep chatted with her casually while he waited but not enough to be a nuisance. She reluctantly allowed him into the doc's office as soon as there was a break between patients, realizing she would miss his easy humor when he left.

An hour later, right at closing time, he returned. "Don't know if you remember me—Devin Grimes with Armstead Pharmaceuticals?"

It would take her longer than one hour to forget him.

His flawless white teeth practically sparkled when he flashed a smile. "I hate to bother you again. I seem to have misplaced my pen. Is it possible I left it in the doctor's office? It wouldn't matter except my late mother gave it to me and I'd hate to lose it."

Kara scurried into Dr. Collier's office. Why did she get so flustered whenever a man showed her any attention? Other women could flirt or joke around with a guy. She became tongue-tied, still the awkward little girl her stepfather had berated for every misstep, dropped glass, broken toy, out-grown dress. The one he blamed for his failed marriage as he carried his suitcase out the door.

The silver pen lay on the floor near the visitor's chair. She scooped it up and spun away before the doc could ask any questions.

Devin's fingers brushed hers and he held on a fraction of a second too long as he took the pen from her hand. An electric current shot up her arm but she didn't pull away.

"Wonderful." Devin's eyes lit up the room. "I was so worried I'd lost it. Let me buy you a drink as a thank you. I'm forever in your debt."

Kara's heart froze. She didn't drink. Not that she disapproved—maybe she did a little considering what happened to her stepfather whenever the bottle came out from behind the mantle clock where he hid it from her mother. She'd simply never had the time or inclination to try alcohol. Or the money.

That was worry number one. Worry number two was the biggie.

She couldn't just go out somewhere with a strange man . . . Could she?

Her mouth opened and she had no control over the words that tumbled out.

"Thanks. That would be lovely."

Canned music filled the air—something soft and bluesy—as the hostess led them to a table near the back. Kara tugged at the hem of her dress. If only she'd worn the green one. It was

more flattering. What a joke. None of her dresses were flattering. Some were her much-shorter mother's hand-me-downs while others came from the bargain rack of the thrift store.

All were functional but not much else. Fact was, she'd never paid much attention to the way she looked. When other girls were learning to put on makeup she'd been learning to cook or change her mother's diaper.

Devin smiled at her across the table. His dark hair fell slightly forward and he brushed it back with one sweep of his hand. "What looks good to you?"

You do.

"I've never been here before. What do you suggest?" *Kara gave herself a mental pat on the back. She'd handled that well. She had managed to hide her ignorance while giving him a chance to set a price range.*

"You've never been here? It's in the same building as your office. How long have you worked there?"

They'd barely sat down and she'd already screwed up. Did most people stop at a bar on their way home? They did in TV shows, but they also wore expensive clothes and never scrubbed the toilet.

If she lied and pretended she was new to the job and they started dating—Ha! What a joke—he might find out and never trust her. If she told him how long she'd worked there, he'd think she was a prude or something.

"I've been with the doc almost five years, but most of that time I worked from home." *There. True yet vague.*

A waiter wearing black slacks, white dress shirt, and brocade vest stopped at their table. One glance at her cheap, ill-fitting dress and he ignored her, speaking only to Devin. "Good evening. My name is Josh. I'll be your server tonight. Are you ready to order or do you need a few minutes?"

Kara's tongue stuck to the roof of her mouth. The few times she ate out, she stood in line at the counter and gave her order to someone wearing a paper hat or shouted into a plastic clown's face and received a meal that didn't resemble what she'd asked for.

The posh atmosphere didn't seem to faze Devin. He glanced at the waiter. "Do you have a specialty you'd recommend for my friend? She's not a big drinker."

Her face flushed. How did he know that? She'd never said anything about it.

"Our lemon drop martini is very popular with the ladies."

That actually sounded good. Sophisticated.

Devin nodded. "Excellent. And I'll have your single malt Scotch. The eighteen-year-old one."

Kara sat up straighter. Her chin lifted. The whole evening— the candles on the tables, the snotty waiter, Devin acting so suave and debonair, a martini for goodness sake—made her feel like a princess.

Like something out of a dream.

The martini was delicious. The slightly tart taste was cut by coating the rim of the glass with sugar. Not just any old glass. A specially shaped glass.

The sugar gave her pause for a moment. Licking the edge seemed out of place among the soft music and white tablecloths. She solved the problem by turning the glass slightly with each sip.

By the time her glass was half empty she found talking easier. She never saw Devin order a second drink, but one magically appeared in front of her as she finished the first. A few more sips and she was laughing at Devin's stories and telling some of her own.

Nothing personal, of course. It would take more than two martinis to accomplish that. But she had plenty of anecdotes about clients doing funny things. Fainting when they drew blood. Dragging in a limping husband who thought he could still dunk a basketball like he did twenty years ago. That kid who tried to bite the doc.

"What about you? Do you like calling on doctors?" Ask the man questions to show you're interested—that's what all the magazines said.

"Most of the time. Not all the office managers are as pleasant as you. I'm generally in Houston every other week. I call on doctors in the morning then head in to my office. You know, meetings, paperwork, tutorials on their latest products. Sometimes I spend a day training new hires." He rolled his eyes. "I've tried to tell HR if the applicant can't pronounce the name of the product by the third try, don't send them to me and expect miracles."

"But you called on Dr. Collier in the afternoon." She fought the urge to slap her hand over her mouth. What an idiot,

contradicting him that way.

A flash of fire in his eye hinted he didn't like it, but it was gone before she could be sure, replaced with his million-dollar smile. "Ah, today was the exception. Big meeting with the company execs. Long and boooring. Couldn't wait to get out of there and on the road."

"What do you do when you're not in Houston?" Had she made another mistake? She was only trying to make conversation, not come off like she was interrogating him. This was so hard. She'd never understand how other women made it look so easy.

"I never know for sure. I go wherever I'm needed, although my assigned territory is the south, especially Louisiana. There are little bayou towns with one doctor who's ninety-seven-years-old and never tried a new medication since he got out of med school. Those offices are a challenge and it gives me a thrill to know I've helped the people of that community by bringing their health care into the twenty-first century."

Something warm spread through the inside of her chest. She'd started working for Dr. Collier because she could do it from home while taking care of her mother. Even then, before she ever met a single patient, she'd had the feeling her job was important. That she helped people. But what Devin did… That was truly a service.

A grin that wasn't nervous or forced made its way across her face.

Devin set his glass on the table and reached for her hand.

"This evening with you has been so relaxing and pleasant. I'd love to do it again. Would it be alright if I called you next time I'm in town?"

His invitation came as such a surprise, she knocked over her martini glass, spilling the remnants into the bread basket.

KARA KICKED OFF the blanket and swung her feet over the side of her cot, resting them on the cold concrete floor. That was how it all started—one foolish decision. The desire to feel important for the first time in her life.

And Devin had worked his magic on her. He'd made her feel special.

The next time he was in town, they'd gone out for Italian on Monday night. For Mexican on Tuesday. On Wednesday they'd stayed in and she'd cooked—it was the least she could do after all he'd spent on her—and watched a movie on TV.

He'd stayed over that night and every night he was in town since then. Insisting on marriage took every ounce of determination she could muster, but she couldn't just let him *live* there, could she? She had neighbors and some of them went to her church.

Little by little they'd gone out less and she'd cooked more.

"You're such a great cook and I eat out every night I'm not with you. I hate to waste the little time we have together in a noisy restaurant."

It sounded so logical when he said it.

He made a few comments about her weight, so she lost fifteen pounds, happy to be able to please him. Unfortunately, he found those pounds and a few more—a testament to her skill as a chef, he claimed.

The extra weight led to his diabetes and the diabetes led to medicine that led to more weight which led to lack of energy and pretty soon they didn't go out at all.

He refused to eat right or quit drinking and his blood sugar readings—when he bothered to take them—went up and down like a Disneyland ride. Then he overcompensated with too much or too little insulin.

Yet it was her fault he couldn't "perform" as well as he used to. She was too fat. Too unappealing. Too cold. Too stupid.

He never hit her, per se. Words were his weapon of choice. She was no longer pretty and smart and all things desirable. Yet whenever he was angry, which was often, he managed to push past her and hit her shoulder or grab her arm hard enough to leave a bruise or shove her out of his way.

Looking back, she could see how each step led to the next until she didn't recognize herself any longer.

She gave out a short laugh into the semi-darkness. That's probably what every woman in this place thought.

There was a time when she trusted people. Then she met Devin Grimes. Now, when she trusted no one, Tom Meyers appeared in her life.

She needed to figure out fast if she could depend on him.

Make the wrong choice and she might spend the rest of her life in this place.

She didn't mind for herself, but she wasn't the only one this impacted.

CHAPTER FOUR

Tom

Tom sat across from Kara as she told him an abbreviated version of her courtship and marriage. According to her, they went out a few times, they stayed in a few times, they got married. End of story.

No one's life could be that boring. Well, maybe his was.

"So after only a couple of weeks he asked you to marry him?"

Kara shifted in the hard plastic chair. The movement caused the chains around her ankles to scrape against the concrete with a sound that traveled straight up his body and into his teeth.

The question seemed to take her by surprise. "I guess so. I mean I was brought up in a nice neighborhood. Respectable people. After seeing what happened to my mom, I knew all too well the impact a damaged reputation could have on your life. I told him he couldn't move in unless we were married. He balked at first, but the next weekend we went to the Justice of the Peace. In five minutes it was over and I was Mrs. Devin Grimes."

Definitely a love story for the ages.

She must have thought the same thing because she immediately changed the subject. "Do you think you'll be able to get me out on bail?"

"Hang in there for a few more days. We have a hearing coming up next week. I'm working on something that should help."

Her face fell. Most people were relieved when he suggested they might be released soon. "Something wrong?"

Her head was down and she appeared to be counting on her fingers. She glanced up, her lips compressed into a white line. "Okay. I can wait that long."

Tom drove back to the office with only half his mind on the road—not ideal considering Houston traffic, but doable at two in the afternoon. Any later and rush hour would have started.

Which was why he tried to time his jail visits to immediately after lunch.

For some reason he did his best thinking while driving instead of in his perfectly designed office with its plush carpet and soundproof walls. He found that place too quiet to concentrate.

Give him traffic noise or construction, maybe throw in a little road rage, and his mind when straight to the heart of the problem.

And Kara Grimes was a problem. Both weak and strong. Naïve and competent. But was she good *and* evil? Could she spend the majority of her life tending to her ailing mother then turn around and kill her husband?

A husband who—according to everything she had told him so far—had never done anything to harm her.

It was the things she hadn't told him that weighed on his mind. There were plenty of blanks to fill in.

She seemed perfectly willing to give him a running account of their meeting, their first date, their marriage, but that's all it was. A list of events.

In his experience, the more a client left out, the more important those details became. And without those details, he couldn't plan a defense.

THE TIRES ON Tom's Mercedes squealed as he entered the underground garage, sending the sound reverberating throughout the cavernous area. The three aspirin he'd choked down on the drive hadn't kicked in yet and the vibration hit his ear drums and traveled down his spine hitting every nerve along the way.

Ten minutes of silence with his feet up on his desk, leaning back in his comfortable chair with his eyes closed would do the trick. He'd be a new man.

If only no one stopped him along the way.

The private elevator whisked him to the sixteenth floor, and he sailed past his receptionist without a word. Halfway down the hall he could see the lights were on in his office.

His teeth were on edge before he pushed through the door.

Stretched out across his leather sofa as if she owned it was Fiona Drake, his sometimes PI. She came and went on her own schedule, appearing whenever a case caught her interest.

How she knew was a mystery to him. Either she was clairvoyant, or there was a leak in his staff. Both ideas were preposterous.

He didn't believe in magic, and his staff had been with him for years.

The only other answer—that she had managed to tap his phone and computer—was too frightening to consider.

"Good afternoon, Fiona. Are you comfortable?" He set his briefcase on the corner of his desk and eased into his chair, facing her.

Her hair, never more than three inches long, was a burnished red today and stuck out like an enraged porcupine. On him it would look ridiculous. On her…well, it fit with her tats and her boots, and her torn jeans.

"Absolutely, although you keep the temperature a bit cool for me."

"I'll tell maintenance to get right on that. We wouldn't

want you to catch a cold. Is there anything else I can do for you?" If she wasn't so good at her job, he'd have security toss her out.

Or do it himself.

Not that it would do any good. How she managed to slip past the best security system money could buy remained a mystery.

Fiona swung her legs lazily to the floor but made no effort to stand, as if she were the boss not him. "I've been expecting you to call. I know you need me on the Grimes case if you want any hope of getting the bitch off."

"Why should I bother to call when you know my business better than I do?" Probably the most honest thing he'd said today.

"Tisk, tisk, Tom. Don't be rude. You know you depend on me."

"You're right. Who else would I get to do my dirty work?"

He'd gone too far this time. He could see it in the way her eyes narrowed, turning from blue to fiery green, and in the set of her shoulders, like the muscles had contracted in preparation for a fight. And the way her left hand clinched and unclenched until the knuckles lost all color—her one true tell.

"What I do isn't dirty work and it isn't illegal. The information I dig up is out there for anyone to find. Most people aren't willing to put in the work or don't know how to find it."

He had to make things better or he'd lose her forever.

"Of course not. I wouldn't hire you if I thought you did. I've spent the last two hours in a place where the only visible colors are cement gray and jumpsuit orange, that smells like rancid bacon grease, and sounds like an echo chamber from hell. I've been visiting a woman who tells me only what she thinks I want to know. If I let my frustrations spill over onto you, I sincerely apologize."

Her hand unclenched and he rushed on before she said something he'd regret. "You're here. You know about the case. Do you want in, because I really need you if I want to have—as you so quaintly put it—any hope of getting the bitch off?"

"You know I already don't like her."

"You've made that abundantly clear." She never liked any of his clients, especially anyone who played the victim card. And she was especially hard on women.

"She sank her fangs into a guy she thought would take care of her and when she found out he couldn't, or wouldn't, she offed him. Sure, he was a jerk and he lied to her, but why not walk away and count her losses? She was perfectly capable of taking care of herself. She was doing fine before she met him."

"I don't care if you like her. In fact, I prefer you don't. That way if you find anything that changes your mind I'll know we can convince a jury."

"And if I don't?" Fiona looked as relaxed as she ever did, which on anyone else he'd call hyper-alert.

"Then I'll recommend we plead guilty, try for the best deal I can arrange, and move on to the next case. Which will also involve a cheat, or a thief, or a murderer, or a lowlife of some type. If that bothers you so much, then you're in the wrong line of work."

She ran a hand through her hair, scattering it like stalks of grain in the wind. "I keep hoping one of them will end up innocent."

He almost smiled.

That's exactly what kept him in this business.

CHAPTER FIVE

Fiona

Fiona pocketed the key Tom gave her and drove to the white Craftsman cottage Kara Grimes had shared first with her mother and later her husband.

She'd driven past the house and through the neighborhood several times before approaching Tom.

She liked to get a feel for the defendant before taking a case, but this place gave her the creeps without any hint as to why. Maybe it was simply that so much grief had occurred inside that it left an aura of misery like a dark cloud hovering above the roofline.

The house was modest even for the area which was definitely on the lower rung of middle class. The grass had dried out and the flowers wilted, but what could you expect with one occupant dead and the other incarcerated?

Fiona parked the dusty van she'd named Bluebeard in the driveway and pulled a white cotton jumpsuit over her clothes. Anyone watching out a window would likely assume she was a crime scene technician or a bio cleanup service.

In a way, she was.

Against her better judgment, she dragged the curled hose on the side of the house into the yard and turned on the sprinkler. Not something any police official would do, but she couldn't bear to see anything die. Not even an overgrown lawn.

"Pardon me. What are you doing?"

Fiona glanced over her shoulder in time to see an elderly woman approaching with the speed of glacial ice, propelling her walker like a snail ready for battle.

Ahh. The neighborhood snoop. Every street had one.

"Official business." Fiona held up a laminated badge she'd made at the office supply store. With those glasses, the old woman would never be able to read it. "I have work to do inside the house, but thought I'd water this grass while I was here."

The old biddy shouldn't object to that, not the way a dead lawn affected property values. Wasn't that what snoops always claimed to worry about?

The woman had made it halfway across the yard and was still charging ahead at no-light speed. "Does Kara know you're here?"

Now that was a problem. Not because Fiona had any qualms about lying—she had her own personal standards about when lying was acceptable and when it wasn't—but she didn't know who this lady was trying to protect. Kara? The dead husband? The police? Justice in general?

Best to play it on the safe side and be as vague as possible. "I don't know, but my boss does."

The woman was still ten feet away when she paused and whipped an old flip-phone out of her pocket. "You wait right there. I'm going to call Kara's lawyer and see if you have permission to be here."

"You do that, ma'am. I can give you his number if you need it. Meanwhile, I'm going inside to start work." She pulled out the key Tom had given her.

"Is that Kara's key? I recognize the angel on the key fob. I gave that to her for Christmas the year her mother died." The walker inched closer.

One question answered. The woman seemed to be on Kara's side. Not what she'd expected in a murder investigation. Maybe she could learn something useful. "Yes, she gave it to my boss." Or he got it from the evidence locker or the court or took it from her personal effects at the jail. "You two must be good friends."

"I've known Kara since she was six-years-old."

"Since she and her mother moved in here?"

"Yes. She was such a darling girl. Much too young to have to deal with an ailing mother and that bastard of a step-father. I guess mother and daughter were alike in their poor judgment around men."

This was about to get interesting.

Fiona didn't really want a cup of tea, but she couldn't pass up the chance to learn more about Kara Grimes. Actually, the mango/mint tasted pretty good, especially when paired with a chocolate chip cookie.

Helen Hawkins pushed the plate closer. "I'm sorry I can't offer you homemade but I don't seem to be able to manage holding onto my walker with one hand and a hot cookie sheet with the other."

"That's okay, Mrs. Hawkins. These taste great." Fiona took another just to make the old lady feel better.

"Call me Helen, dear. If you can help Kara, we're going to be great friends."

Friends? Not likely. Fiona didn't have friends. No one liked to be around someone who lied for a living. Someone who could unearth your deepest secrets with a few keystrokes. Someone who had the power to embarrass you.

Or worse, destroy you.

But she was fine alone. She didn't need the burden of friends. She could take care of herself.

"So, you've known Kara for twenty years. That's amazing. I don't think I've known *anyone* for twenty years."

"Really? To me, that's the amazing part. All my friends are old friends. And I don't just mean *old* old, although I have plenty of those also. I still keep in touch with people I knew in school and people I worked with. I used to babysit for Nicole across the street. She moved away for a while then moved back when her mother died. Now she calls me for parenting advice which is a hoot since I never had kids of my own."

The foster kids Fiona grew up with never banded together to improve their situation but acted more as rivals, fighting for every scrap of food, attention, and privilege. If tattling on another kid got you thirty more minutes in front of the TV, or an extra helping of stew, so be it.

Keeping Helen talking was easy. Keeping her on the right subject was harder. The old woman had a tendency to veer off onto other topics. Although the mention of another neighbor reminded Fiona there might be others nearby with useful information.

She wasn't used to talking to actual people. Most of her information was gathered from behind a computer.

"What was Kara like at that age? Did she play with the neighbor kids? I know when I was ten all I wanted to do was play outside." She had wanted to *be* outside, but had she ever in her life played? Certainly not with other children.

"Kara was always a sweet child. Kind and helpful. But she was shy. That happens when you have an abusive step-father. Kara's mother was still working at the time, but that sapped all her energy. Grant, Kara's step-father, insisted she stay in after school and clean the house, do the laundry, cook the meals, wash the dishes. She wasn't allowed to go out or even watch

TV until she finished her chores and her homework. One year Kara wanted to join the math club, but she'd have to stay after school once a week. So on Wednesdays, I'd slip over to their house at noon, clean up a bit, and put something on to cook in the crock pot. Unfortunately, one Wednesday, Grant stayed home with a hangover. When he realized what was going on, he put a stop to it."

Fiona hesitated, unsure how to ask the next question. "So . . . How abusive was Grant? Strict, demanding step-father, or something else?"

Helen kept her eyes down, wiping at an invisible spot on the table. "I never knew for sure. I could hear the yelling, see an occasional bruise. I had an idea when it progressed. Kara came over, crying, asking how to get blood out of her sheets. But no matter how I begged, she wouldn't tell me. Even at thirteen, she knew he'd go to jail and leave them destitute if she told."

How did that figure in to Kara's guilt or innocence on this case? Did it make killing her husband more or less likely? There was a reason Fiona preferred sticking to computer research. When you dealt with people, there was always the danger of becoming emotionally involved.

Besides, people lied, documents didn't.

"But Grant left anyway, didn't he?"

"Yes. The day Sharon wasn't able to work anymore, he packed his bags and left without a word. The first couple of years I helped out as much as I could. I checked on Sharon during the day, took meals over, but eventually Sharon couldn't be left alone at all and Kara had to drop out of school." Helen looked up, her eyes filled with regret. "Funny how things change. Now Kara has to help me. At least on the weeks her no-good excuse for a husband is out of town."

Well damn. There went Helen as a witness. She needed Kara at home, helping her. However, it was the last sentence that caught Fiona's attention.

"Earlier, you made the comment that both Kara and her mother had poor taste in men and now you called Devin a *no-good excuse for a husband.* Would you care to expand on that?"

Helen cocked her head to one side, narrowed her eyes, and studied Fiona. "Who did you say you worked for?"

Maybe the old woman wasn't as far gone as she'd thought. Fiona dug in her back pocket and pulled out a business card she had printed herself. It was an exact replica of Tom's cards, but she'd had her name added to the bottom line as his associate.

"I work for Kara's lawyer. You're welcome to call the number listed here and check on me."

Helen drew the card close and ran her finger over the embossed lettering.

Damn. Good thing I paid extra for the fancy printing.

After a moment, Helen reached into the basket of her walker and pulled out a tablet. She typed faster than Fiona would have guessed possible with her age and eyesight.

She turned the tablet Fiona's direction. You're not listed on his website."

"I'm not a lawyer." Sometimes the truth was actually the

best answer.

"Harrumph." Helen punched the number from the website into her flip phone. She put the phone on speaker when it started to ring.

"Law firm." Fiona recognized the voice of Tom's receptionist although she had never bothered to learn the woman's name.

"What do you mean 'Law Firm'? Whose law firm is this?"

"This is the Meyers Law Firm. Tom Meyers."

"Why didn't you say that in the first place?"

"We have several people working here. Mr. Meyers doesn't want anyone to hang up because they didn't hear the name of the person they were looking for. Whom did you wish to speak with? I'll connect you."

Fiona had always considered the blond receptionist as decoration. Front Desk Barbie. Maybe she'd misjudged the woman.

"Do you have an employee named…" Helen glanced at the card. "…Fiona Drake?"

Shit. Would the woman even know who she was? Had she ever once entered by the front door?

"Fiona? Sure, she works here. She's not in at the moment, but I'll be happy to take a message and have her return your call."

"Can you describe her?"

"I can try. I'm not very good at that type of thing. She's maybe five nine. Slim build. Blue/green eyes. Ultra short hair. It was pink the last time I saw her but it might be any color now. Does that help?"

It had been three weeks since her hair was pink. When had the blond seen her? She tried to keep a low profile, but obviously not low enough—which in this case was a good thing. Maybe she should actually get to know the blond. At least learn her name.

"And Kara Grimes is one of Tom Meyers's clients?"

"I wouldn't be able to discuss Mr. Meyers's clients. If you want to leave your number I can have him call you."

Who knew there was more to being a receptionist than sitting at a desk looking pretty? She was definitely going to have to tell Tom to give that woman a raise.

Helen set her phone down and clasped her hands. "What did you want to know?

CHAPTER SIX

Tom

A thrill of anticipation surged through Tom as he entered the courthouse. This was where he felt most alive.

Anything could happen here.

No matter how hard you prepared and thought you had anticipated every eventuality, the judge or the prosecution or your own client could throw a curve ball that destroyed your entire case. You had to stay alert every second. Never let your guard down.

And that's where he shined.

Tap dancing, pirouetting, reversing, coming at something from a new and unexpected angle. If he failed, his client paid the price.

So, he didn't allow himself to fail.

He flashed his badge at the guard and was waved through

a side entrance.

There'd been a time, his first year in Houston, when he couldn't afford $80 for a pass. One year of waiting in a line that stretched out the door, setting his briefcase on the conveyer belt, emptying his loose change, pens, wallet, cell phone and keys into a basket, and removing his shoes, belt and jacket before stepping through the metal detector had been enough.

The next January he came up with the money, not only for the Harris County pass, but also for Ft. Bend, Montgomery, and Waller Counties.

Now he avoided the line and the scrutiny, although not once had any machine noticed the inserts in his shoes giving him an extra inch in height.

He wasn't vain—okay, maybe he was, a little—but the lifts had nothing to do with vanity. Juries seemed to trust the taller, stronger-looking lawyers, as if this was a battle of might instead of minds.

As usual, a line fifteen deep waited for one of the two elevators. He took the stairs to the fourth floor and Judge Hinson's court. Kara wasn't anywhere near the top of the docket. Depending on how prepared other lawyers were this morning, or what mood the judge was in, he might have to wait half an hour to an hour. Maybe longer.

Tom didn't mind waiting. He loved the smell of old wood, law books, and justice.

He would never risk working on a case in public so this was the one time all day he allowed himself to simply relax and read. Fiction. Anything that didn't contain a lawyer or court scene. Those were too unbelievable.

Forty minutes later the wooden bench dug into his back and he stuffed the book into his briefcase. Within a minute, the bailiff called out, "Kara Grimes, case number 475862, murder in the first degree."

Tom stood. "Tom Meyers for the defense, Your Honor."

A stir filled the courtroom as every spectator and journalist sat up straighter.

This was it. The big time. What everyone had come to see, whether they knew it or not.

A bailiff brought Kara into the courtroom, orange jumpsuit, leg irons, and all. Tom made his way to the defense table and sat beside her. He reached over and patted her hand before standing again.

"Your Honor. We request the defendant be released immediately on her own recognizance."

The judge peered down over half glasses. "Haven't we had this discussion before?"

"No sir. That was her public defender who, I submit, was woefully unprepared, misstated facts, and failed to question the State's use of unsubstantiated evidence."

The ADA, a baby lawyer fresh from her bar exam, jumped to her feet and began to stutter. "Your Honor. I object to the description of the State's case as *unsubstantiated evidence.*"

Tom smiled inwardly, careful not to let the glee show on his face. The DA would never have sent someone so young and inexperienced as a representative if he'd known Tom would make a motion for Kara's release. This hearing was supposed to cover preliminary paperwork, hearing dates, and exchange of evidence. Nothing a new-hire lawyer couldn't handle.

Instead, the poor schmuck was facing Tom Fucking Meyers.

Even the DA should have guessed this wasn't going to be easy.

Twenty minutes later, Tom was signing papers for Kara's release. She would need to wear an ankle bracelet at all times and had a list of restrictions. She could travel back and forth to work, Tom's office, church, her doctor, and a once-a-week trip to the bank and grocery store. That was all.

She couldn't go to a restaurant, movie, shopping center, drink alcohol, use drugs, or leave the parameters of her yard. Monitors could phone her at any time, day or night, and she would be required to answer within three rings. She would be expected to check in once a week and submit to random drug tests.

In other words, not a walk in the park, but better than jail.

Tom heard footsteps and glanced over his shoulder to see the ADA he'd just wiped the floor with.

"Enjoy your victory, asshole. It won't last," she hissed at him.

"Why, Allison. Your language. I don't remember you talking that way at dinner last week."

Her eyes flitted from one side of the room to the other.

"Keep your voice down. I could lose my job if my boss thought I had shared information with you."

Tom swiveled his chair to face her. She was a beautiful woman, but more than that, she was brilliant, having sailed through University of Texas Law School and aced the bar exam.

If she were fifteen years older he might have been interested in her.

"My dear. We did nothing inappropriate. We merely shared a pleasant meal, discussed office politics, local rumors, an interesting Supreme Court decision, and the chances of the Astros winning the Series. Neither of us ever mentioned Kara Grimes and I'll be happy to tell that to your boss if he should ask. In fact, I had no idea you'd be working on her case. You, however, knew exactly what you were doing when you asked to join me."

Allison spun on one heel and stomped out of the room just as the far door opened and Kara Grimes stepped out looking shell-shocked.

"Am I free?" Her voice held a hint of disbelief.

"No, only out on bail. As we discussed, since you don't have five-thousand dollars to pay a bail bondsman, we used your house for collateral. If you skip town or don't show up for trial, you will forfeit your house. Do you agree?"

Kara gave a faint nod. Tom wasn't sure, but he didn't think she'd blinked once since she came through the door.

"I need you to say it out loud so I can be sure you

understand."

She started to speak but only a croak came out. She cleared her throat and tried again. "I'm not planning to run or hide. I want to clear my name. Redeem my reputation. I want to find out what happened to my husband. I'm happy to use my home as collateral for my bail."

"You have some papers to sign, then I need to go over the rules with you. It will take a couple of hours to process everything before you can be released. I'll arrange for an Uber to drive you home. Settle in, get a good night's sleep, and call my office in the morning."

Now the real work began.

But he couldn't help noticing that she'd said *clear my name* before *find out what happened to my husband.*

CHAPTER SEVEN

Kara

The Uber driver dropped Kara at the rear of her driveway so she could slip in the back door and avoid the prying eyes of her neighbors.

Even the short distance to the door felt odd, her new ankle monitor rubbing against her skin with every step.

Her attention on the uncomfortable plastic monitor, Kara had made it four feet into the kitchen before she took in the scene around her.

Drawers and cabinets weren't closed tightly. The pantry door stood slightly ajar. Her coffeepot sat unplugged at the wrong end of the counter.

One chair faced at an angle from the table, its cushion sported a dirty smudge as if someone had stood on it.

She sucked in a breath and tiptoed down the hall, almost

afraid to look into her bedroom.

It had the same *off* feel. A corner of Devin's underwear hung out of a drawer, preventing it from closing all the way. The bed was made, but the comforter wasn't smooth and the pillows were wrong.

Even the mattress looked slightly crooked on its frame.

She'd been surprised the day Baxter and Copperfield arrested her and hadn't cleaned the house first, but no way she'd left it like this.

Someone had searched her house, and they were very sloppy about it.

Even the jail searches hadn't felt this intrusive. Maybe because that hadn't been her home.

She couldn't rip the sheets off the bed fast enough. Without pausing to think, she jammed them in the washer, switched the water temperature to high and slammed the lid.

It didn't help. She still felt dirty.

The whole house gave her the creeps and she'd lived there for ninety percent of her life.

She wanted to get out. Run down the street screaming. But she couldn't leave her yard. However, she could go out *into* her yard and breathe some clean air.

Even that backfired when she saw the sprinkler next to her flowerbed. No way Helen could have moved it and held onto her walker. Some other neighbor might have if they thought a dead lawn detracted from the look of the street.

As if the rest of the neighborhood was so perfect.

"Kara, honey, you're a sight for these old eyes. I've been so worried about you. Did they come to their senses and let you go?" Helen made her way across her yard as fast as her walker allowed.

Kara took a deep breath and blinked away the tears threatening to form. She couldn't let Helen see how upset she was. She pressed her hands against her hip to steady them and tried for a smile.

"I'm not free. Only out on bond." Kara reached the edge of her driveway and stopped, frustrated she couldn't go another couple of steps to meet Helen. "I'm not allowed to leave the four corners of my property except for work or doctor visits." She raised one pant leg and showed off the black ankle monitor.

"I know. I watch all those legal shows. But they can't think you would ever hurt anyone."

"Well, they sure believe I killed Devin. Say, Helen, were you in my house in the last couple of days?"

"Not me. My sciatica's been acting up. Must have been that associate of your lawyer—Fiona. I know she watered your plants and took out your garbage. She was by this morning and I heard her get your Hyundai started—I think it needed a jump—then she drove it around the block a couple of times. She didn't mess with anything, did she?"

Probably. I just haven't found out what yet.

"No. I wanted to thank her…for taking out the garbage."

"Okay, good. She seems real nice, but she is a bit strange."

"Strange?"

"It's just that she comes across so sweet and friendly but after she leaves, you realize you did all the talking. I checked her out and she does work for your lawyer."

Just when she'd started to trust Tom, this Fiona woman had come snooping around. She should have gone with her first instincts.

No harm done so far. She hadn't told him anything and he had gotten her out of jail.

Kara spent the next two hours cleaning the house, removing any trace of a woman who didn't belong there. Then she spent another hour combing every corner for cameras or listening devices.

Even with clean sheets, she couldn't bring herself to climb into her bed. She ended up sleeping on the sofa.

So much for a good night's sleep and enough space to make some heavy decisions.

The luxury of Tom Meyers's office didn't put Kara at ease. It had the opposite effect.

The butterscotch leather sofa, plush carpet, high-end coffee pot, the wraparound view of Houston only made her wonder what secrets were hidden away in those well-disguised file cabinets.

And what it would take to keep them secret.

Would anything she told him—or anything his *investigator*

discovered—end up in one of those drawers?

Tom offered a quick introduction to the woman draped carelessly across his sofa. The woman, Fiona, nodded her direction.

Kara tried on a slight smile. "Are you the one I have to thank for taking out my garbage and watering my plants?" *And for invading my privacy without asking, pawing through my underwear, and climbing up on my chair?*

Tom looked surprised. Had he not known his employee had come into her house uninvited?

If he was caught off guard, he recovered quickly. "Fiona is very thoughtful about helping our clients readjust after incarceration."

Oh yeah. Fiona looked just like Mother Teresa—if the old nun had three-inch long lavender hair, a leather jacket, motorcycle boots, and an attitude that rivaled Mad Max.

Tom straightened the folder centered squarely on his desk. "Before we start, I need to remind you that anything you say to me or Fiona is strictly confidential. We can't and won't repeat it to anyone. That said, it's extremely important you tell us the truth and don't hold anything back. I can't do my job if I get blindsided by the prosecution."

"I understand." She didn't believe him, but she understood.

The investigator, Fiona, pulled her chair next to Tom's desk, facing her. "Before we get into the details of the case, I've been wondering about your husband. Can you tell me a little about him?"

Kara wasn't sure what the woman wanted, or what she should tell her. "I suppose he was a typical salesman. He could talk your ear off when he was 'on,' but after a long day he wanted dinner and a quiet evening at home. He didn't like going out or being around people. He enjoyed watching football and baseball, but I don't think he ever played. Or at least he never mentioned it to me."

"What about his family? Do you think he had a happy childhood?"

Why did that woman care about Devin's childhood?

"He didn't have any family that I ever met. He was the only child of an only child. His father was in the military so I'm guessing on the strict side. I know he was born in Alaska, but I think they moved around a bit. His mother died not long after he graduated from some community college. His father had been gone several years when I met him."

"Do you know where his father is buried?"

"No." This all made her sound like a terrible wife. Maybe she was. There must be something personal she could say about him. "Oh, he was allergic to cats. I had a cat when we got married. He sneezed and his eyes watered so much I had to give the poor thing away."

Fiona smiled. "Maybe you should think of getting one now. It would be good company."

A jolt of something not quite happiness, but close, raced through Kara's body. "That's a good idea. Thanks." As quickly as the feeling came, it faded. She couldn't make a commitment like that. Not until she knew what her plans were. "Not right now. Maybe later."

Fiona and Tom shared a glance before he turned toward her. "It's time for something I call *The Talk*. It's nothing personal. I tell this to all my clients out on bail. If you were to decide you weren't willing to take a chance on a trial and felt your only option was to run, thinking you could disappear and live out your life in obscurity with no one ever knowing who you were, think again. Most people, even career criminals, don't make it twenty-four hours, much less twenty-four years. Once caught, and you would be, no judge or jury would believe a word you said. There would be very little I could do for you."

Fiona tried to look casual as if the thought had just occurred to her. "Did you read that story a couple of weeks ago? A woman out in California escaped thirty years ago. Had a husband and children. Belonged to the PTA. A truck ran into her at a traffic light and knocked her unconscious. By the time she came to in the hospital, she was handcuffed to the bed."

Those two fools. They had no idea. She'd been preparing for the last year. Had a passport and ID in a fake name along with cash—not enough—buried behind Helen's garage.

Tom looked so pleased with himself for his casual lecture it made her sick.

"Let's get started, then," he said. "What can you tell me about your husband's cause of death?"

The five days since Devin's death had passed in a blur, but Kara had finally pulled herself together enough to take the first step forward when she opened her door to find her two least favorite people waiting. Just her luck. If she'd left five minutes earlier she'd have missed them.

"Mrs. Grimes, we have some questions we'd like to ask you."

It was that horrid woman. The one with the slight mustache and one eyebrow. Kara couldn't tell if she was frowning or if that was her natural expression—or maybe her only expression—but something was definitely wrong.

"May we come in?"

Kara's stomach did a back flip. What if she said no? Was that allowed? The two detectives already suspected she had something to do with Devin's death. Now they were trying to prove it, and she didn't plan to help.

"You've already asked me more questions than I can count. Nothing's changed."

"You can refuse, in which case, we'd have to take you down to the station to question you."

Could they do that without a warrant? She couldn't afford to hire a lawyer to find out.

"We'd rather not have to come back with a warrant," the mousey little man spoke up. Was he Detective Copperfield or Baxter? Oh yeah. He was Copperfield. If he wore his name

across the back of his shirt, he'd have to leave off the last few letters. She was Baxter. B for bitch. She'd have room for the entire team roster on the back of her shirt.

Baxter glared down at her partner as if he'd given away a secret. He took a half step back, away from Baxter's laser-beam focus.

"You have five minutes. I'm due at the funeral home. They need someone to identify the body before the cremation." They'd only been married three years and had never gotten around to discussing final wishes. She literally had no idea what he would have wanted, but buying a cemetery plot and spending Sundays carrying flowers to his grave was never going to happen.

Kara pivoted and stomped back to the living room. They could follow or not. She was too flustered to care.

"You might need to put those arrangements on hold." Baxter remained standing while Kara flopped onto the sofa.

"Why? The medical examiner ruled his death from natural causes and gave me permission to proceed with the funeral. Apparently, Devin had a heart condition he didn't know about. Unusual for someone his age, but not unheard of considering his weight gain and the diabetes he had probably developed long before it was diagnosed."

"There's been a change in his report. New evidence has come to light."

Kara felt her jaw drop and quickly snapped it back. She wouldn't give the woman the satisfaction of seeing her shock.

"The toxicology report showed drugs in his system and a

blood sugar level well over 700. When he checked the vial of insulin from your bathroom trash, it contained only water."

FOR A MOMENT, Kara was physically unable to answer Tom's question. Everything inside her had frozen—her heart, her lungs, her brain. The words simply wouldn't form and she couldn't have uttered them if they had.

What did she know about the cause of Devin's death? Probably less than Tom. He'd read the police report.

"Those two detectives, Copperfield and Baxter, came to my house the day I was arrested. They wouldn't believe I didn't know Devin was using drugs, and I did suspect—he'd changed so much in the last year—but I never *saw* him take any and didn't know where he kept them. They did a drug test on me, trying to prove I was taking them with him or that they were my drugs since I work in a doctor's office. I was clean, but that didn't seem to faze them."

Tom leaned forward, his ice-blue eyes studying her. "The drugs were found in a bottle of Excedrin in your bathroom. And your fingerprints were on both the Excedrin and the insulin."

That's why she'd just spent three weeks in jail? "Of course my fingerprints were on them. My fingerprints are probably on everything in that house. Devin left things sitting around and I put them up. And yes, I threw the insulin in the trash, along with his needles, and test kit, and alcohol swabs, and anything else reeking of sickness."

Kara jumped up and crossed the room in three long strides before spinning back again. She couldn't sit still. Her whole body twitched and hummed with nerves. "As for the Excedrin, Devin claimed it was the only thing that helped his headaches, but Excedrin has caffeine, and I suffer from tachycardia. I can't manage any type of stimulant or my heart goes bonkers and I'm bouncing off the ceiling at two in the morning. Check my kitchen. It's full of decaf coffee and tea. I even have a separate coffee pot."

The pacing helped some, but not enough. She placed her hand on the edge of Tom's desk and tried the deep breathing she'd learned watching yoga videos.

If Tom had watched her before, his eyes now bored through her. "How do you explain the water in the insulin vial?"

CHAPTER EIGHT

Fiona

Armstead Pharmaceuticals occupied the seventh floor of a non-descript office building several blocks south of Greenspoint Mall. Even with the cheaper rent the location offered, the building was less than half full, and Armstead only took up a quarter of the floor.

Not the sign of a booming business.

Fiona tried to make herself comfortable in the hard-backed chair Omar Lloyd had dragged into his office for her. His desk was clean except for a slim manila folder he kept straightening.

"I don't know what I can tell you about Devin Grimes. He didn't 'work' for us, per se."

The man made quotation marks with his fingers, causing Fiona to like him even less than when she walked in and saw him roll his eyes at her blue hair.

"Devin technically worked for himself. He was an independent contractor, and he was pretty good at what he did or at least he was until recently. Lately he acted like this was a hobby instead of a job. I'd have fired him, but anything he sold was profit, so what did I care? The thing about Devin, he could be charming when he wanted to, but one time—and it happened so fast I was never sure—I thought I saw a hint of a temper when we didn't have anything for him to push that week."

Fiona pretended to take notes. "So, he showed up when he wanted to and you gave him something to sell? And he went out and sold it?"

He moved the toothpick to the other side of his mouth. "Well, there was a little more to it than that, but yeah."

"Why don't you explain it to me?"

"We aren't exactly a pharmaceutical company."

"Oh?" This promised to be interesting.

"We're a small, independent company. No one here except myself, my secretary, a couple of bookkeepers, and three buyers make a salary. We don't have a corporate office or a fancy R&D lab because we don't actually *make* drugs. We buy overstocks from the big-name companies, and people like Devin sell them to doctors or clinics."

Was that even legal? She'd have to ask Tom, but she'd bet her last nickel overstocks weren't the only thing they bought. Anyone foolish enough to buy from this grifter had better check the expiration date on the box, or maybe even the tamper-proof seal.

Tom knew a guy in the FBI. When this case was over, maybe they should give him a call and drop a hint or two.

She kept her face natural and leaned toward Omar. "I'm only interested in Devin Grimes." She bit her tongue to keep from saying *for now.* "How did he come to work for you? Did he have references?"

"Sort of. He'd worked as a pharmaceutical rep for a company in Vermont for six years, but told me he was sick of cold weather and Yankees. Can you blame him? He already had contacts in Louisiana, so I said sure, why not? It didn't cost me anything to hire him and he lasted longer than most of my employees. It's not like you make a great living selling overstocked drugs." He gave a wink and a chuckle that sent ice cubes rattling down her veins.

Fiona eyed the folder now turned sideways on the man's desk. "You must have some sort of paperwork on him. Maybe a letter of recommendation? Tax information? Dependents? Address, phone number?"

"I never contacted the company he used to work for. He talked a good game and obviously knew the industry. I really didn't care why he left. As for taxes, I emailed him a 1099. Other than that, not my business. I do have the form he filled out when he started. It lists his full name, social security number, address, email, and phone number. The email and phone number were the only information I ever used." He tapped the folder twice then pushed it toward Fiona.

"What about expense reports?" Maybe she could follow where he'd been and learn something.

If possible, Omar's grin grew even bigger. "That's the beauty of this arrangement. I don't keep up with his expenses. They're his problem."

This whole day was a waste. A dead end. She had one last possibility. "How about his contacts? Can you give me a list of the businesses he called on?"

The line between his eyes deepened as his smile fell away. "That's privileged information. You'd need a warrant."

Fiona reminded herself of the one iron-clad principle she lived by as she left Omar's office: *When someone shows you who they are, believe them.*

This case was no exception.

Omar had showed who he was—a dirt-bag with questionable morals. Helen appeared to be an upstanding friend, but she'd been fooled before and it would take more than one visit to convince her.

Tom, on the other hand, was an enigma. She'd met him outside a sandwich shop two years ago when she tried to give a homeless man half her lunch. She'd lived on the street briefly. It was a hard life she wouldn't wish on anyone.

The restaurant owner had come running out threatening to dump a bucket of water over the guy's head if he didn't move along. Tom appeared out of nowhere, never raising his voice, and schooled the owner on the law against assaulting someone.

He then turned to Fiona and asked if she had a nickel.

"I think so." She dug in her pocket and produced the coin.

"Give it to him." Tom nodded toward the homeless man.

She did and Tom held out his hand for the nickel. "Now you're my client. If you have any problems give me a call. When you're ready, I know a group home that owes me a favor. They have rules, but not too onerous." He handed the guy a twenty and his card.

"Do you have an extra one of those cards?" she'd asked.

Two weeks later she'd slipped into his office with beneficial information on his latest case. She'd occasionally worked with him ever since, even if she didn't always approve of his clients.

Kara was one of those clients she had serious questions about, but the more she learned about the woman's husband, the more she suspected the man was not what he seemed.

INSIDE BLUEBEARD WAS stuffy with a lingering aroma of last night's Kung Pao chicken, even though Fiona had been careful to dispose of the leftovers before settling down to read herself to sleep.

She lowered both the driver and passenger side windows as she cruised I-45 back toward Tom's office. The cross breeze allowed the cool air to blow away everything except her confusion.

The single sheet of paper Omar Lloyd had given her was

short on information but long on questions. She had the name, address, social security number, and phone number for Devin Grimes, only none of those things matched the body waiting in the Harris County morgue.

A quick Google search showed the address listed was an extended-stay motel, and his cell number—which didn't match the phone found on his bedside table—rang and rang then cutoff with a brief message claiming his mailbox was full.

As for the social security number, that might take more digging than she could manage while driving through Houston traffic.

An uncharacteristic smile flitted past her face. Could their client be charged with the murder of a person who didn't exist?

A question for Tom, although she suspected the answer was *yes*.

As for Omar Lloyd... She screwed her face into a smirk and imitated his east Texas twang. "*That's privileged information. You'd need a warrant.*"

The hell she would. He hadn't dealt with Fiona Drake before. Anything less than a national security firewall was amateur hour for her.

For now, she was only two blocks from the motel Devin had listed as his address, and while he hadn't lived there lately, he might have at one time.

She put on her blinker and, a block later, turned into the parking lot of SureStay short-term rentals. Either Devin had been operating on a shoestring three years ago, or the place had gone downhill remarkably fast.

Potholes that large didn't develop overnight.

The kid behind the reception desk wasn't much past his teens, with traces of acne still visible.

His eyes lit up like Christmas morning when she walked in, then fell again when she slapped a photo of Devin Grimes on the desk. "Hi, there." She gave him her 500-megawatt smile. He was too young to handle the 1000-watt version. "I was wondering if you recognized this man. He may have stayed here about three years ago."

The kid's eyes narrowed. "You mean Mr. Pryor? He's in 307, but he hasn't been around for a couple of weeks."

Fiona bit back a grin, gave herself a mental high-five, and checked out the kid's name tag. "Curtis, is there any chance you could let me see his room?" She amped her smile up to 750-watts and leaned forward on the counter. Showing cleavage was against her principles, but letting a green kid think she was about to wasn't.

"Why? Is he in trouble?"

What play was most likely to work here? "Only with his wife. She hired me to see if he was cheating on her."

"I'm studying Hotel Management at the University of Houston and they frown on giving out information on guests."

Then you shouldn't have told me what room he rented.

Fiona winked and slipped a hundred dollar bill his direction. "Maybe just this once." She wasn't worried about the money. Tom would reimburse her and call it petty cash. If she got results.

The bill disappeared in a flash. Curtis might be young, but he could have a future as a magician.

"Seeing as how his rent's overdue and the only reason I haven't cleared out his room is I've been too busy…"

Too busy my ass. Too lazy more likely.

Curtis held out a key and Fiona snatched it before he could change his mind.

"It's around here to the left. Let me show you the way."

"I can find it. I'm sure your boss doesn't want the lobby left unattended."

And I don't want you watching me tear the place apart.

"There won't be much to see. Housekeeping has cleaned the room twice since he's been here." Curtis chuckled. "Well, they were supposed to clean it. I doubt they did when it was obvious he hadn't been around."

"Then it won't take me long to look." Fiona swung around and had the door open before he had time to object. She had one foot outside when she twisted back toward Curtis. "I don't suppose you have his registration information?"

Fifty extra dollars later, Fiona stood in the doorway of 307 and did a quick survey of the room—queen-sized bed, miniature kitchen, TV, and a desk with a computer connection. Taped to the wall was the internet password.

A grin spread across her face. This might take all night.

CHAPTER NINE

Tom

Tom strolled down the hall, coffee in one hand, manila folder in the other. Only one more phone call to make.

Unfortunately, the call was to Marcus Bradley, Sr.

He needed to convince Marcus that Mark Jr. should accept a pre-trial diversion for his shenanigans last December when he and a group of friends rearranged a city councilman's Christmas display so that two of the lighted reindeer were in an obscene position, and a third hung upside down from a tree limb, red lights dangling from its neck like blood. Then Marcus could pay a hefty fine and Mark Jr. could take a couple of online courses about learning to be a decent human being and go off to college with a semi-clean record.

Who was he kidding? Marcus would never admit he or anyone related to him had done anything wrong. In that case, he should have taught his son to run faster or not cut the wiring on $2,000 worth of custom lighting.

Tom reached his office and did a double-take, sloshing hot coffee over his hand and onto his chest.

From her seat on the leather sofa, Fiona glanced at the coffee-stain spreading across his white shirt and laughed.

Son-of-a-bitch. How did she do that? He hadn't been away from his desk for five minutes.

"I left some expense reports on your desk. If you could hurry and reimburse me, I'd appreciate it." Fiona yawned and leaned back against the cushion.

No greeting. No please. And likely no report he'd have accepted from any other employee, just *You owe me $$$$$* written on a scrap of paper with no explanation or receipt.

He set the half-gone coffee on his desk and reached for a tissue to wipe off his hand. Yep, written in blue marker on a sheet of computer paper was one line telling how much she wanted.

"You can add $500 to that as an advance for my trip to Louisiana."

Tom bit back the urge to say *Are you planning to hit the casinos, or maybe just vacation at the Hilton?* He knew better than that. If Fiona said she needed to go to Louisiana, she had a reason. Besides, she'd never stay at a Hilton. She'd worry about her van being stolen.

"What's in Louisiana that's worth $500?"

"Ian Pryor."

"Who's that?"

"I don't know, but he looks a lot like this guy." She handed Tom a photo of Devin Grimes. "And he uses the same phone number that's listed on Grimes's employment application at Armstead Pharmaceutical, which, by the way, goes to a phone we haven't found. I'd like to search his car. Have the police returned it yet?"

If the guy had hidden anything in that car larger than a nickel, Fiona would find it. "Not yet. I sent in the paperwork yesterday morning, but haven't heard back. I'll give them a call and see if I can light a fire under somebody's ass. How long will you be gone?"

"Hard to say. I've got some digging to do on the computer tonight, so I won't leave until the morning. Unless I hit the jackpot on the first try, I'd guess at least two days."

Two days. Funny, he often went weeks without seeing her and complained when she showed up unannounced, but knowing she'd be out of town… Well, he'd miss her. "Keep me updated with anything you find. I'll try to have the car back before you get home. And Fiona, whoever killed Ian Pryor—even if it's our own client—might not be too keen on you snooping around. Be careful."

AFTER A FRUSTRATING twenty minutes on the phone with the HPD impound lot trying to get Devin Grimes's car released,

Tom decided face-to-face conversations usually worked best.

Marcus Bradley hadn't risen to the top of Houston's cutthroat oil well supply industry by rolling over, and the man had never mastered separating his business and personal life. He was insisting on taking Mark, Jr.'s youthful prank to court, and a phone call wasn't likely to change his mind.

Instead of heading home, Tom turned south toward Tanglewood. No matter what happened, the trip wouldn't be wasted. Marcus served an excellent single malt scotch that he poured with a heavy hand.

Jenn Bradley wasn't one to stand up to her husband, but if he could get the family all in one room—Marcus, Jenn, and Mark, Jr.—and explain exactly what Mark was facing, maybe she would find the gumption to face down her husband.

Thirty minutes later, he pulled up in front of the Bradley's McMansion. Mark, Jr. answered the door and his face fell when he saw Tom. Who was he expecting at seven-thirty on a school night?

"Dad!" the kid yelled and stomped off to the back of the house, leaving Tom to close the door.

"Tom, come on in." Marcus's voice boomed across the room as Jenn scurried in behind him. He had poured them each a glass of Glenlivet before Tom had time to get comfortable. The first sip went down smooth.

Then Marcus started in on him. "Have you decided to grow a pair and take this thing to trial? I want my boy to have a clean record."

Tom loved nothing better than a well-fought trial, and if he thought he had a snowball's chance of winning, he might consider proceeding. But he'd seen the video of Mark, wearing his Kincaid High School letter jacket with his team number on the shoulder, shooting the bird toward the camera, his face lit by twinkling Christmas lights.

The fact that the destruction was in retaliation against the councilman's cheerleader daughter who had unceremoniously dumped Mark when she found out he'd cheated on her managed to tie up the whole episode with a neat little holiday bow.

"Marcus, we've been over this. We're screwed as long as they have the video."

"Then get it tossed out. That happens all the time."

Yeah, on TV and in the movies.

"People are allowed to have security cameras on their own property. You do." Like logic would make any difference to Marcus.

Marcus twisted and yelled up the stairs so his son could hear. "The little bastard is lucky he wasn't shot. I'd have killed the sons-of-bitches for screwing around in my yard."

Please, not again.

If he made a list of all the hot-headed criminals he'd dealt with over the years—and the list would be long—Marcus Bradley, Sr. would be near the top of those who should never be allowed near a gun. He'd never seen a case yet that couldn't be made worse with the introduction of a gun or a knife, or any deadly weapon.

If people would learn that, his case load would be cut in half.

"We've been over this. Shooting people—bad. Calling police—good."

"I'd be within my rights if they came on my property." Marcus puffed out his chest. A real tough guy.

"Sorry. I didn't realize you'd been to law school. If so, you should sue your professor. That doesn't apply to property damage. It's only if they break into your house and you fear for your life. Are you sure you want to swear in court you were afraid of a couple of teenagers running around your front yard armed with a wire cutter?"

"I'd take my chances."

Not with me as your lawyer.

"Let's get back to deciding what's best for Mark, Jr. We need to make a decision." And get you off the idea of shooting people.

"Okay then. How about we let Mark plead *nolo contendere* or at least accept deferred adjudication?"

More pseudo-intellectual bull from someone who never touched a law book. One was basically Latin for *guilty,* and the other was wasting Mark's last best chance for staying out of jail if he ever got into trouble again, which the entitled, elitist little jerk would as sure as the sun shone in Arizona and rain fell in Seattle. A pre-trial diversion on the other hand, left wiggle room for the kid's next screw-up.

Tom drained his glass and leaned forward to explain the situation for the third time.

An hour later, he smiled as he headed home. This was why he made the big bucks.

When Jenn realized her baby boy faced actual jail time and would forever be branded a criminal, her mamma bear came out.

The transformation was a joy to behold.

If only his mother had cared enough to stand up to his father even once, he might have a better opinion of marriage. Or mothers.

All his life, starting with his own parents, he'd been surrounded by rich pricks who thought money made them above the law, that rules were for suckers, that wealth equaled worth.

Like his father, they often got their comeuppance, but he'd grown tired of dealing with them until they learned. If they ever did.

Lights from office buildings replaced stars as Tom drove home on the not-too-crowded freeway. The almost silent hum of his GLC Mercedes hybrid with soft, light classical music playing on Sirius XM left him feeling like he existed in a bubble, traveling through time and space alone.

He'd be home soon, in a million-dollar condo, professionally decorated so that every throw pillow, every knick-knack, every painting had been chosen to scream elegance and refinement in a welcoming atmosphere, yet no one set foot inside except him and then only to eat and sleep.

Where was Fiona sleeping tonight?

The weather was mild enough to sleep in her van, although she would never admit that's where she lived on all but the coldest nights or hottest days.

Then she occasionally slipped into his office after everyone was gone and slept on his sofa, which was why he kept a cashmere throw tossed casually over the arm.

He also paid for a firm membership to the gym on the first floor, knowing she used it to shower.

She had claimed she needed to work on her computer, so it was possible she would break into his office. No, she'd been there already today so probably wouldn't risk it again. More likely her van was hidden behind the library or a Panera Bread—out of sight but within Wi-Fi range.

With no rain lately and the cooler October nights, mosquitoes had all but disappeared so she should be comfortable. But was she safe?

The woman could take care of herself. Once, when she'd bent over to pick something off the floor, he'd caught a glimpse of a wicked-looking knife tucked into the top of her boot. She was probably as safe as he was behind locked doors and security-alarmed windows.

He only worried because she was an employee and it would look bad for the company if something happened to her. That's what he told himself anyway.

He certainly didn't think of Fiona as the grown-up version

of the little sister he'd lost when he was ten. Even if Marcie had lived, his parents would have squashed that rebellious spirit she showed until she became more like Martha Stewart and less like Wonder Woman.

CHAPTER TEN

Fiona

Autumn brought darkness earlier every night which was fine with Fiona. The office lights were off at SureStay as she drove around back to room 307. She'd returned the key to Curtis, but not before she made a copy.

While most hotels and motels had long since switched to a keycard system that could be reprogramed easily, any place with potholes that size in front of the main entrance wouldn't bother with such a costly upgrade.

Fiona dropped her bag and sat on the bed, bouncing slightly. Firm. Just the way she liked it.

An in-depth search of the room yielded a toothbrush, razor, shaving cream, and deodorant in the bathroom cabinet. A hairbrush sat on the counter. One drawer held sweatpants and a rumpled T-shirt.

Another drawer had a clean pair of underwear, socks, and a freshly folded polo shirt.

On a shelf in the kitchen were three cans of soup—two chicken noodle and one beef stew—a box of Pop-Tarts, and a package of protein bars. The freezer, where she'd hoped to find some sort of hidden clue to the life of Devin Grimes, contained a lone TV dinner.

The soup, protein bars, and Pop-Tarts went into a plastic bag to take out to Bluebeard's pantry. At the last minute she added the hairbrush. Maybe they would need DNA evidence at some point to prove who this man actually was—or had been.

She skipped the frozen dinner since she'd always hated meatloaf, and heated one of the chicken noodle soups. Now to set up her computer and get ready to work.

Best to start with Devin Grimes. She'd skimmed the surface earlier, but hadn't found much. Now, with time, a comfortable desk, and a good Wi-Fi connection, no telling how much deeper she could go.

A few clicks and she had her answer. Not much deeper.

Unless you counted the Devin Grimes who died at age five in Alaska thirty-eight years ago. Which meant he had both the name and birth date of the now deceased Devin Grimes from Houston, Texas. Who coincidentally listed his birthplace as Bethel, Alaska.

Fiona heard footsteps outside her window. She sucked in a breath and didn't move as a woman's voice came closer.

"That's it. Just make yourself at home. Act like you own the place."

Had Bluebeard been noticed and someone was on their way to kick her out? It wasn't the embarrassment—she could live with that—but she had all her notes arranged and she had just gotten into the nitty-gritty of the search.

"Come on out. Don't make me have to climb these stairs after you."

Fiona leaned forward and lifted one slat of the mini-blinds. A heavyset woman stood at the bottom of the stairs, hands on her hips, and stared at 307.

Her body slumped as the weight of every day of the last twenty-nine years settled on her shoulders.

Suddenly, from behind a post, a curly-headed kid exploded in laughter and flew down the stairs into the woman's arms.

"You little stinker. You're gonna make Grandma chase you all over this place, aren't you? Let's go before somebody complains. I made you a batch of those Rice Krispy Treats you like. You can have one and watch Dora the Explorer before bed." The woman ruffled the kid's hair as they started off toward another building, the kid skipping ahead.

A strange, unfamiliar feeling bubbled up somewhere inside Fiona. She'd never had someone make something special just for her or a grandmother who would have given her one. She'd never had anyone who cared if she went to bed on time, or ate right, or did her homework.

She'd never really had a family, although she'd had plenty

of foster ones. Some good, some bad. Some beyond bad, but she never stayed long at those places.

Most were simply collecting a check and marking time until she aged out.

She'd saved them the trouble by taking off at seventeen.

That last place—the worst one—had been twelve years ago. Now she lived alone, which meant she was beholden to no one. She even owned her own home, and could drive it anywhere she wanted at a moment's notice.

But still…

Time to quit this pity party and get back to work. She had a job to do and she was damn good at it. She didn't do it for the paycheck or the tingle of pride when Tom praised her work.

She did it because she'd grown up around people who kept secrets and her future often depended on uncovering them. It was the only time she felt in control. And her Spidey sense said she was about to uncover a doozy.

She dropped back down at the desk and flexed her fingers. Would she find an Ian Pryor who died as a child in some remote corner of the world?

How about Guam, was that remote enough? Because three-year-old Ian Pryor had been dead for thirty-six years when he applied for a social security number and listed his birthplace as Santa Rita, Guam, and his current address as a post office box in Baton Rouge, Louisiana.

Now she had two men who shared a face, a phone number, and the ability to magically appear, fully grown, and with no known background. Were there others?

This was going to be a long night. She glanced longingly at the queen-sized bed. Not much time for that or a nice shower. She'd hoped for a chance to trim her hair and dye it Kelly green.

What were the odds this place would still be empty by the time she got back from Baton Rouge?

By TEN O'CLOCK in the morning, Fiona was passing through Lake Charles. On her right, the casinos glowed gold in the morning sun and much of the traffic turned off the interstate.

Suckers.

She'd meant to leave earlier, but she worked until almost three a.m. and that bed was so comfortable…

To make up time, she didn't stop until she reached Lafayette, and then only to get gas, use the bathroom, and grab a large boudin ball from the attached restaurant. Eating gas station takeout was always risky, but the spices kept her awake all the way to Baton Rouge.

The afternoon sky had turned dark and threatening by the time she reached the post office where Ian Pryor rented a box.

The building wasn't much to look at. The sidewalk in front was cracked and tilted unevenly toward the street. Paint flaked off the building and the USPS sign had a hole leaving it to read US S.

The surrounding area wasn't much better. Several

storefronts had heavy bars across the windows. Others were closed entirely. A faded awning hung precariously over a diner with a flashing *Open* sign.

Parking was limited to a half dozen places on the street.

Fiona pulled into a spot away from the door so Bluebeard wouldn't be easily visible.

She was in luck. The inside hadn't been updated any more recently than the outside. The boxes were the old-fashioned kind with tiny glass windows and locks she could easily pick.

Best forget that idea. She could talk her way out of many things, but commit a federal crime and even Tom would wash his hands of her.

She waited until the clerk was busy and strolled past box 1735. Yes. Several envelopes showed through the window. She didn't have time to aim or focus, but snapped the best picture she could before the clerk finished her conversation with an older man on a walker.

She strolled out through the side door.

Back in Bluebeard, she enlarged the photo until she could read the return address on the top envelope. No name, but a street number in Comeau. She consulted her GPS. She could be there and back before the post office closed.

She drove ten miles above the speed limit—any faster, and Bluebeard would shake her to death—only to find the address led not to a person, but to a tire dealership.

Well, she'd come this far. She might as well try. Maybe Ian/Devin had bought tires here. She put on her game face and strolled in.

The inside had that specific smell that belonged only to a tire store, a clean combination of rubber and chrome with a hint of motor oil.

Behind the counter, a man with *Troy* embroidered on his blue work shirt glanced up from his computer and gave her a patented salesman's smile. "Good morning, miss. You needing some new tires for that classic VW? What is it, about a '68 or '69?"

That's why she always tried to park out of the line of sight. Bluebeard was too noticeable. Too memorable. "She's a '70. The last of her kind. That's why I try not to drive her too often. Unfortunately, my Subaru has a flat, hence the visit to you."

"You looking to buy new or repair the one? We don't recommend replacing one. Gives you an uneven ride. If you don't want to go all four, you should buy two."

Troy had to be six-four if he was an inch and the way he looked down on her—like he needed to mansplain tires—chapped her big time, but two could play that game. She bit back her irritation and batted her eyes innocently.

"Truthfully, I don't want to buy any. I was hoping the one that went bad was under warranty. I just bought the car used and was assured the tires were new."

"No problem. Show me the paperwork and we'll get started."

"Well, that's a problem because I can't find the paperwork. It wasn't in the glove compartment like the owner told me.

Plus, I checked out several cars before I settled on it and I can't remember which guy I got it from. If I give you a name, could you check on your computer and maybe I can hunt him down?"

"I suppose I could try." Troy wasn't as enthusiastic as when she came in, but he wasn't uncooperative. There was still the possibility of a sale.

Fiona flipped a coin in her mind. Which name to go with, Ian or Devin? Devin's name was on the job application with the P.O. Box number. "Devin Grimes."

Troy clacked some keys on the computer and shook his head. "Sorry. I don't see where we've done any business with anyone by that name."

"How about Ian Pryor?"

Troy's eyes narrowed to slits. He ran his fingers over the keyboard as if typing. "Nope. Sorry. Looks like I can't help you."

She pulled out a photo of Ian/Devin and slid it across the counter, hoping Troy didn't ask how she happened to have a photo of a man she didn't know. "Maybe you recognize him?"

He pushed the photo back toward her. "Never seen him."

"Can you show the picture to the other people working here in case he came in on your day off?"

"They don't see the customers, just the cars. Besides, it would be a violation of privacy. We're kind of busy here. I need to get back to work. If you decide you want to buy new tires for that Subaru or your old bus, let me know. I'll make you a good deal."

With that, Troy began shuffling papers and ignored her.

Didn't bother Fiona. She'd been thrown out of nicer places than a tire store in Comeau, Louisiana. She only wished she knew if the virtual toss-out was because he knew Ian or because he knew he wasn't making a sale.

Before leaving town, she walked next door to a Dairy Queen, bought a soda, and showed the photo to the kid in the paper hat behind the counter, the couple wrangling two toddlers, and the high school lovebirds in the corner.

No luck.

So, was the tire store ad a fluke? The result of a mass mailing?

She tossed the soda in the trash and tried the Burger King across the street in case Ian/Devin just didn't like Dilly Bars or Blizzards.

Her luck wasn't any better there, and time was running short to make it back before the post office closed. As she pulled out onto Main Street, she caught a glimpse of Troy watching through the window.

Heading back to Baton Rouge, she was already sick of the swampy smell and the Spanish moss. Her skin itched thinking about all the bugs waiting a hundred feet off the roadway into the trees. This whole trip was a waste of time.

She fumbled for her phone and punched in Kara Grimes's number.

Three rings later, her client answered. "Hello?"

"Hi Kara. It's Fiona Drake from Tom Meyers's office."

"Oh. Yes?" Between the sound of wind through the open window, tires on the gravel road, and Bluebeard's normal protests, she could barely hear Kara's answer.

"Have you noticed anything resembling a post office box key among your husband's things?"

"I don't think so, but I'm not sure what one would look like."

"How about any key you don't know what it belongs to?"

"I don't remember one." Kara bit off each word.

"Could you look to see if there's an extra key on his keyring or in the glove box, then call me at this number either way, if you find something or don't?"

After a slight pause, Kara answered. "I suppose I can do that."

Fiona was used to clients resenting her intrusion into their lives, but this woman took the prize. Resentful. Secretive. Frightened. And with a definite chip on her shoulder against her.

Kara disconnected without another word, but by then Fiona was back to Baton Rouge—just in time to see the postal clerk lock the door and walk across the street to the diner.

THE AROMA OF Cajun spices and baked bread filled the diner. The protein bar for breakfast and boudin ball for lunch had long worn off and Fiona's stomach let her know it was empty.

She ordered a shrimp po'boy and a cup of jambalaya and carried her tray to the table where the postal clerk was chowing down on a similar meal.

"May I join you?"

The clerk's eyes narrowed. "I know you?"

"I was in the post office earlier."

"I 'member. We don't get a lot of blue hair 'round here."

"I'm looking for someone who lives in this area."

"Uh huh." The clerk's eyes bored into her, not moving, not blinking.

Fiona stared back. This was who she was more comfortable dealing with and more used to. No smiling face, ready to help. She pulled the photo out of her pocket and slid it across the table. "Do you recognize this man? Know anything about him?"

The woman went back to her jambalaya. "You the police?" her Cajun accent muffled around the shrimp and andouille sausage.

"No. Private Investigator." Something of a stretch. She was private and she was investigating. She could never get a license. Not with her record.

"Didn't think so. If you was the police, you'd know it'd be illegal for me to let you look at anything inside that box you were so interested in earlier."

Fiona dug into her bowl of jambalaya and let the flavors explode in her mouth. Worth every minute of the drive from

Houston. Maybe she had judged Louisiana too harshly. "I'm not asking you to do anything illegal. I'm just asking you—like I would anybody else in this café—if you've seen him. He stole a lot of money from my client." She picked up the woman's check and placed it with her own.

"He don't live 'round here."

"Then you've never seen him?"

"Didn't say that. Seen him plenty of times. Said he don't live 'round here."

"How do you know?"

"If he did, he'd stick out. Wouldn't fit in. Just like you, *chère.*"

Fiona glanced around the diner. Everyone had dark hair and eyes. Warm, leathered skin. Work boots meant for work, not show.

She sat her spoon down and said the first honest thing to come out of her mouth in the last twenty-four hours. "I don't really fit in anywhere."

CHAPTER ELEVEN

Kara

Kara took a deep breath. Everything made her angry now, and that wasn't good…in so many ways.

She gave a weak smile to the tow truck driver as he unhooked Devin's car. None of this was his fault. "Thank you," she called out.

He trudged across her newly watered lawn, clipboard in hand. "I need you to sign this. To say the car isn't damaged and nothing is missing."

How was she supposed to do that? She had no idea what had been in the car when they took it. She scribbled a hasty signature and handed the clipboard back, anxious for him to leave.

Tow truck and driver disappeared from sight before Kara glanced down at the keys in her hand.

Five keys. That seemed like a lot. One was the car key. It had a distinctive shape. One was her house key. She knew that because she'd had it made and given it to him. It was a copper color while the others were silver.

That left three keys. One was smaller. With fewer notches. A mailbox key? Maybe.

The other two were regular, everyday keys. They could be a house key or a locker key or the key to his office or a padlock or a storage shed. The fact that she had no idea sent an icy chill through her veins.

Why had she never noticed before? And worse, what was he hiding?

Forgetting her irritation at the tow truck driver for doing the same thing, she trudged across the damp grass to Devin's car, clicking the key fob to unlock it. The familiar *cheep* sounded faint, but the locks popped open.

She sank into the seat trying to catch a hint of Devin's scent, but the inside was hot and musty. The driver's side seat had been pushed as far back as it would go. Much too far even for Devin's long legs.

Someone she didn't know had been in the car, probably searching for evidence. But evidence of what? Even the police didn't think Devin had committed suicide.

The street felt too open, too exposed for a thorough search. Who knew what neighbors were watching? She turned the key and heard only a muted *click, click* but no engine roar.

She tried again. *Click, click, click.* Nothing.

Her heart began to race and she broke out in a sweat. The car was in the street. Off her property. Just sitting in the car, in the street, off her property, was a violation of her bail. She could go back to jail.

Her hands fumbled for the seatbelt latch. Where was the damn button? Her heart beat faster and faster. She tried to breathe but only a sip of air made it though.

There. That was it. The belt sprang free. She grabbed the door handle and threw herself onto the lawn, tears streaming down her face.

Minutes passed before she felt normal.

She was going crazy. That was the only explanation. No one would put her in jail for trying to move her car into the garage. Would they?

That lady detective didn't like her. Well, the feeling was mutual.

She picked herself off the grass, ignoring the damp seat of her jeans, and punched in Tom's number.

By the time he answered the phone, she had begun to calm down. Still, best to know the rules.

"Meyers." His voice was completely natural. Not rushed, not angry, not frustrated. Businesslike, she decided.

"Hi Tom. This is Kara Grimes."

"Hi Kara. How are you adjusting to being home?"

"Not all that well. I think I just had a panic attack."

"I'm not surprised. You've had a lot to adjust to this last month. Do you know what brought it on?"

"I was certain that awful detective was going to swoop down and drag me back to jail when I tried to move Devin's car out of the street and into the garage. I kept watching the rearview mirror in terror, expecting to see lights and sirens and an entire SWAT team coming for me."

"They're not going to bust you for a few inches over your property line as long as you don't make a habit of it. Did you get the car moved?"

"No. The battery is dead."

"I'll send someone over to give it a jump."

"That's not all. Your investigator wants me to overnight her a key, but I don't know how to do that, stuck here at home like this." She'd always been so efficient. A problem solver. Now she couldn't even figure out how to get a car started or mail a key. She'd become the thing she most wanted to avoid—a burden.

She tried to hold back the tears but couldn't. Tom must have heard her.

"I'll send a courier to pick up the key. Meanwhile, would you like me to find someone for you to talk to about readjusting to life after all the changes you've been hit with?"

Did she? If he set up a counselor of some type and paid that person, would anything she said still be private? "Let's wait on that. Give me a few days and see how I'm dealing with things. If I have another panic attack, I'll let you know."

"That's fine, but just so you know, you would be the patient and whatever you said would be strictly between the two of you. He or she couldn't repeat it to anyone, not even me. Meanwhile, is there anything else?"

"My house. Your investigator searched it and left things in a mess. It was very upsetting to come home and find evidence of someone snooping around. It made me feel unsafe in my own home." She hadn't meant to tell him, really. She didn't want to be an alarmist, but the words came spewing out and she listed every moved item or open drawer.

"That doesn't sound like Fiona. Are you sure it wasn't the police?"

"I thought they were in earlier."

"Let me call Detective Baxter. They're not supposed to be in your home without a warrant. If it was Fiona, she's only doing her job. She's trying to find evidence I can use to get you off. Now, go put your feet up and relax. You've been through a lot. It's my job to do the worrying."

Why did everything he told her make her worry more, not less?

CHAPTER TWELVE

Tom

Four years of college. Then a master's degree before three years of law school. Almost twenty years slugging it out in the trenches and he'd become a glorified babysitter.

Tom swiveled his chair and gazed out the window at the Houston skyline. Rain tapped against the glass like a wet woodpecker, washing everything clean.

He loved the law, but sometimes the hand-holding got him down.

No, it was more the *predictability* of it all. Kara had been home a little over twenty-four hours, just enough time for the relief of getting out of jail to fade and the realization of the fight ahead to dawn on her.

He'd say this was why he made the big bucks, but she wasn't paying him.

Didn't matter. He had a job to do, and if the police had searched Kara Grimes's house without a warrant or notifying him, there'd be hell to pay.

If Fiona had searched it and left evidence of her presence, that would require a different type of hell.

He'd dealt with Det. Baxter before and found it an unpleasant experience—more for her than for him—which led him to believe she might be willing to cut corners to bring him down, no matter the guilt or innocence of his client.

He strongly suspected she'd pulled some sleight-of-hand the last time they met but had been unable to prove it. The thin blue line could be more like a ten-foot wall when it came to protecting a fellow officer.

Her involvement in Kara's case, and his desire to have a hand in her comeuppance, might even have played a part in piquing his interest.

But for now, dealing with Det. Copperfield was a better bet.

Judging by the road noise, Copperfield was in his car when he answered the phone. "Yeah?" was all he said.

"This is Tom Meyers, attorney for Kara Grimes."

"I know who you are." His voice dripped venom.

That didn't sound promising. "Have you or anyone in your department searched the Grimes home recently?"

"On the last day of September, just like the warrant said. We sent you a copy. As for any evidence we found, you'll get that report when we're required to send it."

Working with Baxter must be wearing off on him. He was almost as surly as she was. "I'm talking about a second time. In the last couple of weeks. Have you been back over there?"

"Nope. If we had, you'd know about it. If you're trying to accuse me of doing something illegal, think again. You're not the only one who knows how to play dirty."

"Whoa, cool it. I'm not trying to jam you up. I'm trying to get my notes in order. Keep the timeline straight. My client claims things in her house were disturbed. I figure she's fragile right now and anything out-of-order is a big deal to her. I wouldn't be doing my job if I didn't check with you. I don't know what Baxter told you about me, but I shoot straight. I might bend the rules occasionally, but I *never* break them. Play fair with me and I'll play fair with you."

He'd spent half his life trying to prove he wasn't his father. He damn sure wasn't planning to follow in his footsteps now. Rules were what kept the world in order. Disregard them and chaos ensued.

"If you say so." Copperfield didn't sound quite as combative. "We went in with a warrant. Searched. Left. I'm not saying we put everything back in order, but we didn't tear the place up."

"That's all I wanted to know. Thanks."

He still didn't know whether he believed the guy, but he'd take him at his word. For now.

Which meant he had another, even more unpleasant, call to make. That one could wait until he got home. The rain picked up and a clap of thunder shook the building.

If he didn't leave now, streets would be flooded.

Tom went from the underground parking at his office to the attached garage of his condo without being touched by a drop of rain, yet the air felt like a wet wool blanket and he couldn't wait to get out of his damp clothes.

He had two phone calls to make and he wasn't looking forward to either one.

Instead, he slipped into exercise shorts and a T-shirt and began his katas of *Shorin Ryu* moves, gliding gracefully from one position to the next while following his reflection in the rain-darkened windows. He worked until sweat dripped from his face and the stress faded from his shoulders.

After a sauna and a shower, he felt better, if not completely calm.

Isabell had been in during the day, and the condo smelled of a mix of pine cleaner and the chicken molè she had left in the crock-pot.

Dinner could wait. The phone calls couldn't. He glanced at the time. A quarter past nine. Maybe the call to his mother could wait after all. She was probably already into her second bottle of wine, making a simple chat nearly impossible.

Whatever minor thing had gone wrong with her day was now a major disaster. And somehow it would be his fault.

He poured himself two fingers of scotch and dialed Fiona

as lightning lit the sky for an instant and was gone.

"Tom! How are things in Houston?" Her voice sounded far away over the rain drumming on the patio outside his window.

"Wet. How are things in Louisiana?" He realized he had no idea what part of the state she was in.

"Dry. And cool. If I don't get eaten by an alligator, this might be a nice place to live. Pappadeaux's restaurant has nothing on the real thing. Boudin balls for lunch, then a cup of jambalaya and a shrimp po'boy for dinner. I may be so fat by the time I get home you'll have to roll me down the hall."

He doubted that. She could put on twenty pounds and still be considered trim.

"When you finished your gastronomical tour of the city, did you have a chance to learn anything about our case?"

"A few things. I'm waiting on a mailbox key from Kara."

"I had my secretary overnight it to you. It should be there by ten a.m. You want to give me a hint as to what you know so far?"

"I hate to say much over the phone, and I'm definitely not putting anything in writing, but Devin Grimes is not who we thought he was."

Tom was careful about what he said in public. He had his phone and office swept for bugs regularly, but Fiona was absolutely paranoid when it came to privacy issues.

"Give me a couple more days of digging and I'll bring it to you. Don't know if it will hurt or help our case, but it'll be interesting. I promise."

If Fiona promised, it would be gold. Now for the part he dreaded.

"One more thing before you go, did you search Kara's house?"

Silence from the other end of the line. Finally, "Why do you ask?"

"Kara was upset when she saw her house. Cabinets were left ajar. Drawers not completely closed. Things moved. It gave her the creeps. It frightened her."

"She saw the house after the police searched, right?"

"They were in there two days before her arrest, according to Copperfield."

"If he was telling the truth, and if things were moved since then… Well, if I'd been there—and I'm not saying I was—she would never know it. You say she was frightened. I say she should be because someone was in her house and it wasn't the police and it wasn't me."

CHAPTER THIRTEEN

Fiona

Ten past seven a.m. and the sun told Fiona to get up and move Bluebeard before someone came to open the beauty salon she had parked behind.

Still three hours to kill until Devin's mailbox key arrived. How best to spend the time?

Wandering around a city the size of Baton Rouge randomly showing people her photo of Devin Grimes seemed fruitless. Until now, the majority of her computer efforts had centered on Devin. Maybe it was time to concentrate on Ian Pryor.

Two blocks away she found a drive-thru that sold chicory coffee and sausage rolls. She parked and piggy-backed off their Wi-Fi while she ate.

After an hour, she decided she would have had better luck accosting strangers. She found several Ian Pryors, but the only one in Louisiana was a WWII vet living in a nursing home in Lake Charles who'd recently celebrated his ninety-seventh birthday.

He did look a bit shady with what had to be a toupee and false teeth, but he wasn't faking the missing leg.

Her guy wasn't on Facebook, Twitter, Instagram, or LinkedIn. He didn't have a police record, utilities deposit, parking ticket, or state-issued driver's license. Wasn't tagged in any photo she could find. Wasn't registered to vote. Didn't own property.

He was a ghost. Something that didn't happen by accident.

She got out of Bluebeard to stretch her legs and throw away her trash when a dirty-brown Ford pickup circled the parking lot. The driver, whose face was hidden behind tinted windows, slowed to check her out.

She was used to being stared at, but that didn't make it any more comfortable. Not uncomfortable enough to let her hair go back to its natural color, whatever that was, but still…

A line of people waited to drop off or pick up packages at the UPS store. When the clerk called out, "Fiona Drake?" she shuddered. Nothing like keeping a low profile.

"Here," she said, shrinking into herself.

The padded envelope contained two keys and a handwritten note from Kara.

To whom it may concern,

I, Kara Grimes, am the surviving spouse of the owner of P.O. Box 1735 and give Fiona Drake my permission to open the mail box and remove the contents.

Fiona gaped at the letter. It wouldn't help her and she didn't plan to show it to anyone unless the police tried to arrest her, but the fact that Kara had taken the time to send it meant something. She wasn't sure what yet, but it was good to have the woman's cooperation.

Fiona parked Bluebeard half a block past the post office and walked back. She waited for several people with packages to enter the building before she slipped in the side door.

The key slid into the lock like it had been used yesterday.

Fiona pulled a handful of mail out of the box and into the waistband of her jeans, under her too-large shirt.

She had her hand on the exit door when a mud-brown pickup rolled slowly by Bluebeard. She waited until it rounded the corner to sprint to the diner where she'd eaten the night before.

She sat facing the window and watched as two brown-ish trucks passed, but neither had a trailer hitch on the back.

"What'll it be, *cherè*?"

Fiona jumped as the waitress slapped a menu on the table.

"We got pecan pancakes or scrambled eggs with sausage if you're hungry."

"Just coffee, please."

The waitress *harrumphed* and left.

Now what? She could watch for a stranger to enter, but everyone was a stranger. She dawdled as long as she could over her coffee. By the time she'd finished, the place was filling up.

Lunch time. She couldn't stay forever.

"Two of your blue-plate specials," a familiar voice called out.

"On the way, Joëlle," the waitress yelled over her shoulder.

The postal clerk dropped into the chair next to her. "I thought you'd be long gone after the trick you pulled in there. Opening other people's mail is a federal offence, *chère*."

"Not if you have their permission." Fiona pulled Kara's crumpled note from her pocket.

Joëlle read the note and passed it back. "Not sure that would hold up in court, but I don't see you do nothing so I don't care."

"Look…Joëlle is it?"

"Call me Jo. Everybody does." When Fiona raised her eyebrow, Jo nodded toward the waitress. "Marta is my *tante* on my *père's* side. She know me all my life."

"Okay…Jo. I'm Fiona. The man who owns that box is dead. I'm not sure what he was up to when he died, but I'm sure it was no good. I'm trying to help his wife."

"He cheat on her?"

"I don't know yet. I do know he was leading some type of double life. You said he didn't live around here. I thought I might drive over a few blocks to the next subdivision and show his photo around."

Marta appeared with two plates of meatloaf, dirty rice, and collard greens. She added a basket of cornbread and filled their water glasses before shuffling back to the kitchen.

Jo grabbed a piece of cornbread and buttered it. "If he a smart man, he wouldn't live so close. I'd try over to Bayou Bend. That's close you know, but not *too* close."

Fiona dug into her meatloaf. If foster mom #3 had made it this good, she might have eaten it and not been sent to her room hungry. "Good idea, and I'll try that if I can figure out how to get away from here."

"What's the problem?"

"I think there's a guy in a brown pickup following me."

"You sure? The world is full of brown pickups."

"This one has a trailer hitch."

Jo rolled her eyes. "That narrows it way down. Everybody and their *oncle* owns a boat here. How long you been hiding out?"

"About an hour. Maybe a little more."

"Parking's tight about here. Be hard to just hang around." Jo slapped a ten-dollar bill on the table and shoved her chair back. "If I see such a thing as a brown pickup with a trailer hitch, I'll turn around and scratch my head. If not, I'll head straight in to work."

Fiona pushed the ten back toward Jo. "I've got lunch. Thanks."

Jo started across the street, stopped and looked both ways, shrugged, and headed into the post office.

CHAPTER FOURTEEN

Kara

Devin's Subaru started on the first try. Why shouldn't it? Kara had let it run in the garage with the door open for almost twenty minutes last night while she searched every corner.

Nada.

Even the trunk was empty. It should have contained Devin's sample kit and boxes of medications. If the police had kept them, she wanted them back. Armstead Pharmaceutical ought to reimburse her for their return.

Between Devin's death and her time at the *Gray-Bar Hotel*, she'd missed almost a month of work. Dr. Collier had paid her salary for the first two weeks and kept her job open by hiring a temp to fill in after that. She appreciated his efforts, but she was still short of money and had plenty of expenses waiting.

She drove the Subaru to the office. It had a full tank of gas while hers was almost empty. Should she sell it because it was worth more than her old Hyundai, or keep it because it might last longer?

She'd have to worry about that tomorrow.

Kara's hand shook and she took two deep breaths before entering her office.

April came around the corner just as the door opened. Her eyes went wide. "Oh Kara! I... It's... Welcome back. Things haven't been the same without you," she finally stammered.

I bet they haven't. You had to actually do your job and you couldn't slip out early.

April took a few steps backward and called over her shoulder. "Doc. Kara's here." She shuffled away, never turning completely around.

Dr. Collier came into the reception area and gave her a half-hearted smile. "Well, Kara. Good. Good." Then, as if he couldn't think of anything else to say, mumbled *good* again before going back into his office.

Within minutes, the phone was ringing, patients were arriving for their appointments, and Kara didn't have time to worry about anything but repairing the damage the temp had done to her records.

April rushed to take first lunch before Kara had a chance to ask. That was fine because it allowed her privacy to call Tom. He answered on the second ring.

"Kara, I'm glad you called. How's your first day back at

work going? Nobody's giving you a hard time I hope."

Her heart settled back into a steady rhythm and she realized she'd been worried he wouldn't want to talk to her after her mini-meltdown the day before.

"No one's been rude to me or said anything nasty if that's what you mean. Doc Collier won't look me in the eye. April avoids being alone in a room with me as if she's afraid I'll slit her throat for losing a file or putting the wrong code on a chart. At least that's more direct than the patients who ask questions like, 'How are you *doing*, Kara?' or saying 'Well, you *look* good.' As if I should be wearing a scarlet *A* on my chest or, in my case, an *M*. And they all, every one, glance down to see if they can spot my ankle monitor."

She hadn't meant to let that all spill out, but keeping up a false façade was exhausting. "I really called to apologize for yesterday. You got me home and all I did was complain. I really do appreciate your efforts." She almost teared up when she realized how much she actually meant those words.

"Think nothing of it. You've been through a lot these last few weeks. I can't even imagine all the adjustments. From what other clients have told me, coming home is almost as big a shock as going in."

"That's what I wanted to ask about. I know you can't give me any guarantees, and I won't hold you to whatever you say, but what do you think my chances are of winning this thing?" She couldn't bring herself to say what the thing was. "And if not, and I'm facing the death penalty, I need to start making some arrangements, like putting my house up for sale and updating my will. I think I'd like to leave everything to a battered women's shelter, or to The Innocence Project."

Tom paused and Kara's heart rate picked up again. When he answered, his voice was smooth and calm. "First of all, you can't sell your house now because you put it up to cover your bail, but don't worry about that because the death penalty is off the table. I can guarantee you that. Even life isn't going to happen. As to our win/loss chances, I can't give you any odds yet because we have very little information to work with so far."

Kara's heart sank. How could she make any decisions without knowing what the future held for her?

"Fiona has already uncovered some interesting facts about Devin. Now she's in Louisiana digging up additional information. When she gets back, we'll put our heads together and plan our defense. Can you let me do the worrying for now? I promise things will look better when we know what we're working with."

Kara looked at the calendar in front of her. Indecision was a weight that made every step a chore, every breath difficult, every minute a year.

"I'll do my best," she said.

She counted seven days in the future and drew a circle around the date.

Not being able to sell her house was a blow. She could have used the money. Now she'd have to sell the Subaru. It would bring in several thousand dollars more than her car.

Her whole life had been one calamity after another.

Her father refused to acknowledge her.

Her stepfather abused her.

Her mother grew weaker and weaker before dying too young.

Her friends, except for Helen, were turning their backs on her.

Her husband, the man who was supposed to cherish her, hadn't.

Her name had become a dirty word all over Houston.

All she'd ever wanted in life was a family of her own. Now, it was almost too late.

If she ran away, changed her identity, left everything she knew behind, would her bad luck follow? Was it attached to her name like a shadow or could she reinvent herself and start over?

She glanced at the mess the temp had made of Doc's books. Anyone with a rudimentary knowledge of accounting could waltz in here and siphon off enough for a small nest egg and he might never know.

CHAPTER FIFTEEN

Tom

Driving in to work, Tom left the sunroof open. The air smelled so cool and clean after last night's rain, he promised himself that for once he'd take an actual break at noon and walk somewhere for lunch.

By one o'clock his desk was buried under paper. Four pink Post-it notes stuck to the edge of his computer listed calls he needed to return.

He reached for the intercom to ask Janice to order his usual Asian stir-fry chicken salad when he remembered his promise. Could he really leave the office for a full hour?

The tinted windows let in only a weak stream of diffused sunshine. Sometimes he thought he was turning into a mole-man, living his life under fluorescent lights, scurrying down crowded hallways, breathing recirculated air.

He left his suit coat on the hanger in the corner and stepped out of his office. Janice gaped in surprise as he passed her desk. "I'm heading out for lunch. If anyone needs me, I'll be back in an hour."

She grabbed for her phone. "Do you need me to make you a reservation?"

"That won't be necessary. Thanks."

And just like that, he was outside. Like a kid cutting school or maybe a convict who tunneled under the wall.

Free.

The sun warmed his face, but the air held a hint of the cool front due later in the week.

The sidewalk was full of people in groups or alone, chatting or studying their phones, rushing or window shopping, men, women, white, black, brown, Asian, in suits or high heels, work shirts and steel-toed boots.

A homeless man huddled near a building. A young couple, t-shirts and torn jeans, played a guitar and sang. He left each a twenty.

A laugh bubbled up in his throat. If he were thirty years younger, he'd swear he was running away from home. But he'd tried that once and it didn't work out so well.

He cut across Texas Ave. and into the church cafeteria at The Cloister for lunch at Treebeards. He was about to dig into a bowl of chili when he smelled perfume.

"We meet at all the best places." Allison Palmary slipped into the chair next to him.

"It's good to see you again, Allison." He tried a bite of chili. Perfection.

She buttered a piece of jalapeño cornbread. "I'm glad. It gives me a chance to apologize for the way I acted the last time we met. I shouldn't have lost my temper simply because you bested me. You taught me a valuable lesson about being prepared. One I won't forget."

"Unfortunately, most good lessons are learned the hard way. I hope that one wasn't too painful."

"Not at all. No one cares if your client got out on bail as long as she ends up in prison."

"A word of friendly advice?"

She speared a chunk of fried catfish. "Certainly."

"Asked to be transferred to another case. A loss won't look good on your record."

"Ah, but a win—against you—will look so good. Another couple of years at the DA's office and I'll be able to write my own ticket."

Tom's phone buzzed with a text from Janice. Time to get back to the office. Vacation was over.

He paused by Allison's chair. "It's your decision, but just as an FYI, your detectives, Copperfield and Baxter... The jury's still out on Copperfield, but Baxter's been known to play fast and loose with the evidence. Keep an eye on her. If she tries to hide anything from me in discovery I'll take her down and you'll end up collateral damage. It'll leave both your careers in tatters. You won't be able to get a job sweeping up in any courthouse in Texas. For your own good, get off this case now, before she ruins both of you."

Allison's eyes narrowed. "Don't give yourself so much credit. If I decided to bury something, you wouldn't find it with a divining rod and a backhoe."

He'd warned her. That was the best he could do.

"JANICE," TOM CALLED as he pushed through the office doors. "Call Kara Grimes. Ask her to search her house carefully. And both her and Devin's cars. Find out if she can think of anything, however small, that might be missing but not included on the inventory sheet Det. Baxter left behind. The prosecution is up to something nasty. They're trying to pull a fast one on us."

He needed to be prepared, not blindsided.

Thank goodness he'd gone out to lunch.

Tom sat at his desk, studying every slip of paper he'd amassed in the short time he'd been Kara's lawyer. This was the most tedious part of his job. Going over and over all the paperwork. Looking for any item that might have significance he'd either missed before, or had become important with new evidence.

It would be buried under mountains of worthless forms, hidden among mundane items, or grouped with similar objects.

Whatever it was, it wouldn't be easy to find.

But Allison Palmary already knew what it was and hadn't been willing to disclose it at Kara's bail hearing.

Janice stood half in and half out of his doorway. "I talked to Kara. She'll look for anything missing. Off the top of her head, she noticed that Devin's sample case was missing from the trunk of his car. She'd hoped to return the contents to his boss for a refund."

Tom grabbed the inventory list Det. Baxter had sent him.

Three full pages, single spaced, of medications. All using the scientific or chemical name. How was he supposed to know what they were?

There was one person who would. Devin's boss. Tom punched in the number and waited.

"Armstead Pharmaceuticals." The person on the other end might as well have been asleep for all the interest he showed.

"May I speak to Omar Lloyd, please?"

"Speaking. Who is this?"

"Tom Meyers. I'm the attorney for Kara Grimes. She's interested in returning for reimbursement the excess product her late husband had in his sample kit."

"Wh... What? Wait." Suddenly Omar sounded more interested. "She can't do that. We don't take back medications that have left the premises. That's not hygienic. Or sanitary."

"Yet you allow salesmen to drive around with them in the trunks of their cars and trot them in and out of various doctor's offices. Does the FDA know that?"

"Listen here. You can't talk to me like that."

Bingo. Must have hit a sore point.

"Let's not worry about that right now. What I'm really interested in is a list of medications Devin had at the time of his death."

"I already told you guys. He was an independent contractor. I don't know what he had at any specific time."

"You mean the HPD detectives?"

"Yeah. Them too. The day before your investigator."

Well, double Bingo if there was such a thing. Baxter *had* been there before him. "We don't need to worry about the FDA. What they allow or don't allow is none of my business. I'm only interested in one thing. Protecting my client. To that end, I'll need a list of every medication you've ever given Devin since he's worked for you."

"I don't keep those kind of records." Omar had started whining. He must really be getting nervous.

"What about the last year? Do you have those records?" He really should call the FDA on this guy. He was a menace to public safety.

"I could probably come up with something. Should I send it to those other guys too?"

"Not unless they ask."

Two hours later, working together, he and Janice had gone through half the medications Det. Baxter had listed. Janice spelled out the chemical name, Tom typed it into his computer, and out came the generic name which he checked off the list Omar emailed him.

Tom's phone rang and he almost let it go to voicemail until he saw the name. "Yes, Kara. Did you find anything?"

"I think they took a bottle of morphine." Her voice caught as if she were about to burst into tears.

Shit. That sounded bad. "You had morphine?"

"Not me. My mother. The hospice nurse took all her medications the day Mom died. A bottle of morphine pills the nurse had ordered earlier was delivered the next day. I didn't know what to do with it. You can't just flush those things down the commode, you know. They get into the water supply."

No, he didn't know that but it sounded logical. "What'd you do with it?"

"Nothing. Tossed it into a basket with other odds and ends under my bathroom counter. Q-tips. Cotton balls. Travel-sized toothpaste the dentist gives you. The container worked its way to the bottom and I forgot about it."

"You never took any or gave any to Devin?"

"No. Never. He wouldn't have known it was there."

Janice underlined an entry on the inventory Det. Baxter had sent over.

Hydromorphone, thirty tablets.

There wasn't any on Omar's list.

"Okay, Kara. Don't worry about it. We've got it handled, but I want you to do something for me. Tomorrow, go over to a lab. I'll text you the address. They'll give you a drug test plus take some of your hair to test for drugs taken over the last few months. If you're telling me the truth, you should come up clean."

"I'm telling you the truth." Her voice sounded stronger.

It took him three phone calls and the threat of a lawsuit, but he had his answer. A courier had delivered a bottle of thirty Hydromorphone pills to Kara's mother the day after she died. The bottle had the name of Kara's mother on the label, but that hadn't bothered Allison or Det. Baxter

He'd warned Allison.

She wasn't the only one who knew how to bury evidence under mounds of documents.

The moment she tried anything underhanded, he had the proof to discredit her entire case.

Kara would look like a saint, and Allison would look like the amateur she was.

Whoever said eating lunch at your desk was the only way to get work done?

CHAPTER SIXTEEN

Fiona

After leaving the diner in a rush, Fiona drove until she found a parking lot with a delivery van stationed in front. She squeezed Bluebeard in beside the van and watched the traffic pass.

After ten minutes she'd seen four brown pickups. One was such a light tan it barely qualified as beige. Two others didn't have a trailer hitch, and the one with a hitch didn't have tinted windows.

She was being paranoid.

Before pulling out, she checked the mail still hidden in her waistband. They were all addressed to Ian Pryor.

The letter she'd seen through the postal box window was an ad for Troy's tire store in Comeau. Inside was an advertisement for a tire sale.

She almost tossed the circular onto the floorboard before she noticed the addition in blue ink. *Come in by the 23rd for the best deal.* That was odd because the sale ended on the 20th.

A second envelope contained a flier for another tire store. That one had a note about a different date. A third tire store didn't bother with claiming a sale, just a message about getting the best deal.

Two doctor's offices sent appointment reminders. One was on a Saturday and the other was with an OB/GYN.

She'd never known anyone to need so many tires, and if this guy was selling expired medications to expectant mothers, she'd dig him up herself and kill him again.

Bluebeard started on the second try and she glanced up in time to see a brown pickup with tinted windows fly by like its tail was on fire.

The truck passed an SUV despite a solid yellow line and Fiona couldn't tell if it had a trailer hitch.

She decided to try the next tire store before driving to Bayou Bend.

"I'M SORRY I can't help you." The young woman behind the counter wore a nametag that read *Catherine*. She had short, curly hair, a baby face, no makeup, and the first genuine smile Fiona had seen in three days. "I'd lose my job if I gave out private information about our customers."

"What about looking at his photo? Can you just tell me if you've seen him around here?" Fiona placed the picture of Ian/ Devin on the counter.

Catherine studied the picture and shrugged. "Maybe. I don't know. I've only been the manager for two weeks. Before that I worked out in the bay and didn't necessarily see the customers."

"What about whoever worked here before you? Can I ask them?"

"I don't think so. He disappeared."

"Disappeared? That's weird." Everything about this case was weird.

"You're telling me." Catherine's eyes went wide. "It was all very strange and hush hush. No one will say exactly what happened but my sister works in the hospital and she said he got beat up pretty bad. The owner claims it was probably muggers, but Evan…" She nodded to a large guy repairing a tire. "…said he heard that Corey liked to bet on football and owed money all over town. No wonder he took off, if those kinds of people were after him."

"Can I ask Evan if he knows this guy?" He had his back turned so only his bald head showed. She'd have trouble recognizing him if she wanted to track him down later, although his abundant size might help.

"Better not. He's great about anything to do with tires, but he's on the spectrum and doesn't talk to anyone he doesn't know really well."

"What about the owner? Can I talk to him?"

"Why? He wouldn't recognize any of the customers. Besides, he lives in Bayou Bend. He owns a bunch of these stores."

Fiona glanced at Catherine's blue work shirt and name tag. Just like the one on the guy in Comeau, but then didn't all work shirts look pretty much the same?

"Thanks, Catherine. Congratulations on the promotion. It's nice to see a woman break through the Good Ol' Boy's network in a place like this." As soon as she said it, Fiona realized she meant it, not just as a way of keeping in Catherine's good graces in case she needed more information.

"Who else were they going to ask? Evan can't handle customers and Simon takes off whenever the fish are biting or during alligator season. From my sister's description, I doubt Corey will ever be back."

Before leaving, Fiona took one of the business cards from a holder on the counter. "Is the web address listed here for this store only or for all the stores in this chain?"

"To tell the truth, I've never looked at the website. Mr. Granger takes care of that stuff. I'm still learning to run this shop."

Back in Bluebeard, Fiona used her phone to check out the website. The owners name wasn't given, but all three tire stores that had sent flyers with hand written notes were listed as part of Specialty Tires, Inc.

She dialed the number listed in minute print at the bottom

of the website. A woman's voice gave a generic greeting with no name or useful information.

After the beep, Fiona started in without giving her name and sticking to the story she'd used before. "Hi Mr. Granger. I'm trying to find one of your customers named Ian Pryor. I bought a car from him and the tires are for shit and he said he got them from you. Would you please give me a call back at this number?"

There was nothing left to do but wait. And she was never very good at that.

AROUND THE CORNER from the tire store was a hamburger joint. Fiona decided if Devin didn't like Dairy Queen, maybe he preferred something local. She went inside, ordered a soda, and showed the now rumpled photo to the counter clerk, a young girl smacking her gum.

"I don't know. He looks kinda familiar but I see so many people in a day… Hey Brandon. This the guy who yelled at you for putting onions on his burger?"

Brandon ambled over and glanced at the photo. "Could be. The guy was a real douche. Wanted me to make him a whole new burger. I took it in the back and scraped off the onions, waited till the meat was cold, and gave it back to him."

I'll bet you spit on it, too.

Was the guy Devin, or just another middle-aged white guy

with a paunch and an attitude? No way of knowing for sure.

She could waste the rest of the day showing his photo around town and still not know.

If she wanted to check out Bayou Bend, she needed to leave now. She could always come back later. Besides, the third tire store was on the way, and it might be interesting to see what kind of reception she got there.

Traffic was light and Fiona had plenty of time to think on the drive. No matter what she found at the third tire store, it wouldn't tell her who Devin Grimes was and what he was up to.

She only had the word of Curtis at SureStay that he was Ian Pryor. If Curtis was mistaken, she'd spent the night in a strange man's bed, eaten his chicken noodle soup, and stolen his Pop Tarts.

Although, the mailbox key on Devin's keychain seemed to confirm they were the same person or at the least working together.

Even if she found someone who said the photo was definitely Ian Pryor, she still wouldn't know what was going on, but she didn't need Spidey sense to know it wasn't good— exactly what kind of no good eluded her.

She turned into the last tire store on the list and parked Bluebeard directly in front. She was finished hiding. Time to stir the hornet's nest.

The door flew open and almost hit the wall as she stormed in and stomped up to the desk. "Where's the owner of this dump? Somebody sold me a load of shit and never delivered. I want my money back."

"I'll be happy to help you, ma'am. Do you have a receipt for the tires?" The man behind the counter had a noticeable paunch and the same blue work shirt and name tag as the last two stores. Only his read *Zach.*

"You're not the son-of-a-bitch who cheated me. Where's this guy?" She slapped down Devin's photo.

Zach's face went white. "Um… Um… I think you've made a mistake. He doesn't work here. I've never seen him before."

Yeah, right. You haven't seen him in a couple of months maybe.

Fiona grabbed the pen out of his hand and scribbled her phone number on one of the business cards displayed on the counter. "Well, somebody around here knows him and they better call me ASAP or I'll drop a dime on this place."

Zach swallowed a couple of times and some of the color returned to his face. "Look, I don't know what you're talking about. Give me your name and I'll pass your message to the owner."

"Fuck that. I know your name—Zach—and that's all you need to worry about."

Back in Bluebeard, Fiona didn't know whether to laugh, cry, or throw up. She did know sitting in front of the store wasn't a good idea.

CHAPTER SEVENTEEN

Kara

The solid *thunk* of the door closing behind her might have been the most comforting sound Kara had ever heard.

Not the metallic *clang* of her jail cell. Not the *whoosh* created by the automatic door of her office.

Her door. Her very own door. The door to her home.

It shut out everything that didn't belong to her. Everything that belonged to the outside world.

She sank into her favorite overstuffed chair and rested her feet on the ottoman. Her head hurt. Her back hurt. Her feet hurt. Her ankles were swollen and hurt where the monitor dug into her skin.

But she was home and that's all that mattered.

The fact that she could have been home an hour earlier wasn't important.

Doc Collier wanted to visit a patient in the hospital and had told her and April they didn't need to stay. April practically beat him to the parking lot, but she'd remained behind.

Whatever idiot the temp agency had sent to fill in while she was *away*—she didn't like to think of it as incarcerated—had screwed the books so completely the whole office set-up was vulnerable.

The janitor could have waltzed in and cleaned them out.

Doc Collier had been good to her when her mother was alive and he'd been good to her again now when her life was falling apart.

He planned to retire when the office lease was up in three years, and whether she stayed another week, six months, or the whole three years, she intended to do her best to see that his retirement went smoothly.

In an hour today, she'd straightened out the books and bank deposits. Tomorrow she'd write out detailed instructions for any other replacement. Maybe she should research temp agencies and find one with a sterling reputation instead of one that came first alphabetically.

When her phone rang she almost didn't answer. She was too tired to deal with anything. When Helen's photo showed on her screen, she hit *accept.*

"How was your first day back at work, dear?" The sound of the old woman's voice was even better than the *thunk* of her door.

"Exhausting. How did I ever do this every day then come

home and cook?"

"You'll be back in the swing of things in no time. Meanwhile, I baked enough lasagna to feed an army. Only trouble is, it's sort of hard to carry with my walker. Do you think you could come over and get it?"

"I'm not allowed to leave my yard, but I can come to the edge of my driveway and take it when you get close." Saying the words caused a jolt of pain through her heart.

Outside, she watched helplessly as Helen inched her way across the lawn.

An ear-splitting roar caused her to jump and twist toward the street. A souped-up Camaro pulled in front of the house across the street and screeched to a stop. Little Tyler Henderson stepped out.

Only he wasn't so little anymore.

Still scrawny, but six feet tall with a heavy scruff.

Last time she'd seen him was when Devin yelled at him for messing around near his car. "You thieving little prick," he'd called across the street. "You'll get your head blown off if you try that again." The car was always locked in the garage after that.

She'd heard he was in rehab for the second time.

Kara's blood froze when Helen called out to him. "Tyler, could you help me carry that dish over to Kara? It's kind of heavy for me."

Tyler shot Kara a *why can't you help her* look and slouched over to Helen.

"Smells good, Mrs. H. Is this your famous lasagna? I haven't had any of this since you used to babysit me when my mom worked the late shift."

"Have you eaten yet? There's plenty here."

"Is that okay, Mrs. Grimes? Mom's gone to Reno with her new boyfriend and she didn't leave much in the house. I've been working at the fried chicken place, and if I never eat another drumstick I won't complain."

Well, damn. Just what she needed when she was so tired she couldn't string two words together. A teenage delinquent dinner guest. "Sure Tyler. Go on in. The back door's open. And call me Kara."

An hour later she was full and happy. The company was exactly what she needed to shake off her doldrums. Tyler's stories of working at The Chicken Shack had her in stitches. She still didn't trust him completely, but she understood him a little better.

His life had been every bit as hard as hers, only in a different way. If he had slipped some growing up, she should be more understanding. It wasn't like she hadn't made plenty of mistakes of her own.

Sometime within the next week she was likely to make another. The biggest one yet.

Life would be so much easier if you always knew the right thing to do.

CHAPTER EIGHTEEN

Fiona

Bayou Bend was a nice town with thriving businesses and some beautiful old homes. Fiona loved the ivy and wrought iron railings, but that wasn't likely to be where she'd find Ian. She drove around the outskirts of town looking for a once nice middle-class area on its way down.

She passed the address listed for one of the doctor's offices that had sent an appointment reminder card. She had no intention of stopping. She simply wanted to see what it looked like and where it was located.

That changed when a middle-aged woman wearing scrubs bustled out of the office.

Fiona parked Bluebeard and rushed to catch up with her.

"Pardon me. Do you work for Dr. Lochte?"

The woman's eyes narrowed. "Why you asking? You

pregnant? Lookin' for a good doctor?"

Fiona's spirits dropped. This woman had seen it all and trusted no one. Impossible to fool. Truth might be her only option. "No. It's not for me. I'm looking for this man." She pulled out the increasingly tattered photo.

The woman's nose wrinkled as if she'd smelled something foul. "What you want wit' him?"

She knew him, or knew of him. There wasn't any doubt. "He got a friend of mine in trouble and disappeared."

"If your friend's in trouble, she should find another doctor. Dat man's no good."

Was she talking about the doctor or Devin? "Not that kind of trouble. Legal trouble."

"Either way, your friend should stay clear. Dat man used to come around some. Late. When the office was closing. Don't know what he and the doctor were up to in that back room. Haven't seen him in maybe a couple of months. Doctor's been acting more nervous than usual. And that's saying a lot."

"Do you have any idea where I might find him? Does he live around here?" He could be anywhere in the state. Stopping strangers was like looking for one particular fish in all the ocean.

"I saw him once a year or so ago. Getting gas at a convenience store about six blocks down and to the left. Had on shorts and a T-shirt so I don't think he was working."

"Can I ask you a question? If you think the doctor's no good, why do you stay?"

"Gotta protect my girls. Some of dem he delivered and now delivering their babies. I do my best to keep an eye on the doc, maybe send dem girls somewhere else if they have any problems. I'd report him, but for what? I don't have proof of anything 'cept sometimes his hands shake."

Maybe she could find something on the old coot. Get his license yanked if nothing else.

THE SUN HAD painted the sky a soft pink by the time Fiona found the area the nurse had mentioned. A neighborhood that had the same feel as Kara's. A place where he'd feel comfortable.

When she spotted the convenience store with gas pumps outside, she stopped and filled up. Once inside she placed three twenties on the counter. "Fill up on pump four."

She'd only used thirty-seven dollars' worth.

The man studied the twenties as she placed the photo on top of them. "I'm looking for this man. He lives around here somewhere."

"Haven't seen him." The man moved the toothpick to the other side of his mouth and reached for the money.

She slapped her hand on the stack. "Are you sure? He deserted his wife and kid and cleaned out the bank account. They're about to be evicted."

It was always good to throw in a kid and some financial shenanigans for good measure.

"Haven't seen him *lately*," the man said. "He used to come in here and buy lottery tickets. We joked about what we'd do if we hit the big one. He said find a good-looking senorita and move to Mexico. Maybe that's where he is."

No. He was in the medical examiner's morgue in downtown Houston.

"Got any idea where he lived?"

"Someplace within walking distance. He had a big hairy dog that he'd walk here, grab a beer and a lotto ticket, and walk home. Dog was old and didn't make a fuss so I didn't complain." The guy chuckled. "Called the dog Marley. I guess after that singer. You know, the one with the dreadlocks?"

Getting closer. According to Kara, Devin wasn't exactly an exercise hound so that probably put him within a three-block area.

She'd cruised for ten minutes when she spotted a house with a chain-link fence. A big hairy dog peered out, too old or tired to bother barking.

It couldn't be that easy, could it? She cruised two more streets but didn't see another hairy dog. Of course, the dog could be inside.

She stopped in front of a dry cleaners to think. No point in going in unprepared.

Night was falling fast. People were always more reluctant to answer the door after dark. She'd take time to do a little research. Find out who lived there. Approach them tomorrow.

After picking up dinner at a drive thru, she found a secluded spot to park Bluebeard and pulled out her laptop. Someone in the neighborhood used Gryffindor as their internet name. She tried several Harry Potter characters and presto, she was in.

People were so easy.

Fiona was deep in her research when headlights shone into the bus, blinding her. Someone banged on the side of the bus. "Police. Open up. You can't park here."

What the hell? She wasn't hurting anyone. Why couldn't people just leave her alone? She closed her laptop and slipped it under a seat cushion, out of sight.

"Now. Open this door now. Show us your hands."

"I'm coming. I'm coming." Good thing she was still dressed.

The moment she slid the door open rough hands grabbed her and threw her to the ground. A sharp-toed boot kicked her in the ribs. Then in the hip.

Bluebeard groaned as someone heavy stepped inside and tossed things around.

She tried to reach for the knife hidden in her boot but the man knelt on her arm and grabbed her chin, twisting until she thought her neck might break. The headlights blinded her, but his voice sounded familiar. "Where is he? Where's the lousy son-of-a-bitch hiding?"

She tried to play dumb. "Who?" How the hell had they found her?

The man kicked her again. "The asshole whose photo you're carrying around."

"I don't know. I don't know where he is. I don't know anything except he owes me money." She didn't have to try hard to sound terrified.

"Little girls like you should learn to stay home and mind their own business. Try to play with the big boys and you're likely to get hurt. Now go back where you came from and you might live another day."

He slammed her face into the mud.

As he stood, his weight pressed down on her arm and she was afraid it might break but it sank into the mud instead.

Another loud crash—her built in kitchen?—and the big guy climbed out, followed by the hiss of propane escaping. He tossed a firecracker at the bus, but it hit the side and fell onto the wet ground.

The tall man kicked at her one last time and she swung the knife at his leg. His jeans ripped but she couldn't tell if she hit flesh. He bellowed and drew back to hit her but laughter floated through the air from somewhere nearby and the fat guy grabbed his arm, pulling him away.

She rolled over toward Bluebeard, covering the firecracker before it had time to ignite the propane fumes.

Her last view as they drove off was of a trailer hitch.

CHAPTER NINETEEN

Tom

The Astros were playing their bitter rival, the Dodgers. Tom had a beer, a pizza, and the game in high definition.

He muted the sound during a commercial and called his mother, catching her well into her first bottle of wine but before she opened the second.

The right amount of wine had put her in an unusually good mood. He listened while she went on about her day. She had played tennis in the morning, then gone to lunch at the country club with friends.

Someone whose name he didn't recognize had an exceptionally juicy piece of gossip. He threw in an occasional *Hmm* or an *Oh my* so she'd know he was still there.

The Dodgers batter swung and missed a fast ball for out two as the crowd in the stands cheered silently.

When she mentioned a name he knew, he sat up. Apparently, the wife of her mortal enemy, the judge who'd forced his father into retirement, had worn something completely inappropriate to a charity event.

What on earth could the poor woman have done, worn pearls when diamonds were required or vice versa?

He'd never understand his mother's resentment of the judge when it was his father who'd skimmed money from a client's account and the judge who'd saved his reputation by giving him the option of retiring early and never again practicing law.

When another call buzzed in, he hesitated. Taking it would anger his mother, but not taking it meant he'd have to keep listening.

Fiona's name appeared on the screen. "I've got to take this, Mom. It's business." Business was something she understood and forgave.

After a quick goodbye, he answered his other line. "What's up, Fiona? Have you solved the case yet?"

The long silence caused something deep inside him to freeze.

"Tom?" The voice on the other end sounded like nothing he'd ever heard from his investigator. Soft, shaky...small.

"I don't know what I found, but I definitely found something. Or it found me."

"What happened? Are you hurt?" The words caught in his throat.

"A little worse for wear, but nothing's broken. Two guys came after me. Wanted me to quit asking questions about Ian Pryor."

"Who is Ian Pryor?" Something didn't make sense.

"Devin Grimes. At least that's his name in Louisiana."

Rage built inside him until even his skin felt stretched to the limit. "Get out of there. Now. Come home. We'll let the police take care of this. Can you drive?" How bad was she hurt? She hadn't said.

"No way. They messed with the wrong woman. They tried to burn down Bluebeard. They'll have to kill me now."

Bluebeard? She was worried about that stupid bus?

"Where are you now?"

"Bayou Bend. A ways out from Baton Rouge."

"Leave right now. Go to the Hilton Hotel on Lafayette. I'll have a room booked for you under Louise Spellman, my mother's maiden name. Have them valet Bluebeard." She wouldn't want anyone else to drive it, but they needed to get that eyesore out of sight before someone came looking for it.

He rushed on before she could object. "I'll meet you there first thing in the morning. Don't open your door to anyone but me."

A four-hour drive to Baton Rouge. In the middle of the night? The Mercedes was a more comfortable ride, but in the Porsche he could make it in three and a half. Maybe even three. If he got a ticket, he'd pay it.

Tom threw some things in a bag, paused, opened the safe

hidden behind an air conditioning vent, and grabbed a few more essentials.

Shortly before midnight, he reached Baton Rouge. Most of the city was asleep, but there was always someone awake and willing to sell him what he needed.

After circling the hotel several times to make sure Bluebeard was well hidden, he checked in and texted her. *I'm next door. Get some sleep. Knock if u need me.*

AT SEVEN A.M., Tom tapped lightly on the connecting door. "Fiona? Are you awake? It's Tom. I have coffee."

She opened the door immediately. If she slept at all, it must have been in her clothes. "I hope it's chicory."

"I got a pot of both. Plus beignets, scrambled eggs, and pastries. I didn't know what you liked."

"Right now I want food and coffee. Then we talk."

Fine with him. He needed a few minutes to adjust to the sight of Fiona barefooted, with a bruised, swollen jaw, and favoring her left arm. A clump of something he hoped was mud caked her left ear.

Good thing he'd made that stop on the seamier side of town last night.

He might have to kill someone.

Fiona wolfed down enough food for a football team. With every bite she looked more herself. Tom stuck to coffee. He needed the caffeine.

When she sat her cup aside and leaned back, Tom raised an eyebrow.

"There were two of them. They jumped me. Banged on the door pretending to be cops and I fell for it. That's a mistake I'll never make again." Her eyes, which had been blue twenty minutes ago, turned a fiery green.

"Did you recognize them?"

"The light was in my eyes. One was tall and the other heavy, I know that much." Her right hand clenched and unclenched.

She was lying. She'd kept enough information from him in the past that he could recognize her unconscious tell. She had a good idea who attacked her.

She'd tell him when she was ready. Or he'd keep an eye on her and find out for himself.

"How about we get you back home to Houston and to a doctor?"

"No way. I'm fine. A little stiff and sore. The only thing that really bothers me is this." She raised her shirt to show a dime-sized burn.

"What happened?" Had the asshats put out a cigarette on her body?

"Fat Boy dumped over my propane tank then tried to light up Bluebeard with a firecracker. Luckily it landed in the mud and I was able to get it out before the fumes got too bad."

"So Tall Guy was the one who did that to your face?"

"He wanted to be sure he had my attention."

I may need to get his soon. "Promise me you'll go to the doctor if that burn looks infected."

"I promise, but I have a good first aid kit in Bluebeard and I've been taking care of it."

The piano wire across Tom's shoulders loosened a millimeter. Fiona had never broken a promise that he knew of. "In that case, tell me about Ian Pryor. Who is he and how'd you find him?"

"It's a long story. I haven't found him yet, but I know where to look and was heading there when those two goons jumped me."

"Start at the beginning. I want every detail." He never knew at the beginning of a case what would turn out to be important later.

"Simply a matter of following the breadcrumbs. The pharmaceutical company where Devin worked had his contact info as a phone number to a phone I haven't found yet, an email I didn't know about, and an address at a long-term rental motel. The guy at the motel, where he still keeps a room, never heard of Devin, but recognized the photo as Ian Pryor who uses a P.O. Box in Baton Rouge."

Breadcrumbs my ass. The woman was a bloodhound who could follow a three-week-old scent through a swamp, across a river, and down a sewer. No one could cover their tracks well enough to throw her off.

"And you're sure Devin Grimes and Ian Pryor are the same person?" He didn't need proof, but Baxter and Copperfield would.

"Ian's mailbox key was on Devin's keyring. People keep recognizing the photo of Devin as Ian. Ian has been missing since Devin died. Yes, it all adds up to they're the same person, but I'll feel better later today when I go to the house where I think he lives."

"When *we* go to the house." She'd been beaten up once already. He wasn't sending her anywhere alone until they had the information they needed to clear Kara Grimes's name.

Fiona reached over to scoop up the last few crumbs of beignet "The two men have something else in common."

"What's that?"

"They're both dead."

What was she talking about? That's why they were here.

"Ian and Devin both have birthdates and hometowns of kids who died at an early age. Devin from Alaska, and Ian from Guam. Ian first showed up about eight years ago. Devin appeared three months before he met Kara."

"Who's the dead man our client is accused of murdering?" He was already trying to figure out if this helped or hurt Kara's case.

Fiona lifted one eyebrow. "That's the question, isn't it?"

"True, but it fits with everything else about this case. I've never seen a sloppier investigation. Or maybe I should say trickier. HPD had Devin's car impounded for almost a month and other than removing the sample kit of medications, I don't think they ever searched it. His driver's license had to be a fake yet no mention of his fingerprints not matching was listed on the evidence sheet."

"If he followed Ian's pattern, he didn't have anything in his name. Not the house or the car or the utilities. There was no one to match him to."

Tom could feel the blood run to his face. His breathing got heavier. Those sons-of-bitches. "They found a suspect and stopped looking."

CHAPTER TWENTY

Fiona

Fiona left Tom in his room working on his laptop, researching the owner of the house on Herron Lane.

She could have found twice as much information in half as much time, but she hadn't and she could kick herself for it. Instead, she'd spent the night curled in a chair, wrapped in a blanket, never taking her eyes off the door.

She wanted to take a shower and change. And she didn't mean only her clothes, but her attitude as well.

The shower was heaven. Hot water streamed over her head, clearing away the inertia that had gripped her since she watched the pickup drive away. Clumps of mud fell to the bottom of the tub and washed down the drain. Lavender scented shampoo calmed her nerves.

Steam coated the glass door and she cleared a spot with

her hand in order to watch the bathroom door. She needed to catch the two bastards who did this to her so she could feel safe again. She'd never trusted many people, yet she'd let those two yahoos fool her with the oldest scam in the world.

Now she couldn't even trust herself.

The coffee had given her an adrenaline jolt, and the shower had loosened her sore muscles. It was time to get to work.

Just because she seldom wore makeup didn't mean she hadn't learned how to apply it. After a heavy coat of foundation to cover the bruising, she chose a pale pink lipstick and dark eyeliner to draw the eye up and away from her jaw.

A mid-length blond wig fell forward covering much of her cheek.

A modest dress that hit just below the knee and ballerina flats completed her outfit.

Tom had fallen asleep in his chair, and from the look on his face when he looked up, her disguise was successful.

"Fiona?"

"Think those two guys will recognize me if we run into them again?"

"I'm not sure your own mother would recognize you." He stopped short, obviously realizing his mistake. "I think you're safe, but remember, your name is Louise Spellman for now."

"I can remember that if you can."

He glanced at the purse over her shoulder. "Are you carrying?"

"Are you?" She knew he wasn't. She'd heard him say a dozen

times, *I have yet to come upon a situation that the presence of guns didn't make worse.*

He didn't answer, so neither did she. She didn't mention the knife strapped to her thigh either. Or the pepper spray in the pocket of her blazer.

"Where to first?" he asked as the valet brought his car around.

"The car rental place." She nodded toward his shiny red Porsche. "If you think Bluebeard attracts attention what do you think that will do?"

Tom groaned as he sent the Porsche back with the valet, but the young man grinned at an opportunity to drive it again. Tom groaned again when she insisted they rent a two-year-old Toyota in gray or black.

When the car arrived, Fiona itched to take the wheel. However, in keeping with their low-profile intent, she let Tom have that honor and she rode shotgun, which left her hands free just in case...

The cream-colored house registered to Maria Longcour looked sad and empty. No light showed through curtained windows. No shaggy dog watched through the chain-link fence. No car waited in the driveway. No children's toys cluttered the front lawn.

What worried her the most was no car in the driveway.

Had the woman been warned she was on their trail and pulled up stakes?

They parked in the driveway, and before they got out, a

huge shaggy gray dog of undetermined origin rounded the corner, padded to the fence and let out one lone *woof*—long, low, and loud, the bassoon grandfather from *Peter and the Wolf*—then plopped down with his head on his paws. His tail wagged one time and rested from the effort.

The family hadn't moved. Whether it was the right family remained to be seen.

Tom leaned close. "What's our play?" he whispered.

"Stick as close to the truth as possible."

He placed his hand lightly on the small of her back as she rang the doorbell. For what…comfort, strength, protection? She shrugged him off. She didn't need any of those things.

A teenaged boy—tall, slim, stringy blond hair and a touch of acne—answered the door. "What?"

She pasted on her sweetest smile. "Is Maria Longcour at home?"

"Mom," he yelled over his shoulder.

A small woman appeared—mousey brown hair, fifteen pounds past big-boned, probably pushing forty, but looked fifty—and tapped her foot impatiently. "What?" she asked. Almost as rude as her son.

"Hi, Mrs. Longcour?"

The woman nodded.

"I'm Louise Spellman. This is my associate, Thomas Ringgold."

Tom made a slight choking sound. Was it because she referred to him as her associate or when he realized she knew his super-secret middle name? If that upset him so much, he'd really choke if he discovered how much else she knew about him.

"We represent a law firm in Texas. We're trying to locate this man." She pulled out the photo of Devin Grimes and handed it to the woman. "Do you know him?"

"What's that bottom-feeding scumbag done now?"

MARIA LONGCOUR DIDN'T offer them coffee, or even water, but she did allow them to come inside and ask questions about the man she identified as Ian Pryor.

Her son, Richie, sulked in the corner and occasionally threw out disparaging remarks.

Fiona shot Tom a *let me handle this* look and leaned forward. "We'd like to be sure we have the correct Ian Pryor. What can you tell us about your husband?"

"Well, first off, he's not my husband. I wasn't stupid enough to marry that grifter."

Too bad Kara was. "What'd you mean?"

"He was all sweetness and light when he showed up, but I recognized a con artist when I saw one. "

"Yet you let him stick around?"

Maria grinned. "Like I said, he could be sweet when he wanted to. My husband had passed away two years before. I was lonesome, broke, and Richie needed a father figure."

"Some *father figure*," Richie spit out. "Once in a blue moon he tossed a ball around with me—"

"He taught you how to throw a curve ball and you better be glad he did."

Richie shrugged. "But the few times he actually came to one of my games we'd get home and he'd start bitching at me for not hustling or missing a catch."

Maria rolled her eyes and twisted back toward Fiona and Tom. "Like I was saying, I checked him out before I let him move in. Didn't want some kind of pedophile around my boy. Richie was only nine at the time. But I never let him around my money."

"Nice to know you cared more about your money than me. But he got some anyway, didn't he?"

"Richie, get upstairs. Go finish your homework."

"Now you care. What about all the times you left me so you could be with *him*?" Richie spun around and stomped up the stairs.

Once the thudding footsteps faded, Maria leaned forward and lowered her voice. "This has hurt Richie something awful. He might act like he hates Ian now, but the boy worshiped him. He could probably live with Ian stealing from me, but embezzling from his college fund? He felt so betrayed."

Fiona's heart ached for the kid. That first betrayal was the hardest. Yet something in his eyes was…disturbing.

"Anyway, Ian had ditched a woman and her kid in Vermont before he moved here. He had a job and paid for all the utilities. My late husband didn't leave much besides debts so I let him move in. Big mistake."

"What exactly happened?" This should be good. Fiona's foot began to jiggle so she crossed her legs at her ankles like one of her foster mothers had insisted was lady-like.

"The first few years were great. I was able to catch up on my debts. Richie loved him no matter what he says now. I was happy. The house and utilities are in my name so when I started getting overdue notices on the electricity and water, I confronted him. He would apologize and say he'd had a bad month or the company was behind on his commission payments. After a while I just started paying them. The last year or so he's had more money but that doesn't mean he paid his fair share."

"Have you got any idea where he got this money? Some of it might legally belong to you."

"I doubt it *legally* belonged to him."

"And that was okay with you?" Fiona wanted to feel sympathetic, but she was pissed. She'd seen too many women who let men get by with things because it was easier to ignore than to confront. Get a backbone or get out.

Maria gave a slight chuckle. "He had a knack. I'll give him that. Whenever I got fed up he'd turn on the charm. Whisk me off for a romantic weekend. Buy me a bit of cheap jewelry. Take Richie to some superhero movie. It got old, though. By the time he disappeared I really didn't care."

"Did you report him missing?"

"No point. It's exactly what he did to that woman in Vermont. Ghosted her. Didn't answer her texts or calls. But that's because she was a manipulative bitch and he loved me now, right? I already suspected he had another woman somewhere. I did his laundry. When he left on his business trips he didn't always come back with the same clothes. Only the last time he left, he ran up my credit card and dipped way into Richie's college fund. Good thing the kid has a wicked curve ball. His only hope now is a scholarship."

Tom's eyes lit up. "And you didn't notify the police?"

"I talked to one guy. He said what Ian did wasn't criminal. That I'd have to file a civil lawsuit. Y'all are lawyers. Is that right?"

Tom cleared his throat. "I'm... We're licensed in Texas. Louisiana laws are completely different. When I get back to my office, I'll send you a list of attorneys who might be able to help you."

"That's the problem. I don't have any money to pay a lawyer." Her shoulders slumped like a whipped puppy.

"These guys won't charge you unless they win. Off the top of my head, I'd say you'll have better luck going after the credit card company and bank for letting him get away with fraud. They might be willing to settle to avoid bad publicity."

Fiona tried to catch Tom's eye. All this was good information but didn't prove Ian was Devin and not some doppelganger clone. "What can you tell me about Ian's life before you met him? Are his parents alive? What about brothers and sisters?

Any look-alike cousins?"

"No family that I know of. Only child of an only child was the way he described himself. An army brat who moved around a lot. Both his parents died when he was in his twenties. Supposedly went to junior college in Vermont but I don't know where."

Tom sat forward on the saggy sofa. "What about his health? Is there a doctor we could check with?"

"Ian's put on weight over the last couple of years. He's been diabetic for the last six months or so. I guess he had a doctor. I've overheard him talk to doctors about appointments, but I don't know who. There should be a record on his phone."

"At this number?" Fiona twisted as she pulled a sheet of paper from her purse with the missing cell phone number, being careful not to expose the pistol inside.

Maria nodded but didn't answer. She was getting tired. Fiona needed to wrap things up before the woman threw them out. "The main reason we're looking for your...*Ian* is his relationship with a man named Devin Grimes. Do you know Mr. Grimes? Ever heard Ian mention him?"

"Who is that? Did Ian owe him money?"

"Possibly. You mention you thought Ian was up to something shady. What do you suppose he was doing?"

"I don't know. I'd say drugs if I had to guess, but only because I think he'd started taking them lately. Several times his eyes were dilated or he zoned out. And then there was his work schedule. When he first moved in, he'd stay here one week then work in Houston one week. Lately he spent less and less time here. Coming on Monday or Tuesday instead of Sunday or leaving on Friday. Twice last year he skipped a whole week."

That was interesting. She'd have to ask Kara if he pulled the same thing on her. "Any idea where he went?"

"A couple of times he had to go back to Vermont to take care of some old customers, but mainly he went to Laredo. He claimed the market there was opening up fast." She hung her head. "That's not all."

This was it. There was always something they hid or were embarrassed to admit.

"Men keep calling, asking for him. They get ugly when I say I don't know where he is or how to reach him. It might be my imagination, but a couple of cars keep driving by. One, a brown pickup, parked across the street several times and waited for hours. Two weeks ago, I came home from work and the house had been broken into. Things messed up but nothing stolen. The police acted like I was crazy. That's why I never reported him missing."

A loud and surprising *meow* tore through the room. A gray cat poked its head around the corner and sprinted to Maria's lap.

"Oh, you have a kitten. Does it get along with your dog okay? I've been afraid to get one in case my dog didn't like it." Devin was allergic. This could blow everything.

"She's called Echo because she answers back when I speak to her." Maria lowered her head. "Meow."

The cat answered between purrs.

"I've only had her a few weeks. She's a stray who showed up on my doorstop one day and decided to adopt us. She and Marley are still getting used to each other. Ian was allergic to cats so we couldn't have one until now."

One more brick in the wall in addition to the photo, the mailbox key, his possibly phony life story, and his diabetes. If only she had fingerprints or DNA.

She could ask to use the bathroom. Steal a toothbrush or comb, but how would she know whose it was? "Did Ian leave anything here?" It was worth a try.

"A few weeks ago, I stuffed everything of his into a plastic bag, but somehow haven't had the nerve to throw it in the trash in case he shows up and wants it back. He's got a mean streak when things don't go his way. I hate to admit it, but I'm afraid of him."

"Then seeing him might be dangerous. No telling what he'd do. Give the bag to us. We'll take it to him when we find him—and we *will* find him. Then we'll let you know where he is in case you want to serve him with papers."

"You'll see that it gets to him so he has no reason to come back here?" The hope in Maria's eyes cut through Fiona like jagged glass.

"Absolutely. He won't be back."

CHAPTER TWENTY-ONE

Tom

Tom carried the over-stuffed trash bag to the car and tossed it into the trunk. Fiona, a few steps behind, had an old gym bag and a plastic grocery sack filled with toiletries and an ancient flip-phone.

He twisted toward her as soon as the front door closed and neither Richie nor Maria could hear him. "What happened to sticking as close to the truth as possible?"

Fiona chucked her bundles in beside his. "It wasn't possible."

He pushed back a pang of annoyance. "At least tell me why we have a trunk full of the man's dirty laundry."

"DNA. Plus I'd like to know what he left behind not knowing he'd never be back. Do you have anyone who might be able to retrieve any information off that old phone?"

"Maybe. I suppose it's worth a try. Is this it? Can we go back to Houston now?" Missing money, drugs, Fiona assaulted. He'd feel better when they were home.

"Not on your life. You can go if you want to, but I've got more investigating to do. Somebody trashed my home and I aim to figure out who it was, why they did it, and how it ties into Devin's murder."

"We have enough. We'll sic the Louisiana police on them. Let them deal with it."

"Are you sure that'll get Kara off?"

No, damn it. It might pull her in deeper. And if Fiona left town, they'd never look for the guys who beat her up. "Okay, so we stay. One more day. What next?"

"There's a tire store I want to visit but let's drive back to our hotel and get your car for this."

The woman was flat-out crazy, sending him all over East Baton Rouge Parish, first in one car then another. He'd come over three-hundred miles through the night to protect her only to become what, a chauffeur, an errand boy?

She must have seen the look on his face. "Don't worry," she said. "There's a diner I know of for lunch that will make the drive worth your while."

Tom and Fiona were sharing an enormous plate of fried catfish, fried okra, onion rings, and hush puppies guaranteed to raise his cholesterol ten points, but so good he didn't care, when a woman wearing a postal uniform came through the door.

The woman sauntered over and plopped into the chair across from him. She glanced from Fiona to him and back. "If you thought a blond wig would make you fit in here, you guessed wrong, *chère.*"

"Couldn't resist the food." Fiona forked the last piece of catfish before he had time to grab it. "Jo, this is my associate, Tom. He drove over from Houston to help me."

Back to errand boy for him. And one without that last piece of catfish his mouth was watering for. "Nice to meet you, Jo." He grabbed the final hush puppy while Fiona wasn't looking. Nothing left on the plate but the aroma. He'd have licked the dish but his mother would feel it back in Dallas and berate him for the next six months.

"Hmmm," the woman grunted toward him before twisting back to Fiona. "You know there's a package in that mailbox you been watching. Kinda big for the box, but I was able to stuff it in. You'd have to go to the counter and show ID if it didn't fit in the box."

The heavyset waitress shuffled to the table. "I already placed your order, Joëlle. You two want dessert? I got pecan pie or bread puddin.'"

Tom's ears perked up but Fiona pushed back her chair. "We have to go. Can you put Jo's bill on our tab?" The look on his face must have given her pause. "And one bread pudding to go, please."

With that she was gone and Tom was left alone with a stranger and the bill for lunch.

Joëlle stared at him for several seconds then shook her head. "And I thought Fiona didn't fit in around here."

As insults went, it wasn't the worst he'd ever had.

He paid up, left a generous tip—although the waitress never cracked a smile—and waited for Fiona at the car.

She emerged from the post office carrying a package the size of a pound of coffee. "Go. Go," she snapped as she slid onto the passenger seat.

Tom set the to-go bag with the bread pudding and two plastic forks on the center console so Fiona couldn't steal it while he was busy driving.

"Where to now?" he asked.

"Comeau. Turn left at the next stop light."

He didn't bother asking why.

She held up the brown paper-wrapped package, palpitated it, shook it, sniffed it, and set it in her lap. "I don't know. It could be money. It could be drugs. It could be an early Christmas present."

"Stuff it under the seat. I don't want it sitting out if we get stopped for any reason." He didn't plan to speed, but that didn't always matter with a bright red sports car.

"You don't think that's the first place someone would look?"

"If it's bad guys, it won't matter what we do with it. If it's the police, I'll say it's yours and you'll say it's mine. They won't be able to prove anything." Dealing with crooks all day was wearing off on him.

And getting old.

Once in Comeau, Fiona had him drive once around a tire store. "We're looking for a mud brown pickup with tinted windows and a trailer hitch."

That was the most information he'd gotten from her since breakfast. He'd learned the hard way not to press her…to allow her to let go of information in dribs and drabs as she saw fit. That didn't make it any easier.

When they didn't find the truck she was looking for she pointed to an empty spot in front of the window. "Park here."

He pulled in, shut off the engine, and twisted to face her, raising his eyebrows but not saying a word.

She hunkered far down in the seat where even the top of her head wasn't visible. "See if there's a tall guy named Troy working there today. If he is, check for a limp."

"That's it? No more instructions? No reason why I'm looking for him?" Tall, injured, and driving a brown pickup? He could guess why.

"You're a big-time lawyer. You're used to thinking on your feet. You'll figure it out."

Yes he was and yes he could. He'd taken enough guff for one day.

He grabbed his phone, punched in Google, and spent all of one minute searching before opening the car door.

The inside felt like...a tire store. Stacks of tires on one side, a four-chair waiting area on the other, a display of rims and assorted polishes near the back.

An average sized guy with *Silva* emblazoned on his blue work shirt pulled his eyes away from the expensive red car parked in front. "Help 'ya?" he asked, his voice full of hope.

"I'm looking for some Kumho, Ecsta V710 racing tires for my Porsche. You got any?"

The guy stuttered. "Well...uh... Not in stock, but I can order them for you. Be here by end of day tomorrow."

Thank goodness. At least he didn't have to spend $1,500 on tires that might not even be street legal.

"Where's Troy? I was told he could help me."

"He's not in today. Not feeling well. But I can take care of you."

Sure you can, buddy. And what would your commission be?

"No. I want Troy. Tell him Ian sent me and I want the stuff that SOB owes me. I'm tired of waiting. I'll be back and I expect product or my money returned."

He yanked the door open so hard the little bell on top flew off.

He sailed out with his head high and a smile on his face. Yeah, baby. That's the way it's done.

Tom Fucking Meyers was back. And through being an errand boy.

CHAPTER TWENTY-TWO

Kara

After three days back at work, Kara's constant headache had disappeared and her nightly exhaustion had diminished. The plastic ankle monitor still felt like a ten-pound weight and itched any time she thought about it, and nightmares continued to haunt her dreams so she spent most nights sleeping in the recliner.

April no longer watched her every move as if her life were in danger any time they were alone.

Doc Collier had cornered her in the file room on her first day back, his head hanging and his shoulders slumped. He looked twenty years older. "I feel wretched about your situation, Kara. If only I'd spoken up at the time, but I didn't realize that's who you'd married."

What the hell was he talking about?

"I knew that guy was a crook the moment he came into my office, selling his bootleg medications. I threw him out after five minutes and forgot about him. If I'd said something at the time, you would have known."

Her mouth opened, but she couldn't think of anything to say.

"Some docs will fall for that kind of thing and maybe they think they're doing the right thing for their patients... patients who don't have any money or insurance. Black market drugs are better than no drugs if you're desperate for insulin or antibiotics or whatever. Others are in it to make a buck for themselves. But no reputable doctor would deal with a scoundrel like him. Always on the look-out for the next sucker."

And she was the sucker he'd found.

After that, Doc Collier had reverted to his old clumsy self, with dad jokes and misplaced charts and his lost glasses on top of his head.

The patients were still a problem. Each new appointment brought uncomfortable stares, but that would go away with time as they got used to her.

Mrs. Jenkins actually seemed happy to see her. "Kara! You're back! We missed you. This place isn't the same with old Grumpy Face behind the desk."

Things might work out after all. Maybe she could keep her job. Live her life.

Go on as if none of this ever happened.

Or maybe not.

Mrs. Skelton, that white-haired old biddy, had taken one look at her, swung around, and left the office. But Mrs. Skelton had hated her since the day she forgot an appointment and Kara insisted she still had to pay.

Doc Collier had taken Mrs. Skelton's side, but the doc was too softhearted. That's why he barely had enough saved to retire in three years. Plus Doc hadn't checked Mrs. Skelton's Facebook profile and learned the woman hadn't forgotten, she'd just decided to have lunch with her daughter instead.

None of that was important. What mattered was that she had called Tom Meyers's office and learned he was out of town.

This was Wednesday. She needed an answer by Friday. Monday at the latest.

She waited until the waiting room was clear, then called the doctor to make an appointment for Tuesday morning, bright and early. She could always cancel if she changed her mind.

KARA CAME IN through the back door, dropped her purse, changed into house shoes, and went out the front door to the curb to check the mail.

A yellow Camaro with a racing stripe roared to a stop across the street. The door flew open and Tyler Henderson, accompanied by ear-splitting heavy metal music, spilled out.

The aroma of fried chicken and teenage hormones wafted her direction.

"Hi, Ms. G. How's it going? Kill anybody today?"

"Not yet, but it's early." Six o'clock and her first laugh of the day.

"Let me know if you change your mind. I'll help you bury the body. I got you something."

"Oh?"

"Yeah. My mom called. She's staying in Reno an extra couple of days. She and the fat-fuck got married. To celebrate, I confiscated enough chicken to feed you, me, Mrs. H., and half the neighborhood. Let me take care of Fang and I'll be right over, okay?"

Kara's stomach rumbled. She'd pay for it tonight with world class heartburn but she was hungry now. "Sure. I'll call Helen."

God, she hoped the kid hadn't been drinking. He hadn't been out of rehab more than a few weeks, but even through the fried grease she caught a whiff of alcohol.

Maybe it was onion rings.

She hadn't had time to warn Helen before Tyler burst through the door with enough sacks to cover her kitchen counter.

Helen eyed the bags with suspicion. "Gracious, son, won't you get in trouble for taking that much food?"

"Probably." He gave a belly laugh. "What are they going to do, fire me?" He laughed again, harder than called for.

She and Helen glanced at each other. She didn't have the

nerve to say anything, but Helen did. "Tyler, have you been drinking?"

"No," he insisted. Then, "Yes. Why not? She doesn't care any more about me than to marry a man who can't stand being in the same room with me. Calls me a loser. Her mistake. A waste of sperm. Why should I even try?"

Kara put her hand on his shoulder. "Because it's your life you're destroying. Not hers. Eat up and I'll take you to a meeting."

What was she saying? She couldn't drive him to a meeting or anywhere. Her ankle monitor saw to that. Helen couldn't take him—she could barely see during the day, much less at night—and he couldn't drive himself. Not after drinking. She'd have to call him an Uber.

By the time they'd finished eating Tyler had sobered up. He dropped his head into his arms. "I can't go to a meeting. I've been gone all day. Fang gets upset if left alone too long. If he messes up anything she'll kick us both out.'

He lifted his head, eyes full of tears, "Can he come over here?"

A dog named Fang? She'd never handled anything bigger than a kitten.

"He's sweet, I promise," Tyler begged. "He's really friendly. Too friendly. He got kicked out of police training for being so friendly. That's the only way I could afford him."

"Bring him over for a few minutes. Let's see if we get along. And Tyler... Take the rest of this chicken with you to the meeting. See if anyone there needs something to eat." The smell was already upsetting her stomach. By morning it would be more than she could handle.

Helen gave her a warm hug. "Someday you're going to be a great mother."

No. That decision had already been made.

CHAPTER TWENTY-THREE

Fiona

Fiona sat quietly on the ride back, reviewing the last two days as magnolia trees and Spanish moss whizzed past. Tom was in a better mood than he'd been in since last year when one of his clients was murdered in jail.

Tom looked up from the road long enough to glance her way. "So, what do we know? What do we think we know? And what can we prove?"

"We know Devin/Ian was a jerk."

"Can we prove that?"

"He stole from a widowed mother and her son."

Tom chuckled. "Okay. You've got me on that one. What else?"

"Hell, I'm not even sure we can prove Devin and Ian are the same person."

"I can convince a judge they're the same person, no problem. The thing we don't know is if they are someone else entirely. Someone we don't know about."

"You're right. We don't even know who he was in Vermont but we know he ditched another woman and kid without a forwarding address so odds are he stole from them like he did here." She needed to put that on her list of things to find out.

"What else ya' got?"

A blue heron sailed effortlessly past, perched on the upper limb of a cypress tree, and surveyed his kingdom like the majestic creature he was. Fiona's eyes stayed on him as long as possible before Tom shifted and she was yanked back to reality. "We *think* he's a drug dealer. Those trips to Laredo are suspicious. We know he's a con man. Could be he tried to con the wrong man."

"Someone he cheated or someone trying to take over his territory?"

"I'd like to know what's in that package he got in the mail." She reached under the seat.

"No. Stop. Don't open that in my car. I don't want to take a chance on anything spilling out. Let's wait till we get back to the hotel."

"And let it spill out there?"

He shrugged. "Their problem."

She glanced back, hoping to catch sight of the heron but he was gone. She spent so much time in the city, inside buildings, smelling air conditioning and car exhaust that losing track of the bird caused a tug on her heart, like a personal loss.

"Okay, he's a bad guy, doing bad things, chased by bad people. Does any of this help Kara?" She didn't like the woman but that was a long way from believing she could commit murder.

Tom rubbed a hand over his chin. "I keep going back to his manner of death. There's no sign these people even knew his Houston identity. Besides, break into his house and swap out his insulin? Drug dealers usually like to make a splash. Let everyone know not to mess with them."

A curve in the road caused Tom to slow and she gazed out through the trees onto still, black water. Anything could live in there. "Lack of insulin causes damage to the organs—especially the heart—but in *one* day? After *one* unhealthy meal? What if the insulin wasn't removed in Houston? What if that was done in Louisiana before he left for Kara's?"

Tom slapped the steering wheel with one hand. "And the bad guys knew where he lived in Louisiana. A rival wanting to take over his territory might not want his death to attract too much attention. It's enough to cause reasonable doubt."

Fiona didn't answer. Something inside didn't feel right. A memory she couldn't extract from the jumble of the last few days. She shivered under the warm sun.

A HOT SHOWER and a change into her normal clothing brought

Fiona back to herself. To hell with pretending to be someone she wasn't just to make other people more comfortable.

Tom tapped on the connecting door and waited for her to answer.

"Come in."

He had ditched his suit and wore slacks with a polo shirt, possibly the first time she'd seen him without at least a long-sleeved dress shirt.

He didn't look nearly as wimpy as she'd imagined.

"Are we ready for the *big reveal?*" He tossed the brown-wrapped package from one hand to the other.

Fiona yanked the plastic liner from a trash can and spread it on the table. "Let's see what we've got."

He placed the package in the center and withdrew a pocket knife smaller than the first two joints of her little finger.

She couldn't help herself. She let out a snort of surprise. He'd have a fit if he knew about the Smith & Wesson double edged blade strapped to her thigh. She'd tried the Marine Ka-Bar, but the S&W was a better fit. "Where'd you get that, a vending machine?"

He flashed a proud smile. "Don't laugh. I can get this thing through any security system without a *beep.* Even a wand or pat down misses it."

He cut carefully around the end, saving the tape and postmark, then down the side. The paper unfolded revealing white powder. "What is it, cocaine?" He reached out his finger to test it.

"Don't!" She slapped his hand away. "Smell that? Just a hint of acrid. I think it's rat poison."

Tom rubbed his hand vigorously against his pant leg although he hadn't actually touched the powder. "How do we know?"

"Find a rat and feed it to him?" She was the poison expert now?

"Then what, wait to see if it dies or gets happy?"

This wasn't funny. They shouldn't make jokes. "You have to have a court order to test kids for drugs, but you can buy home test kits to test surfaces for drugs. I had a foster father who'd whip out his tester and swab down your hands or backpack any time you giggled or laughed. One day I ate a powdered donut just to drive him wild. I thought he was going to have a heart attack." Why was she telling him this? She never talked about her past. "Poisons are different. I'm thinking you'd have to send this stuff to a lab."

Tom sat his mini-knife to the side as he gathered the plastic and twisted it into a knot, sealing the powder inside. "If necessary, I'll do that when we get back to Houston. It should come from the law firm." He carried the package to the room safe and locked it inside.

Fiona pushed away from the table, palming Tom's tiny knife, and paced the floor, thinking as she talked. "So the tire people killed Ian—since that's what he's known as here— because he tried to cut in to their territory or he cheated them—"

"Or they wanted to cut into his territory."

"But he disappeared and they don't know what happened to him."

Tom put his feet on the coffee table. "Why not kill him outright? That insulin swap was tricky in so many ways."

"They didn't want to call attention to themselves. Better for him to die in his own bed of natural causes."

"Okay. I can go for that."

"Then he didn't die and they lost track of him. They don't know about Devin. They're panicking and thinking he might show up and try to kill them." There, she'd figured it out.

"All well and good, and probably correct, but who are these *tire guys* and how do we prove they were involved?"

Damn Tom. He was always so logical. Her knife held a drop of blood from the tall one—Troy?—would that hold up in court?

"Let's check out the tire store employees tomorrow. We can start with Troy and Zach, but also a guy named Granger who owns all the stores." No point in checking on Catherine. As a new manager, she didn't seem to know anything.

If nothing else panned out they could always hunt for the missing Corey. He might be willing to talk.

CHAPTER TWENTY-FOUR

Tom

Tom went back to his room to check his email and make a few calls. Just because he'd left the office didn't mean business waited for him to return.

Fiona had her nose in her computer before he left through the connecting door, already collecting information on the *tire guys*.

Twenty minutes later, a low rumble from his stomach pulled him away from the notes he was making on the Marcus Bradley, Jr. case.

He crossed the room and tapped on Fiona's door. "Ready to eat?"

She never glanced up as she scribbled more notes to add to the pile beside her. "I might order a sandwich from room service later. The ownership of the company that has the three tire stores I checked yesterday is a tangled mess. Nobody named Granger is listed as an officer, but there are two more stores under the corporate umbrella. Another tire store in Lake Charles, and an electronics shop in New Orleans."

"Leave it for an hour. We'll go to a nice restaurant, eat a good meal, and come back with a clear head. I've already called the valet for my car."

"Which one, the red flash or the gray ghost?"

He'd never named his cars but kind of liked the idea. "Which do you think? Come on. I'm hungry and Flash is waiting."

The concierge had recommended a five-star restaurant only a ten-minute drive from the hotel. Low lights, candles on the table, tux-clad waiters. His type of place.

But probably not Fiona's.

One glance around and he realized the ritzy atmosphere might make her uneasy.

"They say you can't get a bad meal in Louisiana. Want to ditch this place and try the one down the street?" This restaurant might be top notch, but the rest of the area wasn't.

She shot him a look that would stop an elephant in its tracks. "What's the matter? Embarrassed to be seen with me? I know which fork to use. Table manners were beaten into me at an early age."

Since he never knew with her if something was literally true or a joke, he decided to go with joke. "Good. You can teach me."

"May I interest you in a bottle of wine?" A waiter with a phony French accent hovered over their table.

Tom raised an eyebrow. "What do you think? One glass shouldn't keep us from working tonight."

She glanced up at the waiter. "Do you have a *Pouilly Fuisse* available by the glass?"

"Yes, Ma'am. The 2018 Louis Latour is an excellent choice."

Every time he was with her, she surprised him. Maybe he'd finally turned into a rich prick who secretly looked down on those less fortunate.

He'd heard people grew more like their parents as they got older. Please God, don't let him become his father.

Sure, he'd never steal from widows and orphans, but was there some little part of him that thought he had better taste in food, music, clothing, than most of the people he met?

He pushed the thought aside and studied the menu.

When they'd been served, he gazed at her crab au gratin. Maybe he'd made a mistake. "Hey, Miss Manners, any chance you'd consider sharing?"

She eyed his *Poisson en Papillote,* the aroma of Cajun spices rising from under the parchment. "Maybe. If no one's looking. I wouldn't want to risk my membership in the etiquette-for-dummies club." She scooped a large helping onto his plate, strings of creamy cheese dangling from her spoon. Then she helped herself to half his fish.

Every bite was better than the last.

The meal, the wine, the conversation, all made for a perfect evening. He hated to see it end. He hadn't enjoyed himself this much in ages, but Fiona was getting antsy. Time to call it a night. "Guess we should get back to work and see if we can clear our client's name."

They had stepped around the corner toward the parking lot when Fiona stumbled over a broken brick in the sidewalk. She leaned on his arm and lifted one foot. "Damn. I broke the heel of my boot."

"Let's see." No streetlights reached them, so he pulled out his phone and used the flashlight to study the heel. It wiggled but wasn't completely broken off. "I think we can fix that with some glue back at the hotel. Wait here while I get the car so you won't make it any worse." He glanced around the empty street. "I hate to leave you in the dark like this."

"Go. Go. I'm fine." She leaned against the wall, disappearing into the shadow of the building.

He could see the parking lot and his car less than half a block away. She wouldn't be alone more than two or three minutes. He speed-walked the rest of the way, keys in his hand.

A panel van raced past him—lights off—as he opened the door to his car. "Fiona, watch out," he yelled, worried she might step into the dark street and be hit.

Brake lights flashed as the van skidded to a halt. A mix of shadows tumbled out the side.

Cold chills ricocheted through his body, landing in his heart. He grabbed the weapon he'd purchased from some street punk last night then abandoned his car with the door standing open as he flew down the street. Traveling on foot was faster than maneuvering out of the parking lot.

Fiona cursed, but the sound was muffled by the number of bodies surrounding her.

Tom had opened the expandable steel baton by the time he reached the van. He'd worked out with swords and batons before, if only for exercise. He knew the damage they could do.

A baton multiplied the force behind it, moving faster than any hand. Its heavy tip landed with a devastating impact. He swung and connected with one of the shadows. By the sound of the crunch and the man's scream, he'd broken the guy's arm.

He swung again. The blow was cushioned by the man's jacket but still managed major damage.

Someone tall swung at him. The blow landed on his shoulder and a bolt of lightning radiated down his arm. He shook it off and lashed out again, earning a yelp of pain in response. Another blow grazed his chin, but he'd seen it coming and turned his head so little damage was done.

Moonlight glinted off a knife in Fiona's hand. Where had she gotten that?

The tall man yanked her arm up high and twisted. The knife clattered to the ground. She was lifted bodily and tossed into the van.

The attackers had closed in too tight for Tom to manage a full swing. Instead, he brought the butt of the handle down onto the nearest head. A smallish guy crumbled, but his friends pulled him into the van and slammed the door.

He had time for one last blow.

The baton hit the side of the van, leaving a long scrape down the side before breaking the tail light. The vehicle pulled away before he could note the license number. He followed around the corner but lost it after two blocks.

Cement pounded under his feet as he raced back to the spot where the attack occurred. All that was left was her broken boot heel. She was gone.

Forget everything he'd ever believed. Next time he'd buy a gun.

"FOR THE FIFTEENTH time, I've told you everything I know." Tom slammed his now cold coffee on the table. "Four guys, one tall, one short, pulled up in a dark panel van, make and license number unknown, grabbed my assistant, and took off."

The older detective, Werner, hitched forward in his chair and eyed the connecting door. "And this woman…" He glanced at his notes as if he didn't already know the answer. "Fiona Drake. She was your assistant?"

"She *is* my assistant." Why were they spending time talking when they should be searching?

"Then why is she registered as Louise Spellman?"

Not again. He dropped his head into his hands.

"Are you married, Mr. Meyers?"

"No."

"Is Miss Drake?"

"No. Neither of us is married. She is my associate. We are here on business. She was assaulted last night and I thought she might be safer using another name until I could get here to protect her."

Phelps, an obvious rookie, flicked his wrist and expanded Tom's baton to its full twenty-six inches then parried it like a light saber, making *Star Wars* sounds under his breath. "And this is what you brought to protect her with?"

"Is that even legal, Mr. Meyers? Where would you buy a thing like that? It could be dangerous."

Of course it was dangerous. Why else would he have brought it? Two detectives. One too old to care. One too young to know better. Showed where Fiona's abduction ranked with the Baton Rouge police department.

Werner took the baton from his partner. "I'll tell you what I think, Mr. Meyers. You and your secretary came here, across the state line—"

"To Louisiana where people like you think anything is allowed," Phelps interrupted.

"For privacy to engage in a little hanky spanky." Werner waved the baton around. "Things got a bit too rough for Miss Drake and she lit out. Now you don't know where she is and you're worried she might cause a stink so you call us and invent this fairytale about a mysterious van and four imaginary shadow people."

"Five people. One was driving."

Phelps stood over him, glaring down. "Perhaps we have it wrong. Maybe you didn't come here together. She got here first and checked in under a fake name. Her van had a tracking device underneath."

So that's how the bastards found us.

"I mean, you did come prepared with a deadly weapon." Phelps nodded toward his baton.

"That's not a deadly weapon. It's a baton I use in my katas." Both of the detective's faces were blank. "Practice moves. I had forgotten it in the car the last time I went to my dojo. I grabbed it when I heard Fiona scream." Screw the truth. Those guys didn't deserve it and would use it against him if he told them.

"Was she hiding from you, Mr. Meyers? Were your attentions unwelcome? You are the one with the black eye, yet you claim to be some type of martial arts expert."

He didn't claim to be anything. *Shorin Ryu* was developed for self-defense. He used it for exercise and to relieve stress.

Werner joined his partner. "Are we looking for a body, or should we check the hospitals?"

Shit. He was going to have to find her himself.

CHAPTER
TWENTY-FIVE

Fiona

The cold steel felt soothing against the road rash on Fiona's cheek—except when they hit a pothole. Which was often. Multiple hands had grabbed her and thrown her onto the floor of the van like a bag of dirty laundry, causing her to hit her head and lose consciousness. When she awoke, her hands and feet were tied and her eyes covered.

They'd taken her S&W double edge on the street. A shift of her hips told her the pistol she carried at the small of her back was gone also. She'd only had the thing twenty-four hours, buying it off a street kid on her way to the hotel last night.

Nothing left but her wits and they weren't feeling too sharp after the blow to her head.

It might be possible to scoot up the blindfold enough to get an idea of her surroundings, but she could learn more by playing possum and listening to their conversation.

She counted three separate voices, but felt the presence of at least one more.

"We need to see a doctor, now. Zach's arm is broken and I'm gonna need stitches."

The voice was high and squeaky with an edge of panic. She didn't recognize it. Were they bringing in hit men just for her? If so, they should pay for better quality.

"I didn't get stiches when the bitch cut me. Suck it up, you pussy. You knew what you were getting into."

That one had to be Troy.

"The jerk who came running down the street with a stick smashed me in the rib cage then conked me over the head. I almost passed out, but you don't hear me complaining. I've stopped the bleeding on Lance's thigh. It wasn't that deep. Zach's arm will be just as broken an hour from now. We have to report this clusterfuck to the boss and see what he wants us to do."

Fiona's heart sank. The voice was no longer soft, feminine, but definitely female. Catherine. The one person she thought had nothing to do with any of this mess. She wasn't only involved, she was the leader.

A moan came from the seat behind her. "An hour, tops. I can't wait any longer. Get me something for the pain. I'm dying here."

Someone tossed what rattled like a bottle of pills. "Here. Only take one. We still have work to do."

"Screw you. This sucker hurts."

She could count Zach out. He wouldn't be worth much in five minutes. Lance wasn't any better. That left Troy and Catherine and someone somewhere in the back she hadn't heard from yet.

A deep voice bellowed from the rear of the van. "Quit bickering or I'm out of here. You two should have settled this the first time. Now the rest of us have to fix it. You better hope the boss doesn't rip you a new one."

Okay, that was five. The four that grabbed her and the one driving. Troy, Catherine, Zach, Lance, and new guy. He was the one who worried her.

She didn't know how old he was, how big he was, or how good he was.

She'd have to take him out first.

The van came to a stop before she had time to act. Everyone piled out, yanking her to her feet last. At least they were untied now. The blindfold had worked up enough that she could see the bottom half of everyone's legs.

Troy—he was obviously tall—and Catherine—she was short—each took one arm and led her up a flagstone walkway lit by the soft glow of solar lanterns. Zach stumbled unsteadily ahead of them. A pair of worn tennis shoes and a pair of lace-up work boots followed behind.

The tennis shoes would be Lance—unprepared, flighty, probably imbibed in their own product.

The work boots worried her—organized, capable, ready

for any eventuality. Or maybe he just thought they made him look cool.

They went up three steps, before ringing the bell. The first notes of *Ode to Joy* chimed somewhere inside. If she tilted her head back just right she could see the bottom edge of an ornate leaded glass door.

Slacks and dress shoes answered the door. Ice from a drink of—she took a deep breath—bourbon sloshed in a glass. She could use a nip about now. "What the hell are you doing here? My wife is watching TV upstairs."

"You said to find out what she knew," Troy stammered.

"Yeah. For *you* to find out what she knew. Not to drag me into this." The boss hissed, barely above a whisper. "And did you? Find out?"

"Not yet. We needed a quiet place to work on her."

"And you thought my house with my wife and kids was that place? How do you even know where I live? Did you tell them after I told you not to?"

Was this Granger, the boss Catherine mentioned? He twisted toward Catherine's feet and Fiona felt her flinch. *That bitch. She's in this up to her pert little nose. Acting all innocent. She needs to go down. Right after Work Boots.*

The man gulped down the rest of his drink and tossed the ice on the ground. "Never mind that for now, just get her out of here. Find out what she knows and feed her to the varmints where you left Corey. We can't have her running around talking, or the badgers will be after us."

Troy took a step forward and lowered his voice. "What about her friend? He broke Zach's arm and dislocated my shoulder."

"This just gets better and better. I guess I don't have to ask if he saw you." He spit the words out. "I thought you promised to clean this up with no more problems."

Catherine sputtered, indignation causing her voice to take on an unpleasant pitch. "He said you told him to bring her to you for questioning."

"And you believed him? You're just as big an idiot as the rest of them. Now scram and take care of her before I decide to be rid of the lot of you. I have to go upstairs and lie to Heidi about who was at the door this late."

While he was still issuing orders, Fiona managed to trip herself and fall on the brick steps. Troy yanked her upright. He was close enough to see part of his face and one arm held against his body with a belt. This time she managed to protect her head as they tossed her into the van.

She huddled in a fetal position as Catherine tied her feet.

THE VAN BOUNCED and jolted over rough roads and Fiona could smell the swamp. No street lights or passing cars lit the inside. They had left civilization and any hope of help behind.

No one spoke for at least twenty minutes, but Zach snored on the seat above her.

Good. That gave her time to maneuver Tom's mini-knife from the top of her boot and begin sawing the twine around her ankles.

Only one strand held the rope in place when the van pulled to the side of the road and stopped.

Catherine twisted in her seat and leaned over Fiona. "Look. This was all a big mistake. These guys went too far. We only wanted to find Ian. He disappeared with something that belongs to us. If you'll tell us where he is, I'll give you Troy's share to make up for the harm he caused and we'll call it even. Deal?"

"Wait a minute. Make Granger pay her. I earned my share."

Fiona could imagine the *shut up you fool* look Catherine shot Troy.

"I don't know where he is." That sounded pathetic even to her own ears. "I've been looking for him too. Cut me loose and I'll help you."

"What good are you if you don't know? Are you sure you don't have any information to share?"

"Let me have her. I'll get her to talk." Work Boots's voice carried more than a hint of excitement at the prospect. A jolt of fear shot from her head to her gut and back.

Between the damage she and Tom had done, she was dealing with a bunch of cripples. Work Boots was the only exception. If she could avoid him, she had a good chance of getting away. But if she didn't make it, she refused to sic them on Kara. That woman wouldn't have a chance, even against a gang of cripples. "I know he went to Laredo and then on to Hidalgo. I have a couple of sources down there. My Spanish is pretty good. Let me go. I'll find him. One of you can go with me if you don't trust me."

"We know about the source in Laredo," Troy scoffed at her. "Mr. Granger already sent somebody down there looking for him and to Houston."

Troy yelped as Catherine punched his sore arm. The bitch couldn't even pretend they'd let Fiona go now. Troy had said Granger's name twice. Plus they knew about Houston. That put Kara in danger.

One more thing to try. "Okay. Okay. I have a package of coke back at my hotel."

Someone snorted. Lance? "Did you get it from his post office box? You go right ahead and keep that. Try some on us."

She was down to her least favorite option.

Work Boots slid the side door open and climbed out.

She kicked both feet forward as hard as she could, plunging them into Work Boots's stomach.

He let out an *ooof* and doubled over.

This was it. Do or die. Literally. The last thread of twine around her ankles parted as she scrambled out of the van. The blindfold had come off and she could see him for the first time.

And there was a lot to see. Big. Bald. Muscular. Missing teeth. A malevolent jack-o-lantern glaring at her with murder in his eyes.

The sight froze her in place.

Evan, from Catherine's garage. He might be mentally disturbed, but he wasn't on the spectrum. Not unless there was a spectrum for evil.

Still doubled over, he made a grab for her arm. She jabbed Tom's toy knife in his neck. The blade broke off but not before the rope around her wrists was coated in blood.

CHAPTER TWENTY-SIX

Kara

Exhaustion hit Kara like a slap in the face. It slipped up on her unannounced. She'd stayed late to do the monthly inventory hundreds of times. Why was this time so different?

Maybe because it wasn't exactly a *monthly* inventory if no one had done it since Devin died. Closer to quarterly.

April's husband picked her up with the kids in the car and they went out for hamburgers. Only she and Doc Collier were left.

He spent most of the evening in his office reading up on the latest information about Alzheimer's, only coming out when he ordered them each a Cobb salad from the restaurant downstairs.

Lisa Dunwood had brought her husband in earlier for

their annual flu shot, then left him in the front office while she talked to the doc. Mr. Dunwood, Hugh, had proceeded to tell Kara about a fishing trip he'd taken with his dad in 1941.

The same story he'd told her when they arrived.

Only the second time, he seemed to think she was his daughter and had gone on the trip with him.

The story left a hollow space in Kara's heart. The Dunwoods had been coming to the office since she first worked on the doc's books from home. She even remembered their daughter, Heather, before a truck hit her, killing her instantly.

Sometimes life was so damn sad she didn't see the point of it.

"How's it going, Kara?" She glanced up to see the doc standing by her desk. "Do we have enough supplies to last till the end of the month?"

"Not hardly. We're barely going to make it to the end of the week. The company is in California so if I email this order form to them in the next twenty minutes we can have the order by Monday. Otherwise it might be Wednesday."

She had purchased twice as much as necessary in case she wasn't here to make next month's order.

"What if I agree to pay for expedited shipping and we both go home? You can finish in the morning."

That sounded like heaven.

"Grab your purse and I'll walk you to your car. A beautiful young woman like you shouldn't be traipsing around a dark parking lot alone."

Doc Collier was sixty-seven, with white hair and glasses. He had ramrod posture. Except tonight when his shoulders slumped.

Had time slipped up on him also while she wasn't looking, or did today's visit with the Dunwoods drag him down?

"Don't worry about me. Tortellini's is still open. I'll ask the valet to keep an eye on me until I'm in my car."

For five dollars the valet was happy to stand in the same spot and not move while she walked six cars down to Devin's Subaru. She even waved to him as she drove off.

She was almost home when her phone rang. Helen's name showed on the ID.

"Are you at home?"

"Not yet. This was inventory night. I'll be there in ten minutes."

"I think someone may have been in your house."

"What'd you mean?" Her heart rate kicked up a notch.

"The lights were on earlier when I went out to get my mail. Now they're off. Do you have them on a timer?"

No, damnit. She meant to get one now that she lived alone, but she kept forgetting until she walked into a dark house.

"It's likely nothing. Don't go in there, Helen. Not before I get home."

"So it's safe for you but not for me?"

What was the old woman going to do, throw her walker at a burglar?

"Wait for me, okay? I'm only a block away."

She rounded the corner with tires squealing and pulled into her driveway. Helen stood in the front yard.

Great place to wait, Helen. Maybe you can trip anyone who runs out the front door.

"I called 911." Helen maneuvered her walker across the grass. "So there's no need for you to go inside."

"For a possible burglary? We'll be waiting here all night."

Helen grinned. "Well… I may have suggested they could still be in there."

Sirens sounded in the distance and Kara slumped against the cool metal of her car door. More strangers traipsing through her house.

The first batch of uniformed officers may have been strangers, but Baxter and Copperfield showed up half an hour later. Neither looked happy about being called out after eight at night.

They all sat around Helen's table, out of place in the cheery yellow kitchen.

Baxter scowled, knitting her eyes so tight together she had only one long eyebrow to match her Hitler mustache. "No one was in the house. The back door may or may not have been tampered with. While the house was disheveled, I've seen bigger messes without a break-in. Since nothing was missing, we can't be sure anything happened."

"I didn't leave my house in that state this morning. I always make my bed." She hadn't actually slept in her bed but they didn't have to know that. "Anyway, how do you explain the photo of my husband that's missing from the mantel?"

"Maybe you were in a rush this morning and forgot. You might have moved the photo when you were dusting? At any rate, there were plenty of things in the house worth more than that silver frame."

Helen *harrumphed* and straightened in her chair. Fire lit her eyes. "How do you explain the lights that were off, then on, then off again?"

Copperfield glanced from his partner to Helen and back. "Timers? Lots of people use them to make a house look like someone's home."

"Did you *see* any timers?" It seemed impossible, but Helen's spine stretched even taller.

Baxter's eyes bored into Kara. "Maybe they were removed before we got here?"

Kara was afraid Helen might explode. "I told you. She wasn't home yet from work when I called you and she didn't set foot in that house until you walked through it with her."

How many times had she teased Helen about all the true crime shows she watched on TV? They were certainly paying off now. She might have to start watching if she were going to keep dealing with the police.

"One phone call to my boss, Dr. Eugene Collier, will tell you what time I left work. The valet at Tortellini's can confirm what time I got to my car, and I'm sure Helen's phone will show when she called me and 911. If you doubt all of them..." She pulled up her pant leg. "…the court will have a record of where I was at any minute of the day."

For once her ankle monitor didn't seem so intrusive.

CHAPTER TWENTY-SEVEN

Tom

Getting rid of two detectives wasn't easy, but they had no evidence, and Tom refused to go with them willingly.

"We'll expect you at the station by eight to make a statement," Werner demanded.

"Make it nine. I don't get up early." If he hadn't found Fiona by that time she was probably dead.

He watched from his third-floor window as they exited the hotel and approached their unmarked sedan. The car was parked slightly past the glow of the marquee, making it almost invisible if he hadn't known where to look.

Not something that had happened by accident.

No overhead light came on as they opened the doors. After several minutes, the sedan hadn't moved. They were waiting.

And keeping an eye on the hotel entrance in case he left.

They could watch all night, and he hoped they would. They'd never see him.

Tom took a moment to scan the research Fiona had gathered, making note of any address, then took the stairs down to the first floor and out the service entrance.

Fiona's van was too distinctive, and his rented Toyota was parked in the garage. If he left in it he'd have to drive directly past the waiting detectives.

Werner and Phelps had insisted he ride back to the hotel with them, so his Porsche still sat in the parking lot near Fiona's abduction—if no one had tried to steal it.

He jogged the whole way, keeping to the shadows to avoid any prying eyes. He'd had enough trouble for one day. The sight of Flash, all in one piece, allowed him to breathe for the first time in hours.

Where to first?

If he were a cop, he'd have checked all over the city for security cameras. But he wasn't a cop and Dumb and Dumber hadn't bothered.

He did know which way the van had headed and that's where he went.

Two miles later he had a decision to make. Bayou Bend or the Comeau tire store?

The tire store was dark inside but well-lit outside. No van with a broken tail light or brown pickup with tinted windows and a trailer hitch graced the parking lot. He circled to the back, but no sign of them there either.

Windows on the big bay doors were located near the top. Tom pulled Flash as close to the center door as possible and climbed on the roof to peer inside. Scratches on the roof were the least of his worries.

The bay was empty.

No point in cruising by Troy's place. He lived in a third-floor apartment. Hard to get an uncooperative hostage up three flights of stairs unnoticed.

And Fiona would be uncooperative. He refused to believe anything else.

The next store listed in Fiona's notes was near Bayou Bend. A detour to check it out didn't slow him down. At least that one didn't require him climbing on top of Flash. Windows in the store allowed him to see through to three empty bays.

Like Troy, checking Zach's house wasn't worth his time. Zach lived at home with his parents and little sister. Not even those idiots would risk taking Fiona there.

Tom sailed into Bayou Bend at three in the morning. The town was still and silent. Closed stores. Empty streets. Lights circling from green to yellow to red for no reason.

Maria Longcour's house was as dark as the rest of the town. That didn't faze him. He banged on her door, counted to ten, banged again.

The porch light flicked on. A female voice shouted, "Who's there?"

"Tom… Thomas Ringgold. We spoke earlier."

"What the hell do you want at this time of the morning?"

"I'm looking for my associate, Louise Spellman. Have you seen her?"

"I'm sorry if your lady friend got drunk and ditched you but she's not here and I don't have any idea where she would have gone. Now go home and sleep it off. I have to get up for work in two hours. "

He banged again. Harder. "Some of Ian's friends grabbed her off the street and shoved her in a van. They had weapons. If you have any guess where they might have taken her I want to know. *Now!* Open this door and let me in."

The door cracked open the length of a chain. The barrel of a gun peeked out. "Are you alone?"

Tom scooted back so she could see him. He held his arms out to the side and twisted in a circle. "There's no one here but me and I'm unarmed. Let me in so we can talk."

The door closed and the chain came off before it swung open. "I don't know what you think I can tell you. No one's been here. I haven't seen that brown truck again. I don't know who those people are or where to find them."

Tom shoved past her into the house. Things looked much the same as when he'd seen her earlier: messy, disheveled, but not as if anything untoward had happened.

The aroma of whatever she had fixed for supper hung in the air, but not in a good way.

"Where's Richie? Get him down here. I'll bet he knows something he hasn't told us."

"You leave my son alone. He's not in on this. I hope your

friend is okay. I really do. But you won't find your answer here."

"Maybe. Maybe not. Either way, I intend to see what your son knows about Ian Pryor and what he's been up to." Tom pushed past Maria and headed for the stairs.

She grabbed his shirt and tugged. "No. Stop. You can't." She broke into sobs. "He's not up there. He left right after you were here and hasn't come back."

Tom's heart softened for an instant then hardened again. "Has he done this often? Stayed out all night?" He couldn't afford empathy for this woman while Fiona was in danger.

Maria sagged back onto the sofa, her face in her hands. "Only recently. He's changed the last few months. He used to be so sweet. Now he's always angry."

"Just since Ian disappeared?"

"It started before. That's why I thought Ian had been giving him drugs. It's worse now. He comes and goes as he wants. Skips school. I don't know where he is half the time. I have gas card charges from all over. Last summer he was supposed to go to the beach at Gulf Shores with some friends for the weekend. He didn't come back for over a week. I call everywhere and his friends had no idea where he was. Later I found credit card charges from spots along the coast almost to Canada. What the hell was he doing there? Even in August the water's too cold to swim. Now he's running to New Orleans and Lake Charles and Houston."

The fear for Fiona's safety stayed, but the anger at Maria melted. "All the more reason I should search his room. The answer may be in there somewhere."

He started up the stairs again. This time Maria didn't stop him.

TOM DIDN'T HAVE kids or siblings so he had no basis for comparison. Growing up, a maid had kept his room spotless and his natural inclination was to be neat and orderly.

None of those adjectives applied to Richie's room although it probably resembled the living space of most normal seventeen-year-old boys.

The bed was unmade. Dirty clothes covered most of the available floor space. Dirty dishes covered the rest.

A six-inch stick propped open the only window. A saucer decorated with pink roses sat in the sill, serving as an overflowing ash tray. Tom didn't have to get any closer to smell marijuana.

A thorough search failed to turn up any harder drugs.

All this he expected. What he didn't expect was the gun under the mattress.

At least the boy hadn't taken it with him wherever he went. He reached out to pick up the weapon but stopped, his hand inches away. He needed to be able to swear he'd never touched the gun.

Instead, he leaned closer, trying to catch a whiff of gunpowder in case the weapon had been fired recently. The odor of gym socks, last week's pizza, weed, and teenage hormones was too strong for him to know for certain.

He'd give the kid his patented talk on the dangers of carrying a gun but none of his clients listened to him so why should a boy who already resented him?

What Tom needed was an address, a phone number, the names of friends. Anything that led him to someone or someplace to search next.

Schoolwork cluttered the small desk. Tom flicked on the computer and waited while it booted up. The machine didn't seem to be password protected as it lit up showing an essay on Herman Melville.

A wicked curve ball wasn't going to get the kid into college unless he learned basic grammar and spelling.

More pages. More schoolwork. Math seemed to be his best subject. A little porn—not too much. Not many emails—most kids texted. He'd need the boy's phone to learn more.

He was about to give up when he found a folder labeled *Homework.* Inside was a list of names and photos. The first showed Lucian Archer, a red-headed pre-teen with freckles, braces, and an address in Winooski, Vermont. The date on the school photo was ten years earlier.

He should probably have Fiona check the kid out later, but one thing he knew for certain—Lucian hadn't driven down from Vermont to kidnap Fiona and that's all he cared about tonight.

Another photo was of Devin Grimes along with his

address in Houston and Kara Grimes with her phone number, and what appeared to be Devin and Kara's wedding photo.

Sometimes he hated to be right. Richie definitely knew more about Devin's background than he had admitted.

The last entry was a faded photo of a young boy in a baseball uniform, his dark hair falling onto his forehead. With the notation Baumholder Army base, Baumholder, Germany.

No name or date was listed under the last photo, but if Richie could find it, so could he.

All this was useful information, but didn't move him one inch closer to finding Fiona.

CHAPTER TWENTY-EIGHT

Kara

Kara stood on her front lawn and watched the Not-So-Dynamic Duo depart. She wanted to make sure they were well and truly gone.

No prowler waited, hidden, in her house. She knew that. But it didn't keep that uneasy feeling of ants crawling down her arms at bay.

She couldn't make her feet move toward the front door. Helen had offered her extra bedroom until Kara felt safe again, but that was definitely against the rules without express permission.

What was the old adage about getting back on a horse if it threw you? She'd always thought that was a stupid expression. Why climb up on something so big that didn't want you on there?

Still, if she didn't go back in her house now, she never would. She'd spend the night in Devin's big recliner and have all the locks changed first thing in the morning. An alarm system on all the windows and doors would be a good idea.

That came to a lot of money if she wouldn't be staying much longer.

Decision time was fast approaching and she hadn't been able to reach Tom all day. His secretary claimed he was out of town.

He was supposed to be working on her case, not taking a vacation.

A yellow Camaro with a black stripe roared to a stop across the street. Tyler Henderson rolled out and slammed the door.

"Good evening, Tyler. You worked late tonight." She was killing time. Postponing going inside. So what? She didn't have a curfew.

"I came from a meeting." He didn't look happy about it.

"Good for you. I know it's tough. I'm proud of you for keeping with it."

"I'd rather be there than here." He nodded toward his house. "Mom and fart-face came home last night. He's already slapped me for not taking out the garbage and warned me I better shape up or he'll kick me out. I'd go now if I could afford a place that'd let me bring Fang."

Even in the dark Kara could see the worry on Tyler's face. "Go get Fang and meet me in my kitchen in fifteen minutes. I think I have a solution to both our problems."

KARA HAD A Coke and a plate of cookies waiting for Tyler and a scoop of leftover chicken and rice for Fang.

Fang had disposed of his treat in seconds. Tyler hadn't touched his.

"Live here? What would people think?" Tyler's voice cracked.

"I'm way past worrying about that. I'd feel a lot safer with the two of you around. Someone broke in here today because they knew the house was empty. I don't need Fang to attack anyone, just bark and let them know he's here."

Tyler scratched behind Fang's ear. "Yeah. He's a lover not a fighter. That's why he flunked police academy training."

"I have an extra room that would be all yours and a fenced-in yard for Fang. You'd have to remember to do a few chores though. Like take out the garbage."

"I knew tomorrow was garbage day. I'd have taken it out when I got home from work. I didn't expect them until much later."

"Do you want me to call your mom and talk to her about it?"

"No. She'd make a fuss. Not because she wants me. She doesn't. Because she'd think she ought to. I'm nineteen. I can do what I want."

"Do we have a deal?" She might be able to sleep tonight

after all.

"Sure. If you really want us." He patted Fang's head. "I'll run across the street and get a few things for tonight. I'll get the rest tomorrow."

"No loud music when I'm sleeping and no drinking, okay?"

"Anything you say." His face lit up until he didn't look like the same hang-dog kid who walked in half an hour earlier.

"There is one favor you can do for me. Not tonight. Tomorrow night, after dark."

"What's that?"

"Behind Helen's garage is a large round flagstone that her garbage can sits on."

"You want me to take out her garbage, too? I can do that."

"That would be nice. Neighborly. It's hard for her with her walker. But it's not what I was thinking about. Under the flagstone, about a foot down, is a package in a waterproof container. Take that out, fill in the hole, and put everything back like it was."

"What do you want me to do with the package?"

That was the question. She hated to ask him to retrieve it for her, but if she needed it, she wouldn't have time to waste. She couldn't dig it up herself due to her ankle monitor and she couldn't keep it at home. They'd searched her house three times already. Would they come back? Fang might be a deterrent, but not if they brought a steak bone.

"Take it to Helen's house and ask her to hold it for me."

Tyler's eyes gleamed. "I always wanted to be a secret agent. James Bond Henderson, license for intrigue."

CHAPTER TWENTY-NINE

Fiona

The only light came from the half-hidden moon and the van headlamps, leaving Evan nothing but a shadow on the ground.

Fiona wiggled until both feet touched the ground. Her first step connected with Evan's leg and she nearly tripped. He let out a wail that sounded as if it came from underwater.

Catherine sat in the front on the right side, but twisted the wrong direction. "Hey!" she shouted, but was unable to disentangle herself with any speed.

From the driver's seat, Troy had to reach across his dislocated shoulder to unhook his seatbelt and stumble out the door.

Zach sat up in a daze. "What?"

She didn't know where Lance was, but he hadn't made a

move toward her so far.

Hands still tied, she raced across the road and plunged into the forest. No moonlight made it through the tangled limbs and Spanish moss.

Confused yells came from the van, but they weren't chasing her. Yet.

Catherine's voice floated through the air. Then Troy's. Lance chimed in but was drowned out. They couldn't agree on a plan.

With each step the voices from the van grew fainter.

The forest closed around her like a blanket. The air felt so heavy and damp she had trouble breathing.

A gunshot sounded and a bullet smacked into a tree inches from her head.

She was about to be killed with her own gun.

Maybe Tom was right about them making any situation worse.

She threw herself onto the ground and crawled three feet to the left as two more bullets flew past the spot she'd been moments before.

The pistol she'd bought last night held six bullets. Revolvers didn't have a safety so she'd left one chamber empty as a precaution against shooting herself in the back.

That meant two bullets were left.

Her hand closed on a fist-sized rock. She tossed it as far as she could with both hands tied. It landed in a bush, causing leaves to rustle and fall.

Instantly, one more bullet gone.

Fiona cut to the left, back the way they came. Heading straight would be exactly what they expected. Shrubs and detritus grabbed at her legs. She had trouble running with one heel broken.

A tree loomed up out of nowhere and she smacked into it.

She picked herself up and kept going.

The road curved slightly, and somehow she'd managed to get closer rather than deeper into the woods. She could make out the van through the trees without leaving the shadows. She wasn't as far away as she'd hoped.

Maybe this could help her.

Catherine tucked the pistol into the back of her jeans, glanced briefly at Evan, and began issuing instructions. Headlights danced around as Troy backed the van into a three-point turn until they pointed the direction Fiona had escaped. From the way the lights lifted and fell and Zach screamed, Fiona guessed Troy had run over Evan.

While everyone's attention was turned the direction she fled, Fiona darted across the road to the other side. The trees were thinner, which made traveling easier but left her more exposed.

She moved slower, more carefully, in order to make less noise. As near as she could tell, they were still searching on the wrong side of the road.

How much longer that would last, she didn't know.

The forest floor suddenly slanted downward. She stumbled

and rolled several feet until something soft stopped her fall.

A putrid odor filled the air. She pushed back to get away from it. The foul stench rose like a cloud and followed her.

A hint of breeze shifted the clouds. Moonlight lit a distorted lump in a blue work shirt.

Corey. The missing tire salesman.

Shivers raced through her like electricity down a wire. This was the spot they planned to dump her. Deep in the woods where predators could feast on her bones, leaving nothing to identify.

Her breath came in short, rapid gasps. Fear threatened to overtake her. She pushed it away and replaced it with anger. They weren't going to get away with this.

Not if she could help it.

Every instinct sang out to bolt. Run away. Her brain said wait. Think. Running with tied hands slowed her. Left her off balance. Unable to protect herself.

Her teeth gnawed at the rope. The taste of blood made her gag. She spit and kept going. The rope loosened. She managed a better grip with her teeth and tugged again. It loosened more.

She shook the rope until it fell at her feet.

Overhead, a jet pulled away from the airport, making its way to New Orleans, or Houston, or Santa Fe. Anywhere but here. Using the sound for cover, she slammed her boot against a tree until the lone heel broke free.

Now what? Was there any chance Corey had some type of weapon on his body? Holding her breath against the stench of rotting flesh, she searched his pockets.

No phone. No flashlight. No knife. No identification except his name embroidered on his shirt.

Traveling was easier with both heels gone, but it still made for an uncomfortable gait. She had no way to estimate the time, but it would have to be hours before the sun made its way through the trees.

Exhaustion swept over her. Her head ached and her ears rang. Her stomach rolled uneasily, disapproving of the crab au gratin she'd eaten with Tom earlier in the evening.

The lump on her forehead felt damp with blood. Hers or Evan's?

She wanted to rest. To lie down on a soft bed.

She couldn't stop. If Catherine and her cohorts found her, she'd join Corey forever in the woods. If they didn't find her, vicious Louisiana rodents would.

Tom would never know what happened to her. If he was still alive.

She forced herself to go on, expecting a snake to sink its fangs into her ankle at any moment.

Mosquitoes made a feast of her face and arms. Spider webs caught in her hair. She could almost feel the creepy buggers crawling down her back.

The moon disappeared behind a cloud, leaving her in total darkness, like being deep in a cave when the lights went out. Only now she could hear animals moving through the leaves.

Hands out in front of her, she felt her way forward, each

step a thrust into the unknown.

She didn't know if she'd walked for hours or minutes when the sound of running water caught her ear. She edged that direction. A slow-moving bayou inched its way forward. She decided to follow it, otherwise she might walk in circles all night and end up back at the van.

A pale light reflected off the ripples as a fish or turtle jumped in the water.

She refused to think about alligators.

CHAPTER THIRTY

Tom

Tom sat in his car, at a loss about what to do next.

Richie obviously knew more about Ian's life than anyone had guessed. He needed to talk to the boy. So did the police. But none of this told him where to find Fiona.

He shuffled through Fiona's notes again. He'd already checked both tire stores she'd listed. He could go to Troy's or Zach's place and bang on their doors.

Neither one lived close to Bayou Bend and that's where he was now. Fiona had mentioned a man named Granger who owned all the stores plus a few more. She hadn't tracked him down yet when he'd pulled her away for dinner.

Why hadn't he left her alone to do what she was so good at?

So far, she had his last name only and the idea that he

lived in Bayou Bend. He could call the main office when they opened, but that was hours away.

Maria Longcour was scared enough she might call him if Richie returned, and he didn't want to be too far away when that happened.

Driving around aimlessly seemed foolish, but was the only plan he could come up with. Traffic was almost nonexistent at this hour of the night. A brown pickup with a trailer hitch or a dark van with a broken tail light would be easier to spot now than two hours later.

If they carried Fiona to see their boss or ask his instructions on what to do with her, this is where they'd be.

But not in this neighborhood.

He needed to find a more affluent area.

Thirty minutes later he reconsidered. This was the dumbest idea he'd had since second grade when he'd read *Call of the Wild* and convinced Joey Hinton, whose home life was almost as lonely as his, that they should run away to Alaska and pan for gold.

Joey's parents missed him after a couple of hours. His were surprised when the police brought him home.

Tom turned right at the next corner, heading back toward Baton Rouge. That's when he saw it. A brown pickup with a trailer hitch parked in front of a 24-Hour Emergency Clinic. He couldn't tell if the windows were tinted.

The large parking lot appeared empty except for the pickup, and parked in the adjacent slot, a neon blue piece-of-crap Nissan. What were the odds of two strangers parking so close together?

Fiona might be the whiz with a computer, but he had more money and contacts he could pay to do the work for him.

He drove another block then pulled over where he had a view of the clinic and the two cars. He grabbed his phone. Under contacts he punched the listing for Texas Poison Control.

He'd only used the number a couple of times and only for background information. He hadn't needed it since Fiona came to work for him.

The sleepy voice that answered was none too happy at the intrusion. "What? You know my hours."

Yes, he did. Noon to three a.m. It was now four-forty. "This is an emergency."

"And it'll cost like one. What 'ya got?"

"Two license plate numbers."

"What state?"

"Louisiana."

"What all do you want?"

"Just the basics. Quick and dirty."

"Give me fifteen minutes."

He called back in ten. "2017 Canyon Ridge brown pickup belonging to Troy Martin at Oak Ridge Apartments, Unit 3B, Comeau, Louisiana. Next is an Electric Blue Metallic 2006 Nissan, registered to Dwight York. Do you need the address?"

Zach's car was still in his father's name. What a loser. "No,

I have it. How much do I owe you?"

"I'll make it easy on you, $2,000. I needed to take a piss anyway. Make sure it's in my account by end of day or your number will be blocked."

"Make it $3,000. I have one more job for you. It'll be tougher than the last two. A man named Granger. He owns several tire stores in Louisiana. He may live in or around Bayou Bend."

"That's it? Save your money. I'll have the information within ten minutes or you don't owe me a thing."

"I'll go ahead and deposit your fee. It might be harder than you think." If Fiona couldn't find Granger, he was well hidden.

With that, the man whose name he'd never known disconnected.

Tom slipped out of Flash and made his way to the clinic on foot, avoiding security cameras. He kept his head low and approached Zach's car. One glance to make sure no one could see him and he let half the air out of the rear passenger side tire.

Surely the kid wouldn't be stupid enough to keep driving on it for long.

He hoofed it back to Flash and waited. After twenty minutes, he started to sweat. Had they left their rides at the clinic and gone home with someone else?

Every second he wasted was one Fiona couldn't afford.

His only choice was to go into the clinic and see if they were there. He could complain of chest pains and try to look around. Then what, say *never mind, I feel better?*

He reached for the door handle when the clinic door opened and two men—one tall and slim, one short and dumpy—came out.

Troy and Zach.

Troy held his left arm still and close to his body. Zach had his right arm in a cast.

They stood on the sidewalk and talked for a moment. Troy slapped Zach on the shoulder and climbed into his truck. Zach watched, then stumbled to his car. From the way he walked, he had no business driving.

Troy was half a block away by the time Zach had his car started.

Tom watched as Zach jerked into reverse and then forward. He pulled onto the street after Troy who was well out of sight. Tom counted to fifty before following.

Ten miles out of town, Zach began to slow. He stopped the car half on and half off the road.

By the time Tom reached him, Zach stood staring at his tire as if he'd never seen a flat before. Tom pulled behind the Nissan, letting his brights shine in Zach's face and called out his window. "Sumpen' wrong, buddy?"

"My tire." Zach's voice slurred. He lifted his broken arm and shrugged.

"Looks like you've got a problem. What the hell. I broke my arm once. Hurt like the devil at dawn. I have time. I'll help you."

He walked to the back of the Nissan and kicked the tire. "Yep, it's a goner. You got a spare?"

"In my trunk."

Tom had allowed the two cops to confiscate his baton. Arguing would have taken time and with Fiona missing, time was something he couldn't afford to lose.

That left him weaponless. A quick search of the hotel room had offered him only a plastic knife.

He waited behind Zach as the man unlocked the trunk of his car. The moment the lid popped up, Tom closed the distance between them.

His left hand grabbed Zach's chin, pulling it up and back. With his right hand he placed the plastic knife against Zach's throat, moving it slightly so the serrated edge scraped against his skin.

Pressing the knife tight enough to keep Zach from moving, but not so tight the flimsy plastic snapped was tricky, but Tom kept one finger on top of the blade to give it support.

Zach yelped. "Take my wallet, man. It's in my back pocket. Don't hurt me. I won't say a word."

Tom lowered his voice to a raspy growl. "You're gonna wish money was all I'm after. What'd you do with Fiona?"

"Who?"

Did the fool not even know her name or was this part of the act? Didn't matter.

"The woman you abducted earlier tonight."

"It wasn't me, man. You can see. I've got a broken arm. I

couldn't hurt anybody."

"I saw you, asshole. Who do you think gave you that broken arm? Now, where is she?"

The blade swayed on the knife. Should he press harder or let up?

"She's okay. She's okay. We didn't hurt her."

Tom wanted to believe him, but couldn't. She'd have called by now if she could. He slid the knife across Zach's throat. The night was too dark to see if he drew blood but it got Zach's attention. "I'm not going to ask again. Where is she?"

"I don't know, man. She got away from us. I think she killed Evan."

"You don't seem to understand how little I care about you or Evan. Tell me how to find her. Now."

"Go a ways outside the city and there's an old road that heads off to the east. I don't know the name of it. Nobody uses it anymore since they put in the highway. It's supposed to be blocked off, but fishermen and gator hunters like it so they moved the barricade and nobody put it back. That's where she jumped out of the truck and ran off in the woods. We gave up looking after an hour. It's dangerous out there."

Rage started like a hot stone in his chest and spread over his body until even his eyes burned. Fiona. Out in those woods. Alone. All night.

He increased the pressure against Zach's throat only to hear a loud *crack*.

CHAPTER THIRTY-ONE

Kara

Kara opened the door to reveal a hesitant Tyler, a plastic garbage bag of belongings over one shoulder, a fifteen-pound bag of dog food at his feet, and Fang at his side. The dog's tail wagged so hard it hit the door post with a steady *thump, thump, thump.*

"Come on in, roomie. Or should I say roomies?" Fang wagged even harder.

Kara stepped aside and waved them in.

"Are you sure this is okay?" Tyler asked. "I wouldn't want to get you in any trouble."

"With who? The police? They don't care who I ask into my home. I wouldn't want to cause any problems between you and your mother, though. What did she say about you staying over here?"

"You couldn't hear her from across the street?"

This could be a mistake. An angry neighbor might make up all kinds of stories to tell the cops. "Do you want me to call her, ask her permission?" Was it too late for that?

"Not unless you like being called a string of obscene names."

Shoot. She had a knack alright. A knack of making a bad situation worse. "What about your stepfather? I thought he wanted you to leave."

Tyler swung his bag down onto the floor. Fang made himself comfortable on the sofa. "He said to take everything I owned because, if I left, I wasn't ever coming back to their house."

This was supposed to be the answer to both their problems. Instead, she'd caused a split in an already fragile family. "Go on back now before something drastic happens and you can't."

"Fart-face already hit me. That's about as drastic as I plan to put up with."

"Did you get everything you needed?" The garbage bag wasn't very large for all his belongings.

"Yeah, I didn't have much. I hope you don't mind my car in front of your house. He made me move it. Said he didn't want that piece of crap bringing down their property value."

From the look on Tyler's face, that hurt worse than the punch to the face.

She glanced out the window at the yellow Camaro, not ten feet from where it was before, now parked by her curb instead of across the street. "That's fine. I'd say put it in the driveway, but I leave early for work and I don't want to get blocked in. Now, Fang had a scoop of chicken and rice earlier. Was that enough for his dinner?" The dog was huge. He glanced at her and drooled as if he knew what she was saying.

"No. I thought maybe you should do it so he gets used to you."

Great. Now she had a broken boy and a pet dog to take care of.

KARA STOOD AT the door to the guest bedroom. "Do you need anything else? An extra blanket? Another pillow?"

"No ma'am. This is great. Thanks." Tyler looked happier than she'd ever seen him.

"How about Fang? Where does he usually sleep?"

"I put a pallet on the floor in the front hall. That way he can keep an eye on the whole house. He'll let us know if anyone tries to get in."

The dog might be a big sissy, but he was the size of a well-fed wolf and had a deep bark. He'd do until she had an alarm system installed.

She closed Tyler's door and made her way back to her bedroom. With Tyler and Fang asleep down the hall, maybe she could actually sleep in her own bed.

The exhaustion that had begun when Baxter and

Copperfield showed up at her door, suspicions in tow, had reached its peak. In four days, she'd have made her decision and acted upon it. Now was the time to get ready.

She'd changed her mind at the last minute and had Tyler bring her the buried package. Someone had already searched her house today. It should be safe for one night. She could give it to Helen tomorrow.

Tonight, she wanted to double-check the contents. She wasn't worried about anything going missing. It was more about dampness ruining the documents.

When she'd told Devin she wanted a divorce over a year ago, he'd choked her and threatened to kill her if she left him.

So, she'd used the time to prepare.

She had a passport and a driver's license from Missouri with a fake name and address—those had cost her plenty—$500 in twenties, her mother's gold wedding ring, a pair of earrings with diamonds the size of grains of sand that her stepfather had given her for being 'such a good girl,' and a broken brooch covered with seed pearls that supposedly belonged to a grandmother she'd never met.

More important than anything else in the package were two photos of her mother. She would never leave those behind.

Closing two bank accounts might set off alarm bells. She'd planned to solve that problem by making ATM withdrawals of forty to fifty dollars every few days until her secret savings account contained a little over fifty bucks. The other she'd empty on her way out of town, before Devin could stop her.

Her plan was almost perfect. Until it wasn't.

She'd cried for hours the day she discovered she was pregnant. The only thing she'd ever wanted in life—a family—was now the thing that would trap her forever.

If Devin wouldn't let her leave alone, he'd never let go of his child. And she wouldn't subject any child to him as a father.

Hiding would be tougher with a baby. She had to escape before he knew.

As soon as Devin left on his next business trip, she'd planned to be gone. She'd leave a note for Doc Collier, thanking him for all his help, but not mention where she was headed. That way, when Devin called, he could say he didn't know where she was.

Only Devin had died instead.

His death not only didn't solve her problems, it created new ones.

She never expected to be charged with murder. If she had, she wouldn't have called 911. She'd have packed her clothes and driven away.

Now she had a dilemma. She could face the years in prison on her own, but she refused to bring a baby into the world while incarcerated, allowing it to believe its mother had killed its father.

For now, she had three options, but time was getting short.

She'd given Tom until Monday to convince her he could get her off. If he did, she'd stay and fight.

The moon cast its familiar shadow on her wall as she lay in

bed, staring at the ceiling. She'd been a fool to ever think she'd sleep tonight.

If Tom couldn't convince her he had enough evidence to clear her, she still had two options left. One was bad, the other worse.

And that decision had to be made by Tuesday.

CHAPTER THIRTY-TWO

Fiona

The moon played hide-and-seek behind the clouds, giving Fiona light, then taking it away again. She would manage a few steps, stop, then move forward, her feet sinking into mud or leaves, or tangled in tree roots.

Progress was slow, but since she didn't know where she was going, it didn't matter. She wouldn't admit she was lost. Not as long as she kept following the stream. It had to lead somewhere.

Her eyes ached from straining to see. Her legs trembled. The constant sound of rushing water made her thirst unbearable.

At one point she nearly drank from the bayou. If it made her sick, she'd take antibiotics when she reached civilization. She hesitated. Lost as she was, there was every chance she wouldn't make it out of the swamp tonight. Or tomorrow.

In that case, she might be too sick to keep moving.

An owl hooted somewhere off to her left, reminding her she wasn't alone. The rustle of leaves as it sailed overhead startled her. What had it seen? What was it after? Hopefully nothing large.

A high-pitched squeal split the night. What the hell kind of animal made a sound like that? The owl flew back again, carrying its prey.

She couldn't think about not finding her way out. She had to keep going before she became prey for something larger and meaner than the owl.

Something armed with teeth, or fangs, or guns.

She hadn't gone far when she heard a baby crying in terror. Were there people nearby? Would it be safe to approach them? It could be Catherine and her crew, waiting, with one last bullet just for her.

Even Catherine wasn't stupid enough to bring a baby out to hunt through the woods.

Maybe there was a campground ahead. Safety in numbers.

She stumbled a few feet forward and stopped. There it was again. This time it didn't sound as much like a baby. More like Maria Loncour's cat. Only ten times bigger.

What kind of cat lived around here? Jaguar? No, of course not. Mountain Lion? Possibly. More likely a bobcat. How big did they get?

She didn't plan to stick around and find out.

At first, anger fueled her determination. Anger at Troy and Zach for attacking her, not once but twice. Anger at Catherine for conning her with that innocent act. Anger at herself for letting those numb-nuts get the best of her.

As angry as she was at those who'd abducted her and thrown her headfirst into a van, she saved that red hot nugget of fury for the man whose only worry was that her kidnappers would disturb his wife—and who'd sent them off with instructions to get rid of her.

Granger.

She would live long enough to find him. Destroy him.

Anger could only take you so far. Now she was running on muscle memory, placing one foot in front of the other.

Somewhere in the dark, a large animal crashed through the underbrush. She'd seen photos of the wild boar that had taken over much of the area. Four-hundred-pound beasts with curved tusks and the attitude of a charging rhino. Best to believe it was a deer.

Ahead, the stream curved. The moon peeked out long enough for her to see a tree stump. A good place to sit. Rest a few minutes. Wait for daylight.

She took a deep breath. The air was thick and heavy. Every inhale felt like a bucket of scummy water filled her lungs.

No. She couldn't stop. Not even for a minute. Once she sat, she might never get up.

Tom needed her. If he was hurt or bleeding, no one would

know. He'd count on her to send help.

She touched the stump as she passed and kept moving, onward into the darkness.

CHAPTER THIRTY-THREE

Tom

Tom pulled into a parking lot and stopped under a security light. He took out Fiona's notes and went over them again. Maybe he'd missed some hint that might help.

He'd wasted half the night searching for the mysterious blocked road that Zach told him about with no luck. He might have to go back, let the guy out of his trunk, and make him navigate.

If no one had found him yet.

He'd left the lights on, the flashers blinking, and the keys to the blue Nissan on the dash before leaving. He'd also used Zach's own phone to film him confessing to any number of things. Unfortunately, Devin Grimes's murder wasn't one of them.

The question had been who to send the video to. Certainly

not Phelps and Werner. Those two cops couldn't be trusted.

If they found Zach first, they were likely to spirit him away or finish him off.

And with the way they'd zeroed in on him as the main suspect in Fiona's disappearance, he'd likely end up charged with kidnapping while Zach got away clean.

Yep, once you started breaking rules, the world dissolved into chaos. But if that's what it took to protect Fiona, then chaos it was. He'd put her in danger, it was up to him to save her.

He'd made sure he wasn't visible on the video, wiped his fingerprints off the car, and held the video as a last resort.

If he found Fiona—make that *when* he found her—and she testified against Zach, the video wouldn't be needed. If she wasn't found, or, God forbid, incapable of testifying, he was the one facing prison.

Then it would be his word against Zach's.

Zach might look like a chubby goofball, but he was no angel. Not with a record for possession with intent to sell and a couple of DUIs.

For now, he had to concentrate on finding Fiona. He'd worry about the consequences later.

Fiona's notes were of no more use than Zach's directions. Why hadn't he insisted on landmarks? *On your left* depended on which way you were heading.

He might as well spend the next hour retracing his steps. A pale glow in the east indicated morning was approaching and with it more traffic. More busybodies wondering what that red Porsche was doing, cruising the streets of their little town.

He U-turned across the road and his headlights caught a yellow flash. A safety reflector, one of two on a sawhorse mostly hidden by vines and weeds, and meant to block the entrance to a two-lane, potholed street leading to nowhere good.

Thirty minutes later he'd never have seen it.

He eased Flash around the barricade and down the lonely road. After a quarter of a mile, the trees closed in on him, and any lights from the city disappeared.

No wonder they had picked this site.

Not knowing what lay ahead was a huge handicap. His headlights lit the area straight in front of him, but not to the side.

As near as he could tell during the melee at the restaurant, four people had poured out of the van and attacked Fiona. One had stayed in the van, driving.

Five assailants in total.

Subtract Troy and Zach, the walking wounded, and that left three. Fiona's knife had slashed down, possibly injuring another one, and he'd connected with someone's rib cage hard enough to cause damage.

He couldn't count on those two being out of commission, but hopefully they'd been slowed down.

If they were waiting up the road somewhere, doing whatever they intended, they would see him first.

And all he had was half a broken plastic knife.

Too bad.

He pressed down on the accelerator and Flash lived up to her name.

Twenty miles. Thirty minutes. Nothing to show for it but bugs on his windshield.

Tom drummed his fingers on the center console. The road had dead-ended with another sawhorse barrier and a washed-out bridge.

Sort of like his options.

The sky had brightened by several shades. Soon he'd be able to see without headlights. He'd try the road again, slower, just in case he'd missed something, but he didn't hold out much hope.

His phone rang in the middle of his three-point turn. It better not be those two clowns, Phelps and Werner. He had two and a half hours before he was due at the police station.

Not that he had any plans to show up. Still, they could cause the kind of trouble that would slow him down, and he wasn't stopping until he found Fiona.

He glanced at the caller ID and chuckled. Texas Poison Control. His hacker had taken way longer than ten minutes to track down Granger.

Tom punched *accept*. "What 'ya got for me?"

"Damn. I should have charged by the hour. Your guy is

well hidden."

"Can't say I didn't warn you. You did find him though, didn't you?" He'd never known the guy to fail, but there was always a first time.

"I've got the basics, but I plan to keep digging till I uncover all his dirty secrets."

"Easy. I don't know how much I'm willing to pay for this." With the basics, Fiona could find the rest.

"No charge. This is personal. Sucker tried to hide from *me*? I'll crush him like the nasty little bug he is."

This day was improving already. "Okay. Hit me with it."

"I'll be texting you his address, phone number, make, model, and license plate of his car. Make that cars, plural. His name is Homer Hayes Humphry."

"Not Granger?" No wonder Fiona had trouble finding him.

"Granger is his wife's maiden name."

"And that's the name he uses?"

"Only in his illegal pursuits. All the money is hers. Her daddy owned the tire stores and the house they live in. Daddy died mysteriously several years after she married dear Homer. Something I might decide to look into on my own."

"He goes by his own name. The other is just like…code? To keep his identity hidden when he's up to no good?"

"And with the tire company main office so customers will think the old man is still in charge. Only the old man was a marketing genius. He worked it every day, not like our

Homer. He'd pop into a store unannounced. See how they were doing. Glad-hand the customers. Support Little League teams. Advertise in the high school newspaper."

"Let me guess. Homer thinks he's above all that." Tom shifted Flash into park and took his foot off the brake. Things were getting interesting.

"Now guess what's happened to the business since Daddy died?"

"Nothing good."

"In the tank. Homer was in charge of the Belle Mer store when he got caught skimming the profits."

Tom glanced at Fiona's notes. No Belle Mer store listed. When he finished here, he'd have to check it out. Maybe that's where they stashed the van with a broken tail light. He'd better find it fast, before they had time to replace it.

They wouldn't be able to replace the scratch down the side that easily.

"When Daddy found out his son-in-law was stealing from him, the retreads hit the fan. Homer was due to be fired if not sent to jail except for the old man's daughter, Heidi—named their kids Holden and Heather. Ain't that cute? Homer must think he's related to the Kardashians. He certainly spends like one."

"Tell me about the spending later. I want to know what happed when Daddy caught Homer with his hand in the till."

"Darling daughter went to Daddy with tears in her eyes and the next thing you know it was all an innocent bookkeeping error. Homer gave his two weeks' notice to 'pursue other options.' Only before the two weeks were up, Daddy was dead."

These people were their own mini crime syndicate. "The cops weren't all over that?"

"A detective named Werner and his partner Denham checked it out and declared it a tragic accident. Denham is now retired and living the good life in a five-thousand square foot lake house in the Ozarks. Werner has a couple of years until retirement, but he and wife number three are doing well on a cop's salary. Just bought a new boat that sleeps four. Haven't found anything on the new partner—Phelps—yet, but I'll keep looking."

He knew he was right not to trust those two clowns. "Let's go back to the spending part. The business is falling off, but Homer keeps spending?"

"And the wife. She likes to shop. He likes to gamble. They're on a first-name basis at all the local casinos—Shreveport, Biloxi, Lake Charles. Plus trips to Las Vegas. The Bellagio is their favorite."

"If the stores are losing money, where's he getting the cash?" Now they were down to the part Fiona had stumbled into.

"He supplements his income by selling a little weed, a bit of cocaine. Not personally, of course. Does it through the stores. But business keeps falling and his side gig's profits are small because he has to pay off the help. And the cops. Now money's getting really tight. His only option is to expand."

"And what's the point of having friends in low places if you can't use them to your advantage?"

"Right again. Only bigger fish than him already have those areas covered."

Tom took a sip from his water bottle and checked the time. A quarter after seven. He needed to keep searching for Fiona, but this information was too valuable to ignore. "How does he plan to cut into that market?"

"He had a guy who could score modest amounts of product from a source down near the border in Texas. Guy swore he would help them break into the big time for a cut of the profits, so they gave him a shit-ton of cash to make a big buy. Turns out the guy couldn't make good on his promise. Now Granger's in trouble with people he borrowed the money from, the people he promised product, and the crowd he was trying to squeeze out."

This was the big one. This was what he needed to know. "So, who killed my guy?"

"Your guy the go-between?"

"Yeah."

"Does it matter? Could have been any one of those three groups. Can't you sow enough doubt so they can't convict your client?"

He could, but proof was better. "Send me everything you've got that can be proven. I'll take it from there. I'll send you an interesting video I took last night that might help you in your search. Now I've got to get moving. Granger's hired help abducted my assistant last night."

"Fiona? They got her? I thought this sounded close to home."

He'd never used her name. "You know Fiona?"

"Not personally, but I know her work. She's good. In a lot of ways. She wouldn't have gone down easy."

"I'm out searching for her now." Tom smacked his head. "Shit. I need to get someone in my office to start contacting area hospitals. I should have done that first."

"Leave it to me. I've got a program that can cover every hospital from Baton Rouge to Bayou Bend in less time than your secretary could make one call. I'll let you know if I find anything."

"Thanks, man. You've been a great help."

"Anytime. It's a pleasure doing business with you. You in that flashy red Porsche? Be careful. You're gonna stand out like a Clydesdale at a cat show."

He didn't know who the guy was or where he hung out, but this was a reminder the guy not only knew his name, but where he lived, worked, the car he drove, and probably what he had for breakfast.

Good thing he'd already sent in that payment.

CHAPTER THIRTY-FOUR

Fiona

A squawk overhead woke Fiona. She opened her eyes in time to see a blue heron spread its majestic wings and fly down the bayou, while an alligator sank back into the water with no breakfast.

If she wasn't lost, alone, and with killers stalking her, she might wish to be awakened like this every morning.

The solitary dock had appeared welcoming under the pale moonlight, like a suite at the finest hotel. Instead, daybreak showed it to be a rickety death trap with missing boards, sagging to one side.

Her brief nap had caused every muscle in her body to stiffen while offering little rest.

She forced herself to her feet, only to regret it instantly. Her blisters had formed blisters while she slept. Maybe she could take her boots off and soak her feet in the cool water? No, she might not be able to get them back on.

Not to mention a hungry alligator nearby.

She licked her sandpaper lips and tried to swallow. Nothing happened. Which had swollen more, her parched throat or her aching feet?

Her first step caused the dock to sway. She grabbed a post to keep herself from falling through a broken plank.

Maybe if she sat here for a while someone would find her. People fished early in the morning, didn't they? If she waited, help might come to her instead of her searching for it.

The morning mist cleared fast as the sun rose. She searched both directions as her visibility increased and saw…nothing of any use.

Trees dripping with Spanish moss. A muddy bank that sucked at your feet and made traveling difficult. Slow moving water that hid dangerous snags, tree roots, and predators.

Dampness had penetrated her clothes and the cold October breeze caused her to shiver as realization dawned on her.

The owner of the dock wasn't planning to repair it. He'd probably been dead for twenty years. No fisherman would magically appear. No helicopter would swoop her to safety.

Even if Tom was alive and had notified the police, they wouldn't have any idea where to look.

The only people likely to arrive were Catherine and her cohorts, coming to finish what they started last night.

She was lost, alone, and frightened but she knew three things.

If they found her, she didn't have the strength to fight them.

If she remained where she was, she would end up dead.

If she wanted to live, she had to pull herself together.

MOVIES MADE BUILDING a raft look easy. It wasn't.

Fiona worked her fingers between the rotten boards, trying to pry them up in one piece. The planks came up off the old dock easily enough, but broke in half unless she used finesse. Others had rusty nails ready to impale her at every opportunity.

She had to guess at the number of boards it would take to support her weight. Did dried-out wood float better or worse? Better she thought, but what if she was wrong?

She pulled up a couple more, just in case.

The trees were full of vines and moss. In any show she'd ever watched, the hero had a machete that he swung and chopped and vines fell at his feet. She had an old board with a bent nail sticking out of the end, and the forest clung to its treasure like King Solomon.

She tugged and yanked and jumped up to grab a handful and hung on, letting her body weight pull them loose.

Then fell on her butt when they did.

Once down, she needed to cut them into usable lengths. This involved pricking at the vine with a rusty nail or pounding on it with the sharp edge of a rock which sent an echoing noise down the bayou.

At any moment she expected to see her abductors sail around the bend or burst through the woods to grab her.

Despite the chilly air, sweat dripped into her eyes.

She wrapped the vines over and under, around and through the planks. When she reached the end, she discovered vines don't like to be tied into knots. Too bad. She did her best. Then she did the same with long strings of moss.

It wasn't as strong, but might help keep the vines from unraveling.

When she was satisfied with her work, she learned another hard lesson: build the raft closer to the water.

After struggling to slide the raft to the bank, she stood it on one edge and maneuvered it around rocks and tree roots to the edge of the water.

Fiona tested the water by tossing in a dead branch. The current picked it up immediately and swept it downstream. What if it did the same to the raft before she had time to get on?

She worked the front end of the raft into the water.

Okay, now what? Just shove it the rest of the way in and jump on, hoping it went where she wanted?

She needed a paddle or rudder or something to steer with. She ran back up the bank and dug through the broken, discarded boards until she found one that would work.

One last look back at the comparative safety of the woods and she heaved until the raft floated in the water. She climbed on and grabbed the paddle, ready to steer.

Nothing.

The back edge of the raft had sunk into the mud.

She climbed off and tried again, determined not to think about the alligator she'd seen nearby. Splashing out until the water was above her knees. The current grabbed the raft and nearly yanked it out of her hands. She hung on and crawled aboard.

The raft began to spin in circles as it drifted down the bayou.

If this kept up she'd be sick at her stomach.

She grabbed the extra plank and stuck it in the water. The current nearly ripped it out of her hands.

How could water that moved so slow be so strong?

She hung on until the raft stopped spinning. Water splashed up between the boards and occasionally over the top, but it didn't sink.

Now if only the vines held.

Ten minutes later, she blew out a sigh of relief and relaxed her shoulders. Steering wasn't so hard once you got the hang of it. Much easier than trying to run through thick woods in the dead of night.

She glanced up in time to see a dead branch ahead, caught up on a rock and stretching halfway across the bayou. Water foamed and boiled around it.

The raft began to buck as it got closer. She sat up on her knees and used the paddle to push away from the obstacle.

One branch, hidden underwater, snagged on the raft.

The jolt threw her onto her side.

Her heart skittered around her chest when she looked down.

The paddle had broken off in her hand, leaving a board only a foot long—

and the vines were starting to unravel.

Wispy green tendrils trailed in the water. The next board was held by only the moss.

One board had come loose. She grabbed it before it floated away.

Now she had a paddle, if only she still had a raft. She fished the vine out of the water and retied it.

All the boards were looser and spread apart. Water sloshed up from underneath, making the surface slippery. The dried wood was now saturated, causing it to float lower in the water.

Fiona hung on, checking her knots constantly.

Now the knots on the other side pulled apart.

The current slowed and she searched the bank ahead for a spot to land before the bayou pulled her under.

There, on her right. A flat area. She dug the paddle deep into the water and heaved, but the raft didn't respond. Another board broke away. The current claimed it and it disappeared in the murky water.

Her paddle hit a rock and the raft swung around. She jumped off and swam like mad for the shore as what was left of the raft disintegrated.

Wet, exhausted, her arms and legs trembling, she clawed her way up the bank. She lay flat on the forest floor, among the leaves and twigs and bugs, trying to suck air into lungs too tired to expand.

Finally, she forced herself to sit up.

She had no idea how far she'd come, but she had to be close to civilization by now, right?

A sound floated through the air. Please let that be a car, traffic, people. She could make it. She had to.

She held onto a tree for support and placed one foot in front of the other.

After a dozen steps, then a dozen more, she glanced down.

No. No. No. No.

Her legs buckled and she fell to the ground, sobbing.

In front of her was the decomposing body of Corey and the fresh body of Evan.

Tom's toy knife was still implanted in his neck.

CHAPTER THIRTY-FIVE

Tom

The top half of the sun had managed to peek over the horizon. Another fifteen minutes and he'd be able to see without headlights.

Tom decided to wait it out. He needed the best visibility possible.

His phone vibrated. Before he could answer, it vibrated again, and then again. Had he been in a dead spot where messages couldn't reach him? He sent out a silent prayer the calls were from someone, anyone, who had news about Fiona.

They weren't.

Marcus Bradley wanted to talk to him about a new idea he had for Mark, Jr.'s case. Tom deleted the text before he lost control and told the man where to stick Mark's case.

A second text came in from his secretary warning him that

a police detective from Louisiana had called for information about him and his practice and his assistant. Did the guy mean Fiona? Not to worry. She hadn't told him anything.

The third text came from Kara Grimes, wanting to know whether she needed to notify the court if she had someone move in with her.

If that woman had a boyfriend and had let him move in with her while she was being investigated for the murder of her husband, he was dropping her as a client. Although, it wouldn't be the stupidest thing a client had ever done.

A former client hinted he might have a new problem that would require Tom's help.

Former clients. They were some of his best new clients. They kept coming back. Seemed they never learned. It's what made him rich. It also made him sad.

The last two calls were from Detective Phelps reminding him about his nine a.m. appointment at the station. The second call was more insistent.

Tom deleted both messages. They'd have to find him first.

His spirits had spiked when he saw all the missed calls. Now his hopes dashed again. Did silence mean she was dead or still hiding?

Either way, he wasn't ready to give up searching.

He started the engine and lowered all four windows. His ears needed to work as hard as his eyes.

He let Flash creep down the road, his eyes flitting from one side to the other. Every fifty feet he'd blare out three long blasts on the horn, wait a minute, stick his head out the window, and call Fiona's name.

Progress was slow, but he didn't want to chance missing anything.

It might have been the position of the sun, casting its light in an angle horizontal to the road, or it might have been his imagination, but he thought he saw ruts on the shoulder.

Was that dark spot a shadow from the trees towering overhead or an oil stain on the asphalt?

He shut off the engine and dashed over to the marks. Someone had definitely pulled off onto the grass to park. Shorter, deeper marks perpendicular to the road resembled an attempt to turn around. The tire tread was wide, like a van or truck.

He held his breath as he studied the oil stain. It gleamed in the sunlight. Still damp. He bent to touch it and his heart froze.

No. It couldn't be.

Blood. Not oil.

And fresh.

He flew back to the car, leaned in the window and pressed on the horn. A steady pulse. *Beeep. Beeep. Beeep. Beeep.*

Where was she?

He cupped his hands around his mouth and yelled. "Fiona. Fiona. Where are you? It's me, Tom."

The tire tracks were on the north side of the road so that's the direction he went, plunging through the trees in his good slacks and dress shoes from last night.

The leather soles slipped on wet leaves and mud. Twigs and branches reached out to grab him but he didn't slow down.

There. Was that a footprint? He reached out to touch it. His finger sank into the damp earth. Did that mean the print was fresh?

Of course it did. Who else would be walking through this tangled mess of trees and brush and snakes and spiders and predators with two legs or four?

The air hung heavy with the stench of mold, dead fish, and scummy water.

He brushed back a limb and forged ahead. A slight path had been tamped down ahead, showing a trail as if something heavy had been dragged.

He swallowed and forced himself forward. He didn't know what the path meant. It could be anything. A fallen tree. A deer. The wind. Just because he used to watch cowboy movies on TV didn't make him a tracker.

Another footprint, off to one side. He was sure of it.

But was it Fiona's or her abductor's?

He called out again. "Fiona. Can you hear me?"

The buzz of flies brought him to a halt, allowing the fetid air to fill his nose. A few more steps and he saw it. Two bodies.

One stinking of decay. The other bloody, with his own knife implanted in his neck.

He walked in circles for the next twenty minutes, searching, but no Fiona and no more footprints. He even made it to the bayou. Claw marks on the side of the embankment showed where an alligator had pulled himself onto dry land.

If they'd thrown Fiona's body into the water, she might never be found.

CHAPTER THIRTY-SIX

Fiona

The sound of traffic should have been comforting to Fiona, but it wasn't. How could she know who was out there?

The same people who brought her here were the only ones who knew where she was. This was Friday. If it were a weekend there might be fishermen or hunters.

So far, the only hunters she'd seen were hunting her.

And she'd stumbled right back to the first place they'd look.

She had to get away from here…fast. She'd walked hours last night through the woods, yet covered the same distance over water in a fraction of the time.

She sat, paralyzed, knowing what she had to do but dreading it. The sound of a car, then voices spurred her.

Her feet moved of their own accord. She made her way back to the bayou and slithered down the bank.

Two boards had snagged on a root at the bend where she made her way to ground. They hung there, just out of reach. She waded into the murky water and grabbed them before they floated away.

I'll only stay on for a few minutes. Just until I'm far enough away that they won't see me.

Then she could work her way back toward the road and try to get a glimpse of the vehicle making all that noise.

No, not the vehicle, the people. They could have changed cars.

They could have changed people, too. She would recognize Catherine and Troy and Zach, but she'd never seen Lance's face.

How many other people did Granger have working for him?

She couldn't trust anyone. She'd have to make it all the way back to town and go into a store or business of some kind and call the police.

She wrapped her arms around the two boards and kicked off. Most of her body was out of the water, but her feet trailed behind.

Her toothy neighbor from this morning probably wouldn't have followed her this far but he might have friends or family living nearby.

She kicked twice but stopped abruptly. No sense ringing the dinner bell.

The current picked up once she made it around the bend and she moved along at a rapid pace. Almost too fast. She was losing control.

Her grip on the two boards slipped. She moved her hand up and found a nail. Or it found her. Did you really get tetanus from rusty nails or was that an old wives tale?

If she lived, she'd get a shot. If she didn't, well, that was one thing she wouldn't have to worry about.

Something under the surface caused the bayou to form an eddy. The boards began to twist and swirl. She kicked like she was trying out for the Olympics. The nail scraped across her palm and one board floated away only to be sucked under and bob up ten feet away, split in half.

She gave one last heave toward the bank and grabbed a fallen tree limb. It held long enough for her to crawl onto the soggy ground.

Hadn't she been through this once before?

She gagged and threw up a mouthful of bayou water. She couldn't be more than three miles as the heron flew from the nearest Starbucks or Dunkin' Donuts.

The air was still. She sat motionless and strained her ears. No voices. No traffic noises.

If she could find the road, and *if* they had given up the search, she could be drinking a steamed soy milk before lunch.

She felt her pockets. Her credit card was gone, but her emergency twenty was tucked into an inside crevice of her pants. Looking the way she probably did, nobody was going to trust her with anything.

Did they still make pay phones?

CHAPTER THIRTY-SEVEN

Tom

Tom sat in his car and stared straight ahead.

He'd spent the better part of an hour searching both sides of the woods with no luck. Thick as it was in spots, Fiona's body could have been three feet away and he'd never have seen it.

A whole team of searchers with dogs and machetes might not find her.

He couldn't call Werner and Phelps. They'd arrest him on the spot.

He could hear them now. "You put her there. How else would you know where to look?"

Explaining his connection to the two dead men would be tough, but they'd find a way. He was definitely in Houston for the first one, but the second body was fresh and had his knife buried in his neck.

The toy knife he kept as a joke. The one he used as a letter opener or to cut the tape on packages. To clean his fingernails or open the stubborn packet of ketchup at a fast-food place.

The same one he'd have sworn was sitting on the coffee table in Fiona's hotel room.

Fiona's record was sealed. She'd been a juvenile, but she still had one, and Werner was perfectly capable of getting it unsealed if he wanted to. Wouldn't matter what it was—skipping school or lifting a can of soda—Werner would use it to make her look like Lizzie Borden.

He'd contemplated removing the weapon when he first saw it, but couldn't bring himself to do that. He'd never tampered with evidence in his life. He didn't plan to start now. He'd deal with the consequences later.

Zach was another problem. That guy would be only too happy to describe how Tom had held a knife to his throat when he shoved him into the trunk of his car. Insisting the knife was plastic wouldn't be much help.

None of that bothered him. He could fight his way out of any charges they invented. But Fiona might still be alive, and as long as the police had him, they weren't looking for her.

And that would take more than he was capable of managing by himself.

Werner and Phelps might be on the take, but there had to be plenty of honest cops in Baton Rouge.

He had contacts in the FBI. Not friends exactly, but agents

he trusted. Ones he hoped trusted him, too.

His phone blinked and flashed *No Signal.* What the heck? He'd just used it to call Tex, as he'd mentally named the man listed under Texas Poison Control. The signal came through fine then.

But that was where the road ended and the forest opened up. Where a bridge crossed the bayou and nothing blocked the signal.

Bayou Bend sat only a few miles up the road. He could get a signal there. And maybe a cup of coffee. He needed something to clear his head.

He honked one more time and called her name because, why not? He had to do something.

Twice more he honked and yelled before giving up. He checked his phone again. Still no signal. Time to head for town.

Five minutes later, the yellow safety markers winked at him as the morning sun hit them. He stopped the car so he could get out and move the barricade, but he didn't.

He just waited, staring into space.

Leaving felt wrong. Like he was abandoning Fiona.

He'd spent the night hunting for her. He'd honked and yelled until his voice gave out. He'd lied to the police and threatened a man.

He'd broken more rules in the last five hours than in his entire life.

What else could he do?

Something. He had to do something.

Logic said the best way to help was to go into town and call for help. Organize a search party.

He glanced at the Cartier-style clock on Flash's dashboard. Ten after nine. Werner and Phelps probably already had an APB out for him. If he showed his face in town, they'd lock him up without listening to a word he said.

No organizing a search party for him.

If he wasn't there, how could he be sure they'd find the right spot to start searching—if they ever did?

He needed a marker of some kind. The weather had been warm when he left Houston. He didn't bring a scarf or gloves or a cap.

Broken limbs would be difficult to spot among all the other limbs and branches.

His shirt was bright blue. Maybe he could tear a strip off and hang it in a tree.

He swung Flash around and headed back. His conscience was clear.

He was doing the one last thing he could think of to help Fiona, not wasting time or procrastinating because he didn't want to face the shit storm that was about to come his way.

Then why did he feel like a traitor?

Once he'd marked the spot, he'd contact his friend at the FBI, get the name of a local officer he could trust and leave it to them to continue.

Then he'd go after the lowlifes who did this to her.

The sun shone directly into his eyes so he let Flash creep

along. He couldn't afford to miss the spot.

A deer bounded onto the road in front of him. He slammed on his brakes. The deer didn't move. In fact, it came closer.

He squinted and held up one hand to block the glare.

His brain spun and whizzed and clicked. He couldn't register what he saw, but he knew one thing.

It wasn't a deer.

Tom waited while Fiona downed a bottle of water without pausing. She saved the last few drops to pour over her face.

"Feeling better?" he asked.

"Madder. If that's possible. Before, I could only concentrate on getting away and then finding my way out. Now I want to track down those evil bastards and let them spend a night lost in a swamp with gators and mosquitoes and ticks. Oooh, ticks. They should all get ticks on their private parts not to mention chiggers and spider bites. Except Catherine. I'd let her catch a glimpse of a hungry gator then drop her in the stinking bayou and yell 'Swim, baby. Swim.' Let her see what it feels like."

That explained why she was so wet. And smelled so bad. Although, he probably didn't smell much better.

"I can have you back to the hotel for a hot shower and room service in forty-five minutes. If you can hold on a few extra minutes, we could go to a drive-thru now. There's an address near here I'd like to check out."

The Four Seasons concerto played softly in the background. Fiona reached over and changed the station. "Vivaldi might be great for a romantic evening by the fire, but we're gonna need a little Willy, Waylon, and the Boys to get our blood pumping if we want any chance of bringing these assholes down."

They had just pulled into Belle Mer. Stores were open. People were out on the street. Fiona pointed to a dollar store half a block away. "There. Stop there."

He turned in and she was out of the car before he had the engine off. She limped into the store at full speed. Tom did his best to follow behind.

He'd never actually been in a store like this. It looked large and well-lit with some of anything you could want.

Fiona was at a rack of clothing. She already had a T-shirt and hoodie over her arm and was examining sweatpants. She headed for a rack of footwear and grabbed some tennis shoes and a pair of socks before making a bee-line for a restroom clearly marked *Employees Only*.

He tried to act nonchalant, waiting for someone to throw them out. After five minutes he realized no one cared. When he passed a mirror, he stopped with a start.

He didn't look much better than Fiona.

Dirty pants. Dirty shirt. Dirty hair. Too bad. He wasn't buying any clothes here.

A moment later he spied a zip-up sweatshirt with LSU in purple and gold. The temperature had dropped overnight. A sweat shirt would hide most of the dirt and make him look more like a local.

He grabbed it and a pair of socks. His feet were wet and cold.

White socks and dress shoes. His mother would roll over in her grave. She was still very much alive, but she'd hold onto her indignation till she got there if only to have a reason to spin. Meanwhile, he'd just have to hope none of her friends saw him and told her about it.

Back in the car, Fiona gave an almost smile. "Okay. Now for that coffee and I'll be ready to start hunting for those soon-to-be sorry asses."

Fifteen minutes later, Google Maps led him to the address Tex had given him, an elaborate home with a winding sidewalk and leaded glass front door. The house sat on at least two acres with no immediate neighbors.

He discovered his blood was pumping along with something called Imagine Dragons. He was ready to go hunting.

"This is where I was told Granger lived. Let's ring the bell and see what he has to say for himself." Tom started to open his door when Fiona placed her hand on his arm.

"We can't go near there."

"Why not?" He was through being pushed around. Time to confront the lion in his den.

"This is where they brought me when they didn't know what else to do. He told them to get rid of me. I did my best to leave a trace of blood and some skin cells on his front steps. If we go up there now, his lawyers could claim I planted it now, not last night." She held up her arm. The scrape on the side of her wrist was hard to distinguish from the rope burns that circled it.

Tom bit back the urge to smash in that fancy front door and pull the guy out by his hair.

Fiona leaned against the headrest. Exhaustion was evident in the lines on her face. "Let's head back to the hotel and call the police."

"That might be a problem." Tom rubbed the stubble on his chin. "I have it on good authority the guys assigned to our case are in league with Granger. On the take all the way up to their dirty little necks."

Werner was for sure. The jury was still out on Phelps.

Fiona sighed but didn't open her eyes. "Shit. Now what?"

"Don't worry. I have a friend I can call." Not a friend exactly. More of an acquaintance. Someone he'd worked with before and trusted.

And the guy owed him a big favor.

CHAPTER THIRTY-EIGHT

Lincoln

Lincoln Montgomery had gotten an early start, driving from southeast Alabama to his apartment in Houston.

Getting home before dark seemed like a good idea at the time, but now the sun shone directly in his eyes. Sunglasses didn't help. The visor didn't help.

Only the occasional billboard or magnolia tree helped, then only for a few seconds. That was the reason he usually waited a couple of hours before he left.

A tension knot began forming at the base of his neck. The one he'd spent the last four days getting rid of.

He always enjoyed visiting his family—his mother's cooking was great, the laughs were plenty, he'd even come to accept the mandatory fishing trip with his father and brother-in-law—but after a few days he was itching to get home.

No matter how much his father hinted, he didn't plan to ditch his career as a Special Agent for the FBI and come home to help in the family used car business or teach at the local college. His brother could crack J. Edger Hoover jokes all day long and it wouldn't change his mind.

When his mother mentioned that Ashley Lewis was still available, his first thought was, "And she always will be." Probably due to that unfortunate donkey-bray laugh. Among other things.

Living with that for the next fifty years could drive a man to drink.

The road curved slightly and the sun came at him from a new angle instead of straight on. Not better, just different. Maybe worse.

When his phone rang, he didn't answer. He couldn't read the caller ID due to the glare and he didn't like to talk while driving. Especially when he had to struggle to see the road.

Twenty minutes later, a sign advertised a roadside park five miles away and he pulled in to return the call. He didn't care who it was—scammer, old girlfriend, bill collector—it had to be better than facing that sun one more minute.

"Montgomery." He leaned his head back and shut his eyes. He could still see the imprint of the sun, blood red, through his closed lids.

"Hey, Lincoln. It's Tom Meyers."

Damn. He'd been wrong. A bill collector would have been better. "I'm on vacation until Monday morning."

"Good. You'll have time to help me."

If he hung up he'd have to face the sun again.

Besides, he owed the guy. When he was in trouble, Tom had showed up. Although in helping, he'd managed to get a really good deal for a really bad guy. So had Tom helped him or had he helped Tom? "You've got five minutes. I'm in my car on the way back to Houston."

"From Alabama?"

"Yeah." Why would that make the guy sound so relieved?

"Perfect. You're right around the corner."

Around the corner from where? The ask was coming. He could feel it. He counted to ten and waited.

"I've got a client in Houston who's accused of murdering her husband and I sent my investigator, a woman named Fiona Drake, to Louisiana to check out a few iffy things in the dead guy's past. Apparently, the guy was leading a double life and dealing drugs. A local guy may have been murdered. Somebody must not have liked her sniffing around. Last night a bunch of lowlifes bundled her into a van, drove her out to the swamp, and tried to kill her."

This might be interesting after all. His headache was already better. "I'm guessing she got away if you're telling me this story. What's the problem? Go to the local police and report it."

"I did, immediately. They didn't believe me. Tried to say I was involved."

That didn't make any sense. "Why would you kidnap your

own investigator?"

"They came up with some wild theory that we were in a romantic liaison that went south. She either ran away and I was afraid of what she might say or I lost control and killed her then tried to hide the body."

Lincoln couldn't help it. He started laughing. "That's the craziest thing I've ever heard. Do they know who you are? Have they ever met you?" Tom was the most uptight, straight-laced person he'd ever met…besides himself.

"I've just found out that one of the two cops who interviewed me is tied in with the drug cartel we suspect of killing my client's husband. And the two cops in Houston aren't exactly paragons of virtue either."

"Are you telling me you're dealing with dishonest cops in Houston *and* in Louisiana?"

"No. Only the one in Louisiana. The Houston detective, Baxter is her name, has it in for me because I made her look bad on the stand in a previous case. She's not dishonest, but she set her sights on my client from day one and quit looking. I'm afraid she'll ignore any evidence I bring in. I need this stuff to be seen by someone who'll pay attention."

That was a pretty big coincidence. He didn't appreciate lawyers who threw around the term *dirty cops* to get their clients off. He'd only worked with Tom on one case but he'd found the man to be honest. The fact that he'd only called one of the Louisiana cops crooked and neither of the ones in Houston dirty helped. "Where are you now?"

"We're in a little town about 60 miles from Baton Rouge hiding from her assailants. I need to get her somewhere safe but I think there might be an APB out on me already."

Lincoln tried to picture the lawyer in an orange jumpsuit instead of his usual $1,200 pinstripe. Nope. Couldn't manage it. Did not compute.

"And you're calling me because…?"

"Isn't kidnapping federal?" Tom asked.

Ahh. So that's what he wanted. "Only in special circumstances. Otherwise, it's not under our jurisdiction unless requested by the local authorities."

"What if the local cops are involved in covering up the drug dealing and murder?"

"Then you have public corruption plus kidnapping. If the drugs came across state lines, it's a three-fer and you've got yourself a hat trick."

CHAPTER
THIRTY-NINE

Fiona

Fiona finished the last of her coffee and set the empty container in the cup holder. "If we can't go back to the hotel, and we can't call the police, I have one place we can check out while waiting for your friend to call. It's not far in case he wants us to go somewhere in this area."

"Sure. Where's that?"

"One of this guy's tire stores. The van might be hidden there."

"I already checked the places you showed me. Nothing there."

The thought of Tom driving around, hunting for her, warmed a spot in her chest. Had she even thanked him? Admitting she needed help didn't come easy for her. Before the day was over, she had to try. "This is a different place. We didn't go to it yesterday. I didn't think it was important."

"What changed your mind?"

"The woman who ran the store was new. Had only been in charge a couple of weeks. Took over for a guy who went missing. That guy was the older body you found in the woods."

Tom shivered as if remembering the sight of Corey's decomposing body. She wasn't crazy about the memory either. He flipped on his blinker to change lanes. "And you think maybe you misjudged her?"

Like Cleopatra misjudged the asp. Because Catherine was a woman with a sweet smile and soft voice, she'd accepted her explanation. That was as bad as the men who assumed a woman was less intelligent and less capable due to her gender.

It was a mistake that nearly got her killed—one she wouldn't make again.

"She wasn't simply a member of the gang that took me, she was their leader. They took orders from her. And I let her convince me she was a badass for being a woman in charge of a mostly male venue. I didn't realize how bad she was." *Or how much of an ass.*

A light snapped on somewhere in Fiona's brain. "I never checked her out with the others. Lend me your phone. I'll see if I can discover anything about her."

Tom pulled into a small shopping area. "I have a better idea. You lost your phone while on an assignment. Let's get you a new one on the company and put you on our business plan."

The new phone she could go for. Company business was almost the only thing she used it for. Being on the company's plan was another thing. Her whole business depended on privacy. It wasn't that she didn't trust Tom, but why take a chance?

Half an hour later Tom's friend hadn't called back with a workable plan, but she had a sparkling new, up-to-date phone with all her information downloaded from the cloud.

She pointed toward a McDonalds at the end of the street. "Park over there. I can piggy-back off their free Wi-Fi. I want to do some research on Catherine. Something about her doesn't add up."

Tom wove his way through the parking lot to a spot next to the building. "What makes you think that?"

"She hadn't been manager of that place but a couple of weeks yet she was obviously in charge. Lance and Zach are lightweights. No one would put them in charge of a trip to the grocery store much less a kidnapping and murder. Troy seemed fairly capable. Why wasn't he the leader? Which brings me to the dead guy. Corey."

"Wasn't he the original manager of the store? Were they moving drugs then?"

"Yeah, but he didn't like it. He wanted out."

"They killed him to shut him up."

"Except they beat him up first. And that seemed to work. He got scared and clammed up. Supposedly moved to the next town over. Enter Catherine, and *presto!* He's dead and so is

Devin Grimes."

"That's a stretch to put her behind both murders. Why would she want to?"

"I don't know, but I intend to find out."

Her new phone was close enough to the old one that she didn't have to waste time learning to use it. Seven minutes later, she sat back and dropped the phone onto her lap. "So far, all I've learned is that her last name is Holder but she's married to a guy named Phil Woods."

"That doesn't sound suspicious. Lots of women don't take their husband's name these days."

"I agree. I'm just surprised it took me that long to find it. Let's go on and check out the store she manages. I can finish this up after."

"Sounds great. How do I get there?"

"Past the turn-off to the highway and to the right."

South of town and one block off Main Street, they saw a bustling shopping center. At the far end sat the tire store Catherine managed—closed and dark on a busy Saturday morning.

Tom shook his head. "This place was open when you visited yesterday?"

"Open and busy. Cars in each bay and a couple waiting." She got out and pressed her face against the window until she could see into the bay area.

A dark van hugged the far wall. She couldn't tell if it had a broken tail light.

She used the sleeve of her sweatshirt to rub away any marks or fingerprints she'd left on the glass before jumping back in the car. "Let's get out of here. Whatever evidence is in that van, I don't want anyone saying I planted it there."

Tom gave her his *sour attorney* look. She'd seen it before when he had to lecture clients. She didn't like having it directed toward her. "That's fine, but if asked anything about this stop, don't lie. Don't even avoid. Nothing makes you look guilty like being caught in a lie."

Something had preyed on her mind for the last hour. Might as well confront him. If he could lecture her, she could question him.

"Your friend, the FBI agent?"

"Yes?"

"You trust him. We're not sitting ducks here waiting for someone to swoop in and get us?"

"By someone do you mean Granger's thugs or dirty cops?"

"Aren't they the same thing?"

Tom took too long answering for her to be comfortable. "He won't knowingly betray us to either one. It's the unknowingly that worries me. We have no idea how deep this thing goes."

"Yet here we sit, in a bright red sports car, while Granger's goons are probably prowling around looking for us."

"Shit. You're right. We're sitting ducks. We have to ditch this car." The engine roared to life and Tom peeled onto the street.

Fiona hung on to the door handle. "Try not to kill us first."

CHAPTER FORTY

Fiona

Fiona kept her eyes flicking from one end of the street to the other—watching. For what exactly, she wasn't sure, but like the old saying, she'd know it when she saw it.

And she planned to be prepared.

She fought back a shiver. An autumn breeze, fresh and clean after a night spent in the woods and a morning swimming in dark, murky water, had a definite nip to it. Especially since her underwear was still damp and clingy, the one thing she wasn't willing to buy at the dollar store.

Although she hadn't been too proud to pocket a steak knife when Tom wasn't looking.

The handle felt flimsy and the blade dull, but she'd been attacked twice since arriving in Louisiana and going unarmed wasn't an option.

Tom had hidden the car inside a broken carwash located behind a gas station. He'd slipped the clerk on duty twenty bucks not to notice anything. He'd also bought them both gimme caps.

His said *John Deere* and was dark green with gold lettering. Hers was pink with *Super Bitch* in rhinestones. She planned to shove that cap up somebody's ass if they commented.

But the caps covered their hair, probably the most notable thing about both of them.

Somewhere along the way Tom had acquired a cane. As part of his disguise or as a weapon? She wasn't sure, but she'd seen the damage he'd inflicted while on that dark sidewalk so it should work either way.

Tom fidgeted. "Are you sure we're doing the right thing, sitting out here in the open?"

The wrought iron table and chairs were down a side alley between a sandwich shop and an ice cream parlor. The awning left them in shadow but offered her a decent view of Main Street.

She glanced at Tom and smiled. "Trust me on this. I've had more experience blending in than you have. Our best bet is to stay here in public." With that hair and those eyes he would never look pedestrian but he was definitely trying.

After eighteen hours on the run she was famished, the boost from that early morning coffee long gone.

The sandwich shop had only been open a few minutes when they went in so they didn't have to worry about prying eyes. Tom ordered a quiche with fresh fruit on the side. She went straight for the double cheeseburger and fries.

Nothing had ever tasted so good in her life.

She wolfed down half the burger then dug back into searching for information on Catherine. In no time things started to get interesting.

Tom finished the last of his fruit and pushed his plate back. "Find anything?"

"Looks like Catherine's husband has a drug problem that he supports as a two-bit robber. He breaks into houses when the owners are at work and lifts whatever is easy to pawn."

"Burglar."

"What?" What the hell was Tom talking about?

"Robbery is a violent crime. Burglary isn't. A good burglar never lets his victim see him."

"He must not have been a good one because he got caught. He's in jail right now. In fact, he's in the prison hospital. Another inmate cut him pretty bad a few days after Catherine stepped into her new job."

Tom played with his water glass, making circles with the condensation. "Now that's quite a coincidence."

It sure was. "Especially when you consider Catherine sold her car and closed out their bank account a few days after he got caught."

"Trying to pay off his debts? Are you thinking some good old-fashioned blackmail? Get your wife to do this little favor for us and we'll forget what you owe us? Sounds a bit far-fetched. Selling drugs is one thing, but murder is a big step to ask of a common car mechanic."

"What if I told you Catherine is a vet? Four years in the army. Two in Afghanistan."

Tom gnawed on his lip. "Closer, but still a stretch."

He was playing lawyer. Wanting proof. She could understand that. "Then there's the fact that she's diabetic. Takes the same meds Devin Grimes does. Or did." Getting that information hadn't been easy.

"Okay. You've got my interest. Who's she working for? This Granger guy or the other guys? The ones who don't want Granger to take over."

Now she was confused. "How did that help the other guys?"

"If, and that's a big if, it was her, she took out their conduit to the drugs then increased police scrutiny by abducting you."

"But that put her right in the middle of everything. I'm sure she loves her husband, but enough to go to jail herself for a murder?"

"No one would suspect her. You didn't."

He didn't have to rub that mistake in her face. "So which group is behind this?"

"Doesn't matter. If we can get out of here, the police can handle it. All we're interested in is getting our client off and I think we can show other people had motive, opportunity, and the will to kill."

That didn't feel right to her. Just because there were others who wanted Devin Grimes dead didn't mean his wife didn't want it more. Without proof they might never know for sure.

Tom stopped and studied her. "Do you still believe Kara is guilty?"

Did she? Catherine had certainly proved she wasn't above using murder to solve her problems. The thought of her calmly telling Evan, 'Get her out of here.' caused a fist-sized knot to form in her stomach. She shoved the remaining burger to the side, unable to swallow another bite.

Damn. Now she needed to investigate Evan. He seemed quite willing to do Catherine's bidding. "I don't know about Kara. It's her attitude. She's secretive and uncooperative. Definitely hiding something from us."

"I've never had a client yet that didn't hide things from me. If you come up with something concrete, let me know. Then I'll think about how I need to handle it."

Fiona noticed it first, but her brain didn't want to accept the message her eyes were sending. Tom squirmed. He definitely saw it also.

A shit-brown pickup with a trailer hitch turning down the road-to-nowhere that had almost been the site of her death.

Worries about evidence and justice disappeared. Fear and anger fought for prominence. Anger won.

The tinted windows prevented her from seeing the driver but she had no doubt Troy sat behind the wheel. How many others were in the extended cab was another question.

One she wasn't anxious to have answered.

Tom lowered his head. "Now what?"

"Sit still until they're out of sight. If we get up now, they'll notice us."

"Last time I saw Troy, his arm was in a sling so probably dislocated, not broken. Zach's was in a cast so definitely broken. He wasn't in any condition to harm a flea. If he's even been found yet. I don't know about the others that jumped us." Tom's voice held steady, showing no sign of nerves.

Good. They couldn't afford any of those. "Catherine has broken ribs. That won't slow her down too much. I cut Lance on the hip. Not bad but he carried on whining like I'd preformed an appendectomy without anesthesia. Evan was the dangerous one and he's dead. So basically, a bunch of cripples."

"Unless they brought reinforcements."

Leave it to Tom to mention the one bad scenario she hadn't considered. "Whatever. If they're looking for me, they'll be back in those woods for a while."

"If they just want to get rid of Evan and Corey, all they have to do is drag their bodies a few hundred feet to the bayou and push them into the water, something they should have done in the first place. You said you'd seen at least one alligator. Odds are he has friends."

Damn, he'd done it again. That blow on the head and night in the swamp had taken more out of her than she'd realized. She couldn't afford to be this slow on the uptake.

He placed his hand on top of hers. It was probably the first time he'd ever actually touched her on purpose. He better not think she was weak and in need of his protection.

His voice was low, urgent. "We need to make a decision. We can stay here—you're right, they'll likely be a while and we're pretty well hidden—and wait for Lincoln to call us. Or we can get back to the car and take our chances in Baton Rouge. Whichever we decide, we need to make that decision now. We're fairly safe here in town but I don't want to be caught on the open road with them on our tail and no one else around."

Before she could answer, Tom's phone rang. He closed his eyes for one brief second, took a deep breath, and pressed *accept*.

CHAPTER
FORTY-ONE

Tom

The phone lay on the table between them. Tom put it on *speaker* so they could both hear but lowered the volume so others couldn't.

Fiona leaned her head forward until it almost touched his. She smelled better than when he first found her, but not a lot better.

He probably wasn't any bed of roses himself.

Swamp. Sweat. Fear. Fatigue. Not to mention dirty hair. Dirty face. Dirty fingernails. Him with a black eye. Fiona with scratches and a few flecks of blood here and there.

It's a wonder the clerk was willing to serve them at all. In fact, the kid almost jumped for joy when they asked for an outside table despite the chilly breeze.

The Caller ID said Special Agent L.SMontgomery. Relief

swept over him like a warm shower. "Lincoln? Do you have any news for us?"

"Some good. Some bad."

He wasn't sure he could take any bad news. "Shoot." A poor choice of words considering all they'd been through the last two days.

"I can't be involved in anything in Houston between you and Baxter."

Damn. He'd been counting on Lincoln's help.

Lincoln's voice still had the deep rumble he'd come to recognize, even with the volume lowered. "We have too many things connecting us. Baxter could throw a lot of smoke making us both look bad. Anything I said would be compromised."

The guy was right. That didn't make it any easier to hear.

"There's a homicide detective I've worked with in a little town in northeast Louisiana. She'll look after you and make sure every bit of evidence is logged in and examined."

Fiona leaned even closer to the phone. "That sounds great, but what about now? We're exposed here. The guys who abducted me just drove past. They could be back at any time. Is anyone coming to get us?"

"That's the bad news. She can't come get you, but if you can get to her, she'll make sure nothing happens to you. If you swing way east before you start north, you can bypass Baton Rouge and cut through Mississippi. Nobody's looking for you in Mississippi, are they?"

"No." The guy didn't have to get sarcastic about it.

"Then you could be there in about three, three and a half hours."

Tom didn't like it, but they could do that if necessary.

"Or I have another option for you. Not sure how you'll feel about it."

"What's that?" If Lincoln thought they were going to turn themselves in he was dead wrong. The sight of that brown pickup sealed off that idea.

"Like I said, kidnapping isn't federal unless it's across state lines, or involves minors, or a couple of other categories. I have to make sure we're on the same page here. They didn't take you across state lines did they, Fiona?"

She didn't look any too happy about the choices they were being given. "No. I drove here myself."

"But add kidnapping to the sale of drugs, which had to come over some border, either state or international, plus add in corrupt officials, and my boss is interested. You're sure about the dirty cops, Tom?"

"Yes. I'm sure." No, he wasn't, but Tex was and that guy didn't make mistakes. For now he'd give the go ahead and apologize later if necessary.

"Okay then. I'm on my way and should reach Baton Rouge in an hour and a half."

"I don't think we can drive through the middle of Baton Rouge to the Federal Building without getting stopped first." Werner would have every cop in town watching for him by now.

"Don't worry. There's a suburb called Westminster before you get to Baton Rouge."

"Yeah. I saw it."

"I'll meet you there at the Holiday Inn on the south side of town. Park in the back and call when you get there."

The temperature had dropped several degrees since they sat at the little outdoor café. His arms rested on the metal table and he could feel the cold travel up them even through his fleece jacket. Beside him, Fiona had started to shiver.

One way or the other, it was time to move. They couldn't hide here any longer.

TOM DROVE WHILE Fiona worked her phone.

This was the time they were most at risk. Most exposed. Most vulnerable.

He needed to concentrate on the road.

The next town was thirty miles away. If a brown pickup showed up behind them, there was no open store or busy parking lot full of people for cover.

The road was built up to prevent flooding during bad weather, leaving a deep ditch on either side. One well-placed tap on his rear bumper by a larger, heavier vehicle could send them tumbling.

From time to time, Fiona would shout out newly

discovered bits of information. "Evan's last name is Evans. Are you shitting me? They named their kid Evan Evans? No wonder he turned out so screwed up."

Five minutes later, "He was born in Gulf Shores, Alabama."

Later still, "He went into the Army straight out of high school. Well, it would have been straight out of high school if he had actually graduated."

Then, "He has a juvie record. Don't know if I can get into that. At least not now. Maybe when I get back to my computer. I'll have a better connection then."

A bend in the road left everything in shadow. Towering cypress trees blocked the sun. Spanish moss swayed in the breeze causing what light there was to flicker and dance.

He had to slow Flash to a crawl. Anything could dart across the road and he might not have time to react. Even something small like a fox or raccoon could cause him to run off the road or have a flat. A deer or bobcat would wreck his car, leaving them stranded on this little-traveled back road.

He refused to think about black bear, which the pamphlet in his hotel room claimed had recently been taken off the endangered species list.

They had another hour until they reached the outskirts of Baton Rouge. His nerves might not last that long, but they'd flipped a coin and decided this was better than trying to make it farther north and depending on a stranger.

They drove for ten more minutes, in and out of shadow,

when a car came around the next curve and flew past them going the opposite direction.

The steering wheel turned to ice under his hands.

"Fiona, listen to me."

She must have heard the urgency in his voice because her head, which had been bent over her phone, popped up. "Yes?"

"You don't talk. You need a hospital. Some people you don't know abducted you. You escaped and hid in the woods all night. You would have died if I hadn't found you. You're not up to giving a statement. You want a lawyer."

"I don't need a hospital. What are you talking about?"

The flashing red lights behind them answered her question.

"Promise me you'll remember what I told you."

"You mean don't blurt out that I killed a guy?"

"Yes, except I'm not sure you killed him. You would have been covered in blood if you hit his carotid artery and his body was kind of…mangled."

"Well, I didn't do him any good and I'll have to figure out how to live with that, but I did see them back over him."

Later all this would hit her—hard. For now, he could only do his best to protect her legally. "Let's both keep our mouths shut until we figure out where we stand. Can you manage that?"

She nodded. "I don't say anything except it wasn't you who kidnapped me and I need a hospital. If they pressure me, I ask for a lawyer. What about you. What's going to happen to you?"

"Not much if you convince them I didn't harm you." It wasn't as simple as that. They might eventually let him go, *if* they hadn't found Zach and *if* he wasn't screaming about being locked in the trunk of his car, but it would take hours.

CHAPTER FORTY-TWO

Fiona

Fiona's nerves, starting at the soles of her feet and traveling up her torso and down her arms, were on fire. They twitched and jumped like a kid on a sugar high. Her heart had turned into a Kentucky Derby thoroughbred and galloped across her chest.

This was no time to fall apart. She needed to keep her head.

Tom put on his blinker and coasted to the side of the road. "Move slowly and open my glove compartment. My insurance papers should be on top. See if you can hand them to me without causing these two guys to get jumpy."

Oh yeah. Put that responsibility on me.

The car behind them didn't have any markings and the two men who got out weren't wearing a uniform, but they definitely had the cop accoutrements of lights and siren.

That didn't necessarily make them police officers.

Tom lowered his window as she slipped the paper into his hand which already held his driver's license. How'd he manage that?

She closed the glove compartment with her knee and the *click* sounded like a gunshot in the now silent air.

"Good afternoon, sir. What seems to be the problem? I'm sure I wasn't speeding." Tom sounded like innocence personified.

"Step out of the vehicle and put your hands on the roof of the car."

That might have been the first time she had ever seen Tom completely taken aback. His eyes sized up the man. "May I see some identification please?"

The man wasn't large, but he was bigger and bulkier than Tom. His voice lowered an octave and he spoke slowly, as if to someone of minimal intelligence. "Exit the vehicle, now."

Before Tom could answer, the man had reached through the window and opened the door. He grabbed Tom with one meaty hand and yanked, but Tom still had his seat belt attached.

A gun appeared as if by magic. "Take off your seat belt and exit the vehicle."

The race horse galloping through Fiona's chest reared up. "You have to help us. We're on our way to the hospital. Some dirtbags abducted me last night. I might have died if my boss here hadn't rescued me, but I think I have a concussion. My head is splitting and I have double vision. If you could use your siren and lead the way, we'll follow you."

The second man, this one skinnier and with more hair, opened her door. "Please step out, ma'am."

She released her seatbelt and got out. Tom did the same on his side.

The big man spun Tom around and slapped handcuffs on him as soon as his feet hit the ground. And he wasn't any too gentle about it.

Fiona placed her hand on the smaller man's arm as if to steady herself. "I think I'm gonna be sick. I don't know if it's the double vision or all the swamp water I swallowed, but I'm about to throw up."

She stumbled a few feet into the grass, bent over, and made retching sounds. "I really need to get to the hospital."

The bigger man had shoved Tom into the backseat of his car. He swung around. "I'll take this one in," he called out. "Why don't you take the Porsche and get her to the hospital? Keep a close eye on her. We don't know how she fits into things."

Tom stuck his head out the still open door. "You put a scratch on my car and I'll have you in court."

Fiona wanted to kick him. This wasn't the time to antagonize two men who had them under control. On the other hand, maybe he was trying to show he wasn't afraid. That those guys weren't in complete control.

All she knew was the smaller guy flipped Tom the bird

and raced the engine while she climbed back in and fastened her seatbelt.

She had a feeling they were in for a bumpy ride.

THE RIDE TO the hospital wasn't that bumpy after all.

Once Fiona claimed the only way she could make it to Baton Rouge without throwing up was to stay quiet, lean her head back, and close her eyes, she was left in peace.

The two men had finally identified themselves as undercover narcotics investigators from the capital. This should have made her feel better.

It didn't.

Why were they so far from home searching for them?

Obviously, Werner, the guy Tom claimed was on the take, sent them. How deep did the corruption go? Was Gills, the skinny guy driving her, in on everything or simply a stooge sent to bring them in?

She'd love to get him talking. Get a feel for what he knew. Only if she started a conversation, he'd begin asking her questions and Tom had insisted she keep her mouth shut.

Fiona had never been in the hospital herself, except maybe to be born, she wasn't sure, but she'd visited a foster father in one before. She'd been sent back as soon as he got out because his wife needed to take care of him and *not some snotty-nosed little kid.*

This one smelled just the same—maybe all hospitals did. It contained a mixture of air conditioning, industrial cleaner, medications, and fear. Add an unnerving silence, punctuated by squeaky rubber-soled shoes, unintelligible announcements over the PA, and the distant hum of machinery, and she regretted insisting on being checked out.

She was handed a form asking about her symptoms and she basically checked *yes* to all of them.

Loss of consciousness? Yes.

Headache? Yes.

Double vision? Oh, that sounded good. Yes.

Fatigue? She didn't have to lie to answer yes to that one.

Nausea? Gills was looking over her shoulder so she had to check yes.

Slurred speech? Better say no. She hadn't been using that one.

The doctor who came into her little white cubicle looked so young she wouldn't have served him alcohol without asking for an ID.

He checked her eyes and reflexes and asked most of the same questions she'd already answered on the form in his hand.

When he reached the question about nausea, she paused. "I had it earlier, but I went to sleep in the car and feel better now. The queasiness might have been from all the bayou water I inadvertently swallowed."

When he reached the end of the form, he twisted toward Officer Gills. "I need you to step out of the room now."

Gills sputtered, but did as asked.

The doctor leaned forward and lowered his voice. "I'd like to do a rape test kit on you now. I understand if you're not sure you want to pursue that avenue at this time. We can do the test now and set it aside for later, but if you don't do it today and you change your mind, the evidence will be gone. Will you allow me to proceed?"

How did someone that young learn to be so gentle and caring?

Fiona thought of all the women who sat in little rooms like this and had to answer yes to that question. Her eyes filled with tears. She'd had a lot of bad things happen in her life, but not that one.

"I'm okay, doc. Thanks. Really, I am. They didn't touch me that way."

Gills must have been listening outside the curtain because he came in immediately. "Can I take her to the station now?"

"No. I think we should keep her overnight. We need to clean her up, give her a tetanus shot, do some bloodwork. She'll need lots of rest over the next few days. Maybe a week or longer. She's likely to have memory loss, confusion, headaches. I'd advise against any stress. She's not up to any type of questioning."

No. No. No. She might have overplayed her hand. She needed to find out if Tom was okay then get back to her computer. There were things about Catherine and Evan still to learn. Not to mention Devin who appeared to have at least three names and three families.

No telling what else she might learn now that she knew where he grew up.

She had to ditch Gills and get back to work.

"I have a nice hotel room at the Hilton. Can't I go back there? I'd sleep much better. They have room service if I need anything and my boss is just next door."

The doctor glanced at Gills. "You'll make sure she gets to her room safely, not just drop her off in front?"

Gills nodded. "Sure, Doc. Door to door service."

She left the hospital with salve over the rope burns on her wrists and ankles, cortisone on her bug bites, and ointment on a multitude of scratches. She had pills for her headache, medicine in case her nausea returned, and antibiotics against any parasites she'd picked up either in the water or on the ground.

All in all, she was pleased with the way she'd handled things until she and Gills stepped out of the hospital doors and saw Detective Phelps waiting.

Gills she could handle, but she wasn't confident Phelps wouldn't take her to the station for questioning…or to Granger for disposal.

CHAPTER
FORTY-THREE

Tom

T om had sat in many rooms like this over the years, only he
wasn't usually the one in handcuffs.

He'd often waited an hour or more for the detective to
show up. This time instead of letting Tom stew, Werner made
his appearance in less than fifteen minutes.

The guy was allowing his nerves to get the better of him.

All the better for Tom.

He started in before Werner was seated. "What the hell am
I doing here? And in handcuffs. Now get these off so I can call
my lawyer."

Werner took a key from his pocket and unlocked the cuffs.
He slid them to his side of the table, but left them out as if to
say they could go back on as easily as they came off. "You can
call your lawyer if you want, but we'll both end up sitting here

for hours waiting. Meanwhile, you can answer a few simple questions and maybe we can get this cleared up right now. Let you get back to Houston where no one cares what you do in the privacy of your own home."

This should be good. The guy was already breaking all the rules of interrogation. At this rate, Tom would learn twice as much as Werner. "I'm tired. I've been up all night. I want this over so I can go home. What've you got?"

Werner sat a manila folder on the scarred interview table. "You were due in my office by nine a.m. When you failed to appear—"

"Voluntarily. As a witness," Tom reminded him.

"When you failed to appear, we felt it necessary to bring you in ourselves."

"After you *failed* to do your job and I had to rescue my friend—who was in very bad shape and might have died if I hadn't found her in time."

"Which brings us to an interesting question. How *did* you find her?"

Tom let the righteous indignation he actually felt take over. "I looked! How about you? Did you even try? Or did you just send your minions out to find me, the one who *wasn't kidnapped*?"

"Unless there was no abduction and you found her exactly where you left her." The smirk on Werner's face begged to be wiped out with a fist.

"And why would I do that?"

"Because your *kidnapping* story was full of holes. You knew when we found her you'd be our main suspect." Werner actually made quotation marks with his fingers. Asshole.

"That's ludicrous. Your men heard her say a van full of strangers grabbed her off the street. I know. I was there."

"When she was taken or when she denied it?"

"Both. And she never denied being taken."

"For someone who was there when it happened, you weren't much help were you? Even with all your martial arts training and your fancy folding stick."

That part was true, and it hurt. Bad. "I was half a block away when the van pulled up. By the time I got there the fight was over and they were tossing her into the van like a bag of dirty laundry."

Tom reined in his temper. Now wasn't the time. There were still things to be learned first. "If you don't believe me, why don't you ask her? I'm sure she'll be happy to tell you what happened."

"Don't worry, we'll be questioning her as soon as possible. My partner is on the way to her now. We'll also be checking your bank account to see just how much you paid her to keep her mouth shut. Her story might change when we inform her that lying to the police is a crime."

Exactly why he told her not to say anything without a lawyer present.

If that's all they were worried about, they hadn't found the two bodies in the woods yet, if they were still there after Troy and his friends had returned.

Werner fiddled with the folder in front of him. "I'd like to get back to the question of how you found her."

"I drove around all night. I started with the direction the van was headed when it disappeared. I drove down side streets and dark alleys. Anywhere they could pull off without being noticed. I got farther and farther away from Baton Rouge but that seemed logical because it's too busy here in town. I was about to head back when I saw a side road almost hidden behind a store and a safety barricade that had been moved to the side."

So far, every word he'd said had been true. There were undoubtedly traffic cameras with video of him searching.

"And no one told you where to look?"

Now things were getting tricky. "Who could have told me except the people who took her?"

Werner tapped one finger on the manila folder. "Do you know a man named Fredrick Z. York?"

His heart skipped a beat, maybe two, but he didn't let it register on his face. "I don't think so, why?"

Werner opened the folder and pushed a photo forward. "He says you broke his arm and locked him in the trunk of his car."

This put Tom in a whole new pile of shit. "He looks familiar. Is that the guy from the tire store? I went in to see about racing tires, but they didn't have any. He was pissed because I wasn't willing to wait a week while he ordered some. Is he trying to say I did something to him?"

"No, he's the guy who says you came up behind him, put a knife to his throat and locked him in his trunk. Now *that's* kidnapping."

"Why would I do a thing like that? Because he didn't have the tires I wanted?"

"He claims you were looking for drugs, not tires."

"In the middle of the store in the middle of the afternoon with dozens of people around? That's crazy."

"Last night. Well after midnight. He had a flat and you offered to help, then threatened to kill him if he didn't give you drugs he didn't have."

Talk about a story full of holes. This one was Swiss cheese. Only that wouldn't matter if Werner decided not to let facts get in the way. "So I'm supposed to have happened to drive past and saw him broken down, then what? Decided 'Here's someone I can buy drugs from,' grabbed him by the neck, and pushed him into the trunk?"

He rushed on before Werner could stop him to ask questions. Zach's story might be flimsy, but so was his. "Did anyone find drugs on me? Or a knife? Maybe someone should test *him* for drugs. While you're at it, check his car. I bet you'll find at least some residue in there. If he's the guy from the tire store, he was high when I saw him yesterday. I doubt he got in any better shape as the day went on."

He needed to shut this down, fast. "I'm pretty sure we can reenact this guy's little episode and show there's no way he could recognize me in the dark with me behind him. If you're going to try to blame this shit on me, I'm going to need a lawyer. It's time to stop screwing around and let me make my phone call."

A commotion sounded in the hall outside. They both glanced up when the door flew open.

In walked Lincoln Montgomery, wearing a *Black Sabbath* T-shirt, cargo pants, and a sunburn. The FBI credentials hanging on a lanyard around his neck looked like something he'd sent off for in the mail.

CHAPTER FORTY-FOUR

Lincoln

Lincoln was driving his own car, not the black SUV issued him by the FBI. He'd been on vacation after all. The Audi was plenty comfortable, but not as big as his federal ride.

Tom must have liked it. He'd leaned his head back and closed his eyes.

Let the guy rest. He'd had a long couple of days. But when he woke up, he had some questions to answer.

Ten minutes later Tom spoke without opening his eyes. "How'd you find me?"

"I got tired of waiting. I tried calling you twice. When you didn't answer I knew you were in trouble. Some of these local yahoos have an exaggerated opinion of their own importance. A phone call to their boss from the FBI explaining that we're taking over usually dispels them of that idea."

"I can imagine. I saw the look in Werner's eyes. Don't make the mistake of thinking he'll actually step away."

"Don't worry. Others have tried. Generally, we work well with the local police. We have resources they need and they have the manpower we don't. Occasionally you run into a cop who thinks working with us is an insult. If it wasn't for the aggravation, I might even enjoy teaching them that excrement rolls downhill and they're at the bottom of the valley."

"This isn't about power or ego, for Werner, it's about his life. He could end up behind bars himself."

Maybe, but the term *dirty cop* was tossed around a lot more often than proved true. Tom's eyes might not be open, but the guy was definitely awake. "If he's dirty, I'll come down on him with all the power of the federal government. The same goes for you. If you made this whole thing up to get a guilty client off, I'll throw you out of this car and let the gators have you."

The problem was, Lincoln didn't think Tom had made it up.

Not because the evidence was overwhelming. He hadn't looked at the evidence yet. He'd been too busy driving.

Because he knew Tom. Not well, like someone you'd share a beer with or take in a game together. He'd only worked with the guy once, but he'd been impressed.

He seemed more like a person you'd seen in action and knew you could depend on.

Tom was too smart. He didn't need to pull crazy shit to get a client off. And the man would never risk his reputation by doing something illegal.

The fact that Tom paused before answering sent a jolt of ice through his veins. Had he risked his job and future on a rumor?

"I didn't make it up. That I can promise you. I don't have as much proof as I'd like, yet, but that's only because those lowlifes kidnapped my investigator before we finished digging."

The ice thawed…somewhat. "Tell me what you've got so far."

"My client is accused of murdering her husband. I instructed my investigator, Fiona, to dig into the man's past. Took her less than an hour to discover there was something fishy about him. No friends. No past. Not even his employer knew anything about him—had never verified his references— but admitted the guy didn't make enough to live on. Fiona followed his trail to Louisiana and discovered he had a different name, a second family in Baton Rouge, and a third family we haven't checked out yet. That's the part we can prove."

The icy feeling returned. Tom didn't have near enough to warrant calling in the Feds. "That makes the guy a scumbag, but doesn't make his wife innocent. In fact, it gives her more reason to off him."

"I know. I know. Just wait. It gets better."

It would have to.

"Fiona uncovered some iffy ties between our dead guy and three tire stores owned by a guy named Granger. That night two of the tire store guys tried to scare Fiona off. Roughed her up a bit. That's when I showed up and we stirred the pot some more."

That was the time-honored way to get information. Shake the trees and see what fell out. It wasn't proof, but things were getting more interesting. "Werner's boss said they took her to the hospital. Is that why?"

"That happened the second time the guys showed up, with friends. Tossed Fiona in a van and drove her to Granger's house. He told them to get rid of her."

"Okay, we're getting warmer. That's attempted murder. Bad, but still not a federal case. What happened to the drugs and dirty cops?"

By the time they reached the hospital where the Baton Rouge cops had left Tom's car, he'd finished the whole crazy story.

And it was pretty crazy.

The doctor had already released Fiona, so Lincoln followed Tom in his sporty red car back to the hotel where they'd been staying. He spent the drive mulling over everything Tom had told him. By the time he let the valet park his car he'd come to an important conclusion—Tom hadn't told him everything.

And whatever he'd left out was big.

THE SUN CAST a pink glow over the horizon as it set. Lincoln blew out a lengthy breath. A long day finally over. He and Tom reached the hotel room before Fiona.

A flutter of disappointment surprised him. He'd heard so much about this Fiona woman he was anxious to meet her. Everything he'd learned so far left her an enigma, a mystery.

Tom paced the room, obviously worried about his investigator. Supposedly she and Detective Phelps had left the hospital in a BRPD cruiser before they arrived to pick up Tom's car.

Where were they?

If Phelps thought he could play hide-the-suspect he'd better reconsider. Lincoln had the personal cell phone number of both the Chief of Police and the Mayor.

If he used them—and he wouldn't unless absolutely necessary—that would be the end of Phelps's career.

A muffled sound from the next room caused Lincoln to look up from his chair. Tom stopped pacing. They glanced at each other and almost tiptoed to the connecting door.

Voices. More than one. Lincoln eased the knob forward until the lock clicked almost silently into place.

Three seconds later the knob jiggled and the door rattled. He leaned against the wall. Just in time.

When he heard Fiona's side of the door slam and lock, he opened their half again. He pressed his ear against the cold wood, straining to make out any words from the other side.

"There. You…safe now. Don't…behind me. I'll … tomorrow…feel …."

Fiona's voice was easier to understand. She must have

been standing closer to the door. "We'll see. Call me first. If my head's not any clearer by then, there's no point in you coming over. Remember, the doc said it might take several days."

"Do…me…anything?"

"No, but thank you. What I need right now is to sleep for two days straight. Give this fog time to clear."

"Don't…door."

"I won't forget. I'm locking it now. Good night."

The door on the far side opened half an inch and one eye stared out.

Tom pushed past him. "Fiona. Are you okay?"

"I am now. I thought that creep would never leave. He wouldn't tell me anything about you. I was terrified you were in jail, or worse."

"I was, but Lincoln got me out. Fiona, this is Special Agent Lincoln Montgomery of the FBI. Lincoln, this is Fiona Drake, investigator extraordinaire."

She was probably a tall woman, but at the moment she looked small, tired, dirty, and determined.

"Also, fearless trekker and builder of rafts if Tom is to be believed. Nice to meet you, Fiona."

"I wouldn't say fearless. I've been scared out of my gourd since that van pulled up and those people poured out."

If so, she'd handled it better than he could have.

"If you feel up to it, I'd like to take you both to headquarters and get your statements written up."

"Not before I have a bath." She glanced at Tom and he

laughed.

"Me too," Tom added.

Lincoln couldn't argue with that. Neither one of them smelled like spring rain.

She sank into a chair and kicked off one tennis shoe. "After that, I'd like to take some time on the computer. I learned a lot listening to Catherine and her gang talking. I know where to dig for the good stuff now. That way, when we get to your headquarters, we'll have the proof you need."

Lincoln started shaking his head before she finished. "Don't worry about that. We have people who are experts on digging things up and we have resources and records no civilian can match."

He knew instantly he'd insulted her abilities. Didn't matter. She would try to find it herself anyway. "Just give us everything you have. We'll take it from there."

Fiona paused and Tom glanced her way, his eyebrows raised questioningly.

She gave a short shake of her head.

He'd suspected Tom had left out something important. Now he was sure of it.

Whatever they were hiding could change everything.

CHAPTER
FORTY-FIVE

Fiona

A shower had never felt so good in her life.

Fiona avoided looking in the mirror. All the cuts and scratches and bug bites and rope burns were too depressing. Especially if she let herself think what an alligator bite would look like.

She spread antiseptic ointment on the abrasions and cortisone on the bites. Phelps had suggested she get some Benadryl for the itching while they were getting her prescription filled, but she declined. She couldn't afford to take anything that might slow her down.

Once she had on her own clothes, she began to feel like herself again.

She tapped on the connecting door and let herself into Tom's room. He must have showered, too. He looked more like a lawyer and less like a vagrant.

They weren't the only ones who'd been busy.

Lincoln had ordered room service dinner for all three of them. Smoked salmon for Tom, pasta primavera for himself, and braised pork chops with steamed broccoli and garlic mashed potatoes for her.

The last traces of sunshine were gone, leaving only the city lights glowing in the darkness, but the day was finally improving.

Lincoln had the good sense to not start talking until they finished eating.

"Thanks to Tom's excellent directions, a team of FBI investigators was able to find the two bodies he stumbled over while searching for you. They've discovered a third body, an early thirties male with a new cast on his arm. Any idea who that might be?"

She glanced at Tom. She wouldn't have believed it possible, but his face had blanched several shades whiter.

"Maybe Zach. Last time I saw him was inside the van. He complained that his arm was broken, but he didn't have a cast. The way he kept popping pain pills like M&Ms, if any one of them was going to cause trouble, it would be Zach, although Lance wasn't much better."

Even with her thirst for revenge, she couldn't wish anyone dead, however, with Zach gone and unable to testify, Tom was in the clear. That had to be good news.

Tom stood and shut the curtains. "We need to be extra

careful here. They're cleaning up. Right now, they may think Fiona's dead. Not a lot of people could spend the night alone in those woods with alligators and bobcats and who knows what and come out alive. When they realize she's okay, they'll come for her."

She could have gone all evening without hearing that. Especially since Werner knew she was alive and he was likely the one who told them to kill Zach, something that protected him more than it did Tom.

Lincoln glanced at the time. "I think we can postpone a trip to headquarters for tonight. First thing tomorrow we're supposed to meet the crime scene investigator at the site where you escaped. They'll want you to walk them through what happened as much as you can."

A cold sweat formed on her back. She clasped her hands in her lap to keep them from shaking. If just the thought of going back shook her this much, what would she do when she got there?

"When we finish there, I'll take you into headquarters to make a statement. We've put it off as long as we can. You may have a lawyer present if you want, but whatever you do, don't lie. That's a federal offense. Is there anything you haven't mentioned that might help us?"

"Blood." The thought came out of nowhere and flew from her mouth.

Lincoln looked puzzled. "What about it?"

"I may have left some on Granger's front steps. I pretended

to trip and scraped my arm." She held up her arm to show an ugly abrasion. "Don't know if there's enough to show up or if it's still there. And the van. I tried to leave some on the floor inside. Lance probably bled in there, too. I think he was behind the driver."

"We're working on a warrant for the van—should have it shortly—and another one for Granger's house. That'll give us something specific to look for. Thanks."

They spent another thirty minutes going over what happened, what they knew, what they could prove, and what they couldn't.

Finally, Lincoln yawned. "It's getting late and we'll have to leave early to meet up by first light. Let's all hit the sack. Tom's been generous enough to offer me the second bed in his room. The Bureau would reimburse me if I got my own room, but it might take them until Christmas."

I'll bet that's why he wants to stay in the next room with the connecting doors half open. He can't risk one of us bolting during the night or getting together to firm up our story.

Fiona brushed her teeth, slipped on an oversized tee, turned back the bed, and switched off the light. Then she took her computer into the bathroom and eased the door shut.

She had work to do.

AFTER TWO NIGHTS with no sleep to speak of, the four hours

Fiona managed felt like one sip of water to someone dying of thirst…only enough to make her crave more.

But the time spent on her computer had been worth it.

She still couldn't uncover Evan's juvenile records. She hadn't really expected to. She did discover that Evan and Catherine were second cousins. They grew up in the same town. Went to the same high school.

With only thirty-seven in Catherine's graduating class, they had to know each other even if he was a year older.

That was all interesting and possibly useful, yet the information on Catherine made her rethink everything they believed about the woman.

They thought she was trying to help her husband out of a jam, and she was, but it went a lot deeper than that. Her husband was the son of one of the biggest drug lords in the southeast.

He ruled Georgia and Alabama and was making inroads into Louisiana.

She wasn't working for Granger. She was betraying him. Spying for her father-in-law. Trying to bring down the upstart before he got too powerful.

And killing Devin Grimes would stop Granger's supply chain and leave him in debt.

Whether Catherine killed Devin herself or told daddy-in-law where to find him, didn't matter. She moved to the top of the list.

When Lincoln tapped on her door and called out, "Up and

at 'em sleepyhead," she could have punched him.

Still, this might be the day she could put all this behind her.

She threw on last night's clothes, still draped over a chair, and joined the men in the other room.

Lincoln had looked nice the first time she saw him—tall, slim, good hair—if somewhat out of place in his vacation clothes and sunburn.

Now he looked like a for-real FBI agent—suit, tie, even better hair, if that was possible.

Let's see how he fares after an hour tramping through the Louisiana woods.

She grabbed a cup of coffee—dark, aromatic chicory. The good stuff. That should get her heart pumping. "Let's hit the road. I'd like to get this finished so I can have my life back."

"I'll second that," Tom chimed in.

They went in Lincoln's Audi. The rent-a-car people had already picked up Tom's Toyota. He didn't need it anymore, everyone involved knew who he was, and Bluebeard only had seating for two.

They completed the drive mostly in silence.

She debated whether to share the information she'd gleaned last night and decided against it. A secret's value lay both in when it was revealed and what it was worth.

If she disclosed all she knew now, she'd be giving it away for nothing.

She'd wait until it helped Tom's case.

In this instance, she'd learned something new about Lincoln Montgomery.

Last year, the papers had all reported on the sweetheart deal Tom had arranged for a serial killer in return for his testimony against the mob boss who hired him.

When that killer realized he'd have to appear in court and swear to his crimes in front of his mother and other members of the syndicate, he'd panicked and decided to make a run for it.

Tom had used one of his self-defense moves to stop the guy in his tracks, before he'd even gotten out of his chair.

Reading about that incident had piqued her interest in Tom and why she decided it might be fun to work for him.

What she didn't learn until last night was that Lincoln Montgomery was one of the men who'd captured the man.

Now she knew why he trusted Tom. It didn't mean she had to trust him.

Which led directly to the other value of a secret.

Lincoln had been quick to claim the FBI had hackers who could discover all she'd learned last night and more.

Maybe they could. Maybe they couldn't.

What interested her more was if the information highway ran both ways. Would Lincoln tell them what he'd learned?

Which led her back to her original question.

Even if Lincoln meant well, could she trust the big brass of the FBI to protect her and Tom?

The work she'd done last night had laid a trap.

She only hoped the answer wouldn't cost Tom his friend.

THE SOUND OF crickets, the smell of the swamp, the feel of broken twigs under foot hit Fiona like a punch in the gut.

"This is it. Here's where they pulled over. I ran across the road and into the woods here." She refused to look at the dark stain on the asphalt while trying to remember Tom's advice. *Whatever you do, don't lie.*

Lincoln pulled out a small notepad. "They didn't try to chase you?"

"With no lights and only a new moon hidden behind clouds? This place was dark as the bottom of a cave. I ran smack into a tree before I learned to run with my hands out in front." She touched the bruise on her forehead.

"How'd you get out of the van?"

That one was tricky. How much could she tell without incriminating herself but not lying?

"Evan. The big guy. He opened the side door. I had managed to get my ankles free so I lashed out and kicked him in the chest. He went to the ground and I took off. They were all in the front except Zach who had a broken arm and had taken several pain pills."

So far, so good. She'd told the truth, if not the whole truth. Anything she left out could be blamed on the fog of a concussion. She could hug Tom for suggesting she go to the hospital.

"That's it? They couldn't open a door and follow you because it was too dark?"

"I heard a lot of shouting, then the headlights moved back and forth. I think they turned the van so the lights shone into the woods."

The crime scene tech, a bespectacled guy who looked like he belonged behind a desk with a protractor and pocket protector, chimed in. "That jives with what we found." He used a pen to point to tire tracks in the mud.

"I only made it a little way when they all bailed out and tore into the woods where they'd last seen me. That's when I crossed back to this side."

"Can you show me where?" the crime scene guy asked.

Fiona glanced at the ID clipped to his white paper suit. *Byron.* "I don't know. I can try." She started down the road, looking for a gap in the trees.

"I think this is where I crossed."

Byron immediately began taking photos of a footprint. "Do you have the shoes you were wearing? I need them for comparison."

"No. I threw them away along with my clothes when I got the tennis shoes and sweat pants."

Tom spoke up for the first time. "She was wet and a cold and a front was blowing in. Her shoes were broken. The store is on the main drag, on the right as you head into town. I think it was called The Bargain Gusher. If they haven't emptied the trash, they might still be in there."

"You broke your shoes?" Lincoln glanced up from his notes as if he couldn't imagine how someone could break shoes.

"The heel came off my boot after dinner last night. Or was it the night before? I can't remember." And she couldn't. Maybe she did have a concussion. She certainly had the headache, and now, when she needed it the most, her memory decided to play tricks on her.

"The night before last. When that van showed up and those asswipes grabbed her." Tom almost never raised his voice or used profanity. The fact that he'd done both showed how upset he was. Or maybe he was trying to distract Lincoln from asking too many questions.

"That's right. It's why Tom left me alone to get his car."

"So you had one heel on and one heel off?"

So much for distracting Lincoln.

"Only at first. I ripped off the other heel as soon as I could."

"Did that help?"

"Not so much. Want to see my blisters?"

Guess not. He didn't even blink.

"Then what? Did you run straight down the road?"

"Hell no." She wasn't as prudish as Tom. "I went straight over to the other side and into the woods."

"Here it is. I see the spot." Byron was already taking photos.

Lincoln looked back and forth along the road. "Which direction did you go?"

"This way." She pointed left.

"Not toward town?"

"I'd been blindfolded the whole time, remember? I didn't have any idea where to find the nearest town." Why had she gone that direction? Animal instinct? A break in the trees? Dumb luck?

If she'd headed toward town, they probably would have been waiting for her.

"Do you think you can show us the dock you mentioned?"

He's kidding, right? Asking me to go back in there?

"Not on your life. It's down that way. I don't know. A mile? Two miles? I walked all night, but only a few feet at a time, when the moon came out from behind the clouds. There's probably a trail of some sort even if it's overgrown."

Let them find it themselves. At least they had daylight.

An hour later, she'd gone through the story twice more and felt pretty good.

She'd faced the bayou and fought back her terror, she'd gone over what happened without lying, and she'd managed not to incriminate herself or Tom by omitting major details.

This nightmare was almost over.

Lincoln tapped his notepad. "That sounds good. I only have a couple more questions. Can you explain to me again how you were able to get out of the van and why Evan Evans has a knife in his neck?"

"Um… It's kind of foggy. The doc said concussions sometimes scramble the brain and I might not remember everything right away."

Lincoln pulled them both to the side away from the crime scene tech and lowered his voice. "Look, I know it feels risky to trust me right now, but I promise I'm on your side. There are three dead guys in those woods. You were both in Texas for the first one and with me for the third. That leaves the big guy. He must weigh three-hundred pounds bare naked—which he's not, thank goodness, because he looks a lot like Wally the Walrus. There's no way you could have moved him yourself. And from the looks of his body, that dinky little knife in his throat didn't kill him. The tire tracks across his belly say he was run over. More than once. If you don't tell me the whole truth, right now, no one will believe anything you say about the rest of it and those crooks might get away."

She gazed at Tom, waiting for a hint as to what she should do. After a moment he shrugged and gave a curt nod.

"Everything I've told you so far is true."

"I know it is. I'm interested in the stuff you left out."

She started over from the beginning and added every detail she could think of.

Lincoln scribbled in his notebook. When she finished he glanced up. "We've found the van right where Tom said it would be. It has the scratch down the side and the broken passenger side tail light. Forensics will go over the inside and check for DNA. We're in the process of picking up Catherine, Troy, and Lance. I'm sure one of them will turn."

"Start with Lance. He's the weakest. Catherine acted like the leader." She shivered at the thought of Catherine issuing orders.

"I'll let them know, Thanks. What I'm most worried about is Granger and any ties he has to the detectives you thought were dirty. So far, we haven't found anything. As for the blood you might have left on his front steps, we'll try, but it's doubtful. His sprinklers went off early this morning."

The painful road rash on her wrist was for nothing.

Lincoln turned his notepad to a new page. "Can you remember exactly what Granger said that night?"

She had to stop for a moment. Everything jumbled up in her mind. She'd never had a concussion before, but if this was what one felt like, she didn't want another. "Something like, 'Take care of this. Dump her in the same place you left the other guy and the varmints will leave no trace. Otherwise, it'll be us the badgers come after.' He sounded angry that his wife and kids might hear. That's when he shut the door and we left."

Tom closed his eyes and rubbed his forehead. "Wait a minute. Remember that stupid brochure I read at the hotel while I waited for you to change? It didn't mention badgers. Do they live around here?"

All three whipped out their phones.

Lincoln held his phone over his head. "I can't get a signal."

"Neither can I." Tom walked in a circle, his arm outstretched.

Fiona scurried to the forensics van and climbed on top. "I've got one bar."

She typed furiously on her phone. "They live in most of

North America. Here's a list of states. Hmmm. Mainly up north and west, but not all. Okay. Down at the bottom it says they are also found in parts of Tennessee, Kentucky, and Louisiana."

Tom and Lincoln were craning their necks to see her on top of the van. "I know they're fierce suckers," Tom called up to her. "But what'd they eat?"

Her arm was tired from holding the phone above her head but every time she lowered it, the signal dropped. "Almost anything. Roots, worms, mice, eggs, chickens. They're nocturnal, can climb trees, get drunk eating rotten fruit. Looks like they've been known to come into people's houses and eat their mashed potatoes."

Tom held his hands out, palms up. "So what were they planning to do? Find a drunken badger then tie you to a tree and cover you in mashed potatoes? Maybe sprinkle you with chicken feathers?"

Lincoln shook his head. "I don't see how that makes any difference."

She stashed the phone in her pocket and climbed down. "I can't work like that. It makes me dizzy. Let's drive closer to town and see if we get a better signal."

Fifteen minutes later she hit pay dirt. "You're not going to believe this. Detective Werner attended the University of Wisconsin, whose mascot is the badger."

A few more clicks and she started laughing. "He even dressed up as Bucky Badger for football games."

CHAPTER FORTY-SIX

Tom

Tom sighed and rubbed the back of his neck. This day had gone on forever and it wouldn't be dark for another two hours.

If he made it back to the hotel without falling apart he planned to take three aspirin followed by a large scotch.

He was just tired. It wasn't a guilty conscience.

Lawyers usually advised their clients not to talk. But Fiona wasn't technically his client and this wasn't a usual situation.

He felt comfortable he'd made the right decision encouraging her to tell Lincoln everything that happened. After all, she hadn't done anything wrong. She'd be fine.

Unless Lincoln had lied to him, or Werner managed to pull a magic rabbit out of his hat and claimed up was down and right was left and somehow he was the victim while Tom and Fiona were international assassins.

So, nothing to worry about.

His was a different story with plenty to fret about. Even Lincoln couldn't overlook kidnapping.

Everything he'd told the Special Agent was true, yet the multitude of facts he'd omitted were a possible problem.

He kept telling himself not to worry. With Zach dead, who could contradict him?

He'd admitted to seeing Zach on the roadside but claimed the guy was so doped up he couldn't wait to blab about what had happed to Fiona. He'd seen Zach's pinprick pupils. There was no doubt an autopsy would back him up.

As long as no one asked how Zach came to be locked in a car trunk, he was golden.

So why couldn't he relax?

Only Werner could cause trouble, and anything the detective said would confirm he'd been on the take.

Ten minutes later they didn't need confirmation.

They were in Lincoln's car on the way back to the hotel when the agent began receiving a steady stream of texts and phone calls. Apparently, one of Granger's tire stores made monthly payments, listed under *Utilities,* to a company named Badger Trading.

So far, the FBI's experts had traced one large payment to Werner's old partner and the rest to Werner himself. Nothing they found had gone to Phelps.

For some reason, Tom considered this good news. One

less person to put in the naughty column. There were enough in that column already.

His main concern now was Fiona.

She'd seemed so much better, lighter, more herself after their trip to the bayou, as if facing her demons in the daylight had chased them away.

She'd even laughed and smiled when she deciphered Werner's secret code name.

Now she sat in the back seat, keeping her own company. Had the black cloud that hung over her last night returned for good?

They reached the hotel when Lincoln's phone rang again. He pulled over and waved the valet away. "I need to take this. It's my boss in Houston. Go on up to your rooms and I'll meet you there in a few minutes."

Fiona frowned while waiting on the elevator. Maybe the exhaustion that had plagued him all day had finally caught up with her. She'd certainly earned the right to be tired.

She paused at her door, leaning against the frame. "Do you think he's ditched us? Left us to fend for ourselves?"

"Who? Lincoln?" Why would she think that? "No way. Besides, he left a bag in my room. He has his own key, so I'm going to jump in the shower while we wait. The stink of the bayou has decided to cling to my hair and clothes and thinking about those mosquitoes makes me itch."

Tom waited until Fiona was inside her room before pushing into his own. He'd deal with whatever kept bugging her once Lincoln got back.

A SHOWER AND fresh clothes gave Tom a fresh attitude. He only hoped Fiona had managed to change her attitude as well.

Lincoln's bag was packed and sitting on the extra bed when Tom came out of the bathroom.

Fiona and the special agent sat facing each other. Her arms were crossed and her lips pressed into a thin line. So much for a change in attitude.

"Lincoln's heading back to Houston," she said.

"Really?" All the chairs were taken so he perched on the edge of his bed.

"Yes. That was my boss on the phone. Seems I'm supposed to turn this over to the local bureau and head home. I'm due back at work on Monday morning."

Fiona glared at him. Tom wasn't too thrilled himself.

"You two are welcome to leave whenever you want. You shouldn't have to come back unless they need you to testify at trial. That doesn't seem too likely the way those three are jumping all over each other trying to get a deal. You should be proud of yourselves. You've uncovered a group of murderous scum, including a dirty cop, and brought down a local drug dealer."

Lincoln twisted to face Fiona. "As for Evan Evans, the Medical Examiner still has to do an autopsy, but he says there's no way that little knife killed him. It missed everything important, so you're in the clear."

Tom studied Fiona's face. So why didn't she look happier?

Lincoln paused, as if deciding what to do. "I probably shouldn't tell you this, but since we wouldn't have known any of it without you, here goes. It looks like Catherine was in this deeper than any of us suspected. She has ties to a major drug lord who was trying to increase his territory. This has implications throughout the south. If you're sitting home one night soon watching TV and hear of a drug raid worth tens of millions, you can pat yourselves on the back...but don't tell anyone."

Fiona actually smiled. Maybe that's what she needed to hear. Although it seemed as if her change of mood had more to do with Lincoln divulging FBI secrets than catching the scumbags who abducted her.

He could understand that. After trusting the agent with their futures, it was good to see that trust returned. Now for something a little trickier. "We have one problem I forgot to mention. There's a package of white powder we came across with Ian Pryor's name on it. At first we thought it contained cocaine but the acrid smell makes us think it might be rat poison."

Lincoln slapped his knee and laughed. "I hope you didn't try any. Sending rat poison to someone they think double crossed them is an old trick they must have pick up from the movies. Haven't heard of that in years. Don't worry. I'll dispose of the package for you."

There. He'd managed to drop that problem on Lincoln without mentioning how they managed to acquire the package.

"Those guys really were a bunch of amateurs, weren't they? I have to thank you, Fiona, for turning us on to Lance. He couldn't wait to spill everything he knew from using businesses to front their operations and wash their profits to drug orders hidden in coded messages sent through the mail—which knocked things up to federal offenses. It's like they were reading *How to Sell Drugs for Dummies* but skipped that chapter."

Lincoln may have thought that was funny, but it didn't help Tom any. He still had a client in Houston accused of killing her husband. "What about my murder case?"

"I'm sorry. I can't help you too much with that. Lance seems to think Evan killed your guy, but he doesn't know for sure. Catherine claims Evan did, but anything she says is suspect. If we learn anything else, I'll let you know immediately. Meanwhile, my boss is looking golden so I won't have any trouble getting him to lean on your DA if it looks like you're getting short shrifted on the evidence. He'll make sure they keep an open mind and give you the benefit of the doubt whenever possible. Which shouldn't be difficult considering all we know about your dead guy."

One more round of handshakes and Lincoln headed home to Houston, their case still unsolved.

Fiona remained sitting, but her arms had uncrossed and

she didn't seem distressed so he wasn't sure what to think. "Do you want to head home tonight or wait until morning? It'll be dark most of the way and I'm not sure how much damage your van suffered. You can ride back with me and have Bluebeard towed to Houston if you want."

"Bluebeard's fine. She'll need some work, but I can take care of that when we get back."

"No. The firm will take care of it. You were on company business."

Did her smile mean she'd accept his help?

"You should head on home. There's no reason for you to hang around. I'm going to stay tonight at least. I came here to do a job and I haven't finished."

"Kara Grimes? We may never know exactly what happened to her husband, but I promised her I'd let her know by tomorrow what to expect. I believe we can sow enough doubt that she'll never be convicted."

Fiona looked disappointed. "Is that good enough for you?"

Was it? A week ago, a year ago, it would have been. But now? "What do you think you can find out?"

"For starters, I'd like to know who Devin Grimes really is."

So would he. If Kara Grimes was convicted, they should at least know who she killed. "How about I order us some room service dinner and we can work on it together?"

Three hours later they had their answer, and even Fiona didn't care who'd killed him.

MONDAY MORNING DAWNED clear and cool. The overcast sky of Friday night had been pushed aside by Saturday's brisk norther.

Tom parked in front of Maria Loncour's home. Fiona pulled up behind him.

No car sat in the driveway. Marley, in his usual spot behind the chain-link fence, lifted his head once to say *woof* then dropped it again.

"Are you sure she's home?" Fiona asked.

"I called before we left. She's waiting for us. Not sure about Richie." Would it be harder to have her son there to hear the news or tell it to him later? Tom had never spent much time around kids. He had no idea how one would react.

They filed up to the door then rang the bell and waited while footsteps sounded from the back.

Richie threw open the door, as sour-faced as ever. "Mom, they're here," he called over his shoulder.

Guess that answers our first question.

Maria invited them in but offered no coffee, no water, no hospitality. She appeared as sour-faced as her son.

He couldn't blame her. She had a good idea what was coming.

Nothing to do but end the agony. "I'm sorry to tell you this, Maria, but we have reason to believe Ian is dead."

"Are you sure?"

Was he? "It's not official. I have the items you gave me and a DNA test will be done, but yes, I'm sure."

"Where is he?"

"His body is at the morgue in Houston. You're welcome to go there and see for yourself if that makes you more comfortable."

Not a muscle twitched on her face. She didn't look angry or sad or relieved. Just…blank. "Have arrangements been made for a funeral?"

"Not yet. He has a wife there and lived under an assumed name. I can't reveal it to you due to client confidentiality, but I'm fairly certain your son knows what it is."

Richie shifted uncomfortably.

Yes. He knows plenty.

"Once his wife finds out about you and Richie, she might not be as anxious to assume responsibility for his burial. She might be willing to let you take care of it if that's what you want."

The first spark of emotion showed on Maria's face. "Why would I want to do that? He lied to me. Cheated on me. Stole from me. She can have him. All I want is my money back."

Tom removed a card from his pocket. "This is an attorney here in Baton Rouge. I knew her back in Dallas many years ago. I talked to her this morning and explained the situation. She's expecting your call. If you'll gather up all the information on the money Ian stole—bank account numbers, credit card numbers—she will contact the institutions and insist they return all funds taken from you illegally. She'll even ask for interest. She won't get that, but she should be able to get all your money back. Not right away or quickly, but eventually. She won't quit until they cough up the funds."

Maria turned her head slightly and studied him with suspicion. "Will I have to pay her?"

"Not at all. Her fee will be covered by the bank or credit card company."

She still seemed weary. "And I don't have to do a thing?"

"You'll have to gather the necessary information and sign papers giving her the authority to represent you. She may phone you from time to time for information, but that's all."

Tom could almost see the lightbulb light up over her head. "How did he die?"

"His insulin was replaced with water, compounded by his use of narcotics earlier in the evening."

Richie turned his head and began playing with the cat. His stringy blond hair fell over his face like a curtain, hiding any expression.

Maria, on the other hand, looked puzzled. "How could that happen? It wasn't an accident, was it? That's... That's murder." Her voice kicked up a notch. "Who did that to him?"

He glanced at Fiona and let her take over. "That's the sad part, Maria. We may never know. We do know Ian Pryor wasn't his real name."

Fiona paused to look at him, but he didn't answer. If Maria

wanted to know Ian's birth name she should ask her son. He knew everything.

"We also know he was dealing with some unsavory people. People who wouldn't hesitate to kill—who'd killed before and tried to kill again when they were stopped. That's the good news. You and Richie are safe now. The people who threatened you, who broke into your home, have been arrested. They'll never bother you again."

Tom stood. "We'll leave you now. You have a lot to digest. If you have any questions, go through your attorney. She'll let me know, and I'll do my best to answer them."

Tom took Fiona's arm and headed for the door before Maria could stop him.

As one human to another, he'd done all he could for her, but she wasn't his client or his responsibility and he strongly suspected she wasn't particularly torn up about Ian's death.

Her son however, might be a different story. He was a definite enigma.

At the curb, Tom turned toward Fiona. "Do you want to follow me or me follow you?"

"Neither. Your car can move much faster than Bluebeard. It would drive you crazy to go that slow. Besides, I want to stop in Beaumont to pick up a new stove. Don't worry. I plan to send the bill to you."

"Good. Don't take too long. I promised Kara Grimes we'd meet at her house after she got off work."

Fiona whistled. "That's gonna be an interesting meeting."

Tom couldn't help laughing. Yes, it would be. "Are you comfortable letting this go, never knowing for certain who filled Devin Grimes's insulin with tap water?"

"I would be except for one thing."

Tom thought he knew, but had to ask anyway. "What's that?"

Fiona looked him straight in the eye. "The fact that she's gone to so much trouble to keep something secret."

He was afraid that would be her answer because it bothered him too.

CHAPTER FORTY-SEVEN

Kara

All Kara Grimes could see in front of her was a solid line of red tail lights.

She'd never make it home in time.

Fifteen minutes. If she'd left work fifteen minutes earlier, she'd have missed the worst of the traffic. But Doc Collier asked her to stay and she hated to say no since she'd arranged to take tomorrow off.

No, the real reason she'd agreed to stay had more to do with her abject terror at hearing Tom Meyers's news. News that would affect the rest of her life.

A break in the traffic allowed her to zip around the pickup pulling a trailer full of lawn equipment, then between a semi and an Escalade, and make it back into her lane in time for her exit.

She shouldn't be more than five minutes late. Tom would wait.

And there he was, parked in front of her house, behind Tyler's yellow Camaro.

Fiona, in that faded blue van, had parked in front of Helen's.

The gang's all here. Time to face the music.

Her hands shook as she pulled into her driveway. "Sorry I'm late. I got here as fast as I could. Hope you didn't have to wait long."

"Just got here myself." Tom stepped out onto the lawn.

Fiona said nothing as they followed her up the driveway to the back door.

She paused, her hand on the knob. This could be her last few moments of total freedom. If Tom couldn't assure her she wouldn't spend most of her life behind bars, even the next few months would feel like prison.

She opened the door and Fang rushed out. The dog skipped and jumped and barked as if he hadn't seen her for eight weeks instead of eight hours.

When he saw Tom and Fiona, he stopped and then started the process all over again for each one of them.

Some watchdog. No wonder he flunked out of K-9 training. The only way he could catch a criminal was if he drooled on them.

"Don't mind Fang. He's supposed to be my protection since someone broke into my house."

Fiona rolled her eyes. "Yeah. I feel safer already."

Kara sat her purse on the washing machine and dropped into a kitchen chair. "Okay, let's have it. Have you found out anything on my case?"

Tom sat across from her. Fiona on his right. This was the first good look she'd had of the pair and they didn't look that hot. Tom had the remnants of a black eye and Fiona had a knot on her forehead. The one wrist visible under the sleeve of her jacket looked red and raw.

When Tom's secretary claimed he'd gone out of town for the weekend she thought he'd gone to a casino, not a gang fight.

If they'd been working on her case, maybe she should be afraid.

Tom opened his briefcase and took out a stack of papers. "First, let me say you can relax. There's no way anyone in their right mind could convict you of murder. I've filed a request to have the charges dropped."

Kara didn't move. Her body couldn't decide if it wanted to laugh or cry so it froze. Could this really be over? Then the doubts settled in. "How can you be sure? Have you found the person who did this to Devin?"

Five minutes ago she didn't care. Now she did.

What if he said it was over but it wasn't? What if she didn't follow through on the plans she'd made and then they came after her again later? What if the one thing she didn't want to happen, happened?

Tom leaned forward and softened his voice. "That's the bad

news portion of the information Fiona managed to uncover. Devin had dealings with several people who wanted him dead. It would be tough to prove which one actually messed with his insulin."

Fiona? First, she'd resented the woman for intruding in her life, then she'd welcomed her help, now she didn't know. Was she to be left hanging? Always in limbo?

Tom pushed several sheets of paper her direction. "This is a lot to take in at one time. I've printed everything out so you can go over it when you're able to concentrate, then call me or Fiona with any questions. Are you ready? This is going to hurt, but you have a right to know. Let's start at the end and work back to the first. Okay?"

Was that okay? How was she to know?

"First, Devin Grimes wasn't your husband's real name. This puts your marriage in a difficult light. It could be argued either way, but winning will be difficult. You can decide what you want to do about that at a later date."

So she wasn't married, or she was married, or neither? Both?

"Devin used the name Ian Pryor when in Louisiana where he'd lived for the last ten years with a woman named Maria Longcour and her son, Richie. They never married because Maria would have lost her late husband's pension, but Richie definitely thought of Ian as a father figure."

Another family? That explained so much. The blue shirt that had a spot on the sleeve then didn't, then did again. The gray socks that disappeared then appeared again months later. The holidays he missed. No one but nurses and firemen worked that many holidays.

How could she have missed all those signs?

Attached to the papers Tom gave her was a photo of a nondescript woman and a boy with stringy blond hair. The kid had a big grin and a baseball mitt. Devin wasn't in the photo. Maybe he took it.

She slammed the paper over so she wouldn't have to look at it.

Tom waited while her mind caught up, but it might never be able to absorb all this.

She nodded at him to go on. The quicker he finished and left her alone the better.

"Sometime in the last few months, Ian emptied Maria's savings account and Richie's college account."

How could he have done a thing like that?

She shoved back her chair and reached for the bottle of vodka Devin had hidden behind the unused bread maker. "So, this Maria lady probably killed Devin?" At least she had a tangible enemy to focus on. She sat the bottle back, unopened, and paced instead.

Tom glanced at Fiona and she took over.

"We don't know that. She claims to be in the dark about some of his activities and not to have known he stole the money until after he disappeared, although there's no way to prove what she knew or when she knew it. Her son had been investigating on his computer. He'd definitely found some of it, but we'd need a court order to learn when he started looking."

"And the kid's college fund is missing?" Devin had managed to spread disaster everywhere he went.

Tom shook his head. "I set them up with a local lawyer who can get most of it back along with Maria's savings. Meanwhile Devin played baseball growing up and taught Richie to throw a mean curve ball. He has a good chance for an athletic scholarship. They'll be okay."

Good. She was happy for them, Truly. But what about her, would she be okay?

Fiona tried for her smooth and comforting voice, not her strong point—Tom was more adept at that—but Kara had to give the woman props for trying.

"I'm not going to go into all the details here, they're in the sheet Tom gave you, but Devin became mixed up with some very bad people. It was a drug cartel that wanted to expand into new territories, only another cartel didn't want them to. Devin got caught between these two groups. People that haven't hesitated to kill in the past."

She shouldn't have been surprised, really. They'd found drugs in Devin's Excedrin bottle and looking back, she had to admit he'd changed over the last year or so. More erratic. The ups and downs and secrets he'd always kept were more pronounced.

If she'd confronted him, tried to get him help, would it have made any difference?

She glanced at Tom. He tapped one foot nervously as if unsure whether to proceed. She gave him a brief nod. Best to get this over with.

"The people Devin had been dealing with... They kidnapped Fiona off the street looking for him. When she wouldn't help them, they tried to kill her. She was lucky to escape with her life. I'm afraid they might be the ones who broke into your house."

Kara's heart froze, then pounded like the drumline at a football game. Surely they could hear it across the room. She had to sit before her knees gave out. "Am I in danger?"

Tom and Fiona glanced at each other before he answered. "I have to admit I'm glad you have the dog, but no, I don't think you are. Your first break-in was likely Richie, the boy from Louisiana. He's the one who stole your wedding photo. Now that he knows Devin has passed, there's no reason for him to come back. Everyone else involved is dead, arrested, or soon will be. The word is out that Devin is gone so there's no reason for them to come looking for him, either. They have enough problems of their own to worry about."

Could it be true? Was this nightmare really over? Relief shouldn't be the first reaction at hearing people had died. Later, she'd have to check her conscience about that.

"Is there anything else?" She'd had about all she could handle, but there was more to come. She could see it in Fiona's face.

"We need to talk about Devin's early life. Before he moved

to Louisiana and took on a new name."

Do we really need to? I'm happy not knowing.

"He was born Victor Archer. His father was in the army and spent most of his career in Germany."

I'll never be able to think of him as anything but Devin. I already knew his dad was in the army. Maybe this won't be so bad.

"His dad retired as a Master Sergeant and I think probably acted like one at home. There were hints he and his dad didn't get along. They moved to Vermont to a small farm that had been in the family for generations. Devin had chores before school and early one morning he fell from the loft in the barn and messed up his arm. There went any chance of a major league baseball career."

Her eyes snapped open. "Yes. He had a scar on his arm. He'd tell wild stories about how it happened. One time he fought off a great white shark with his bare hands. Another time he was in the rodeo and a bull named Killer Kane threw him. I think there was one about being in a knife fight with bank robbers. It became a running joke. He never told me what actually happened."

There were good times. Especially at the beginning.

If that was pity in Fiona's eyes, she couldn't take it. She snapped her head to the side. Tom must have thought that was his signal to take up the story.

"He went to the local junior college and got a pretty good job as manager of a feed store. His mom had a stroke and they hired a woman to help take care of her. The woman, Sherry Lyn Duval, and her kid, Lucian, lived on the property in a kind of bunkhouse in the back. A year later, Devin married her. He was twenty-five, she was twenty-eight. Lucian was about eight when Devin adopted him."

Kara flipped over a page and saw the next photo. A much younger Devin with a woman on one side and a kid on the other. An old barn sat off to one side. The kid had curly red hair. The woman looked dowdy, tired.

Was that his type? A plain, run-down woman aching for love and who didn't ask too many questions? If so, she fit right in.

Except for the kid. He'd never wanted kids. Maybe he'd learned they were too much trouble.

"Was he at least divorced when he married me?"

Tom wouldn't look at her. "No."

Great. That explained why Tom said her marriage was problematic.

Fiona almost whispered. "There's more."

Of course there was. "Go on."

"About four years later, on Christmas Eve, Devin took Lucian, and ran up to the store for something. He'd been drinking all day and skidded off the road. He and the boy were in the snow for several hours before anyone found them."

No wonder Devin hated the cold and absolutely refused to take her to see snow.

"Lucian needed several surgeries. They charged Devin with

a bunch of things ranging from DUI to child endangerment, but the county paid up anyway. The road hadn't been cleared and sanded and the guard rail was down. Devin missed several weeks of work. That's when the feed store discovered he'd been skimming off the profits. He cashed the check from the county, added it to whatever money he had left from the feed store and disappeared until last year."

She hated to ask—didn't want to know—but she did anyway. "How did they manage without the money?"

Fiona glanced at her notes. "Sherry Lyn received disability payments for Lucian until he was 18. He went to the same junior college as Devin and got an associate degree in accounting. Something he can do with a bum leg."

This was all too much to take in. "So what changed? Why did Devin go back last year if he didn't care about his wife or kid?"

Tom took up the story again. "The statute of limitations ran out on embezzlement. His mom had been gone several years. Sherry Lyn stayed around and took care of his father until he died last February. His dad left the farm, which is now worth about three million dollars, to his daughter-in-law. Devin hadn't visited once in almost thirteen years, but must have kept up with things because he went to Vermont and hired a lawyer to contest the will. He claimed as a blood relative, the farm should go to him alone."

CHAPTER FORTY-EIGHT

Fiona

Fiona hated not knowing exactly what happened to Devin. It felt like reading a book only to discover the last chapter had been ripped out.

Still, she'd come to terms with the fact she never would.

She couldn't bring herself to say he deserved what happened, but he was the Johnny Appleseed of unhappiness, sowing seeds of darkness wherever he went.

Kara showed her and Tom out through the front door. Fang never more than a few inches from her side. She stopped near the curb and tried her best to thank them. "I know how much you both did for me and I appreciate it. Really I do. You literally saved my life. But all of this is too much to comprehend at one time. I just want to crawl into bed, pull the covers over my head, and sleep for a week."

Tom was the one who had experience with moments like this. "Our minds are mysterious things. They only allow us to absorb what we can handle at the time. You said you had the day off tomorrow. Maybe your first impulse is the correct one. Crawl into bed and shut out the world. We can talk next week. Or the week after. Call me when you're ready to decide what you want to do about your marriage."

Tom pulled away in his Mercedes. Back to stiff-necked lawyer for him. Flash put away for his next adventure.

Fiona hesitated, searching for something to say, but there really wasn't anything that could help Kara get through the next few days or weeks.

Fang's ears shot up and the loopy look disappeared from his face. He all but knocked Kara down as he let out a sound somewhere between a whine and a growl and raced to the Subaru she'd left in the driveway.

The dog's neck stretched out its full length and he led with his nose, inspecting every inch of the car. Finally, he let out one lone bark and sat, stone still, by the trunk.

A tingle of excitement started at Fiona's neck and spread over her body. She twisted toward Kara. "Do you have the keys to that car?"

"It's not locked, why? What is the silly dog doing now?"

"Exactly what he was trained to do."

Fiona eased past the dog, worried she might upset him. He didn't move or blink. She felt around for the latch and the trunk popped open.

Nothing inside that she could see. But there wouldn't be, would there?

She pulled out the spare tire and rolled it off to the side.

Fang didn't like that. His head swiveled from the trunk to the tire and back. He whined again then ran to the tire and sat beside it.

Damn. He was better than a metal detector.

Fiona needed twenty minutes and half the tools in her van, but she took the tire apart.

The inside was stuffed with bundles of cash. Tens, twenties, a few fives and dirty, crumpled ones. Those were nice, but it was the stacks of hundreds that interested her the most.

The front door opened and a lanky young man stuck his head out. "You out here, Kara?"

"Who's that?" Fiona whispered.

"Tyler. Fang's owner. His parents threw him out so he and Fang are staying here while he goes to school. They're my protection, or at least my early warning system."

Kara swung around to face him. "Hey, Tyler. This is my friend Fiona. She helped me change a flat."

"Cool. I would have helped if you asked me."

"I'll remember that next time. Did you need something?"

"Yeah. Seeing that car parked out front a few minutes ago reminded me of something. Did that guy ever find Devin?"

Fiona threw a towel over the ripped tire. She kept her voice casual. Just a couple of friends, talking. "What guy was that?"

"Some kid. I saw him standing on your front porch. I told

him you and Devin would be home around five-thirty. I hope that was okay."

Sure. You really like the guy protecting you to tell strangers when you'll be home. "When was this?"

"A while ago. Before I went to rehab. I was higher-'n-hell. Maybe the day Devin died?"

If Tyler wondered what she was doing asking all these questions, he didn't let on. "A skinny kid around seventeen with stringy blond hair?"

"Nah. A couple of years older. Early twenties maybe. Red hair. Walked kinda funny. Used a cane or crutch or something. Oh! License plate was from Vermont. I remember 'cause I thought that was cool. I've never been to Vermont."

Fiona's heart ping-ponged around in her chest. Damn. She should have delved deeper into that family. She sucked in a ragged breath. Would that have changed anything? No. The damage had already been done the day Tom was hired.

Kara's eyes got big. She knew exactly what that meant. "Umm, thanks Tyler. I don't think it was anything. Just a delivery."

Fang pawed at the tire.

"Hey Tyler," Fiona called out. "Could you do us a favor? Fang's in our way. Could you take him for a walk? Tell him he's a good boy?"

As soon as Tyler left, Fiona tossed the tire into the trunk. "Get this car into the garage, then find a bag or something to put the money in."

Thirty minutes later they sat on Kara's bed with the door closed.

"Two hundred and fifty-seven thousand dollars. That's a lot of dough. What'd you plan to do with it?" Fiona had some ideas, but was interested to hear what Kara thought.

"Keep it." Kara sounded sure of herself.

"Devin cheated two families out of money. Should any of it go to them?"

"Not to Lucian. I don't care if Devin stole from him. He doesn't deserve a reward for what he's done. Besides, he and his mother inherited a three-million-dollar farm. Maria Longcour has a pension and gets Social Security payments for her son. You said she would recover the money Devin stole from them. If they don't, you can let me know and we'll make other arrangements. Don't forget, Richie's likely to get a scholarship."

"That's true."

"I won't have a pension or Social Security to help raise this kid." Kara caressed her stomach.

"You're pregnant?" So that was the secret she'd been keeping.

"I'm sorry I didn't tell you sooner. I couldn't have this baby and let it be raised by strangers. There's a guy called The Doctor who helps women in trouble. He's supposed to pick me up in the morning and drive me to a woman's shelter someplace so secret I don't even know where it is except dress warm. This is the last time he'll be in this area for three months. By then it would be too late. The DA might find out and slap me back in jail. I'd have lost my chance."

Fiona's jaw all but dropped. This woman was sneakier than she'd given her credit for. What would she do in that situation?

She'd lived through foster care, but it hadn't been easy and she had some of the better families. Better only in comparison to the bad ones. "You're not going to fight for the farm? Your baby will be the Archers' only blood relative."

Kara pulled the duvet over the money covering her bed. "Do you think Lucian killed Devin?"

"I don't know, but he goes to the top of the list."

"I don't know either, and I'm fine with that. An hour ago I worried I'd spend the rest of my life in prison. Now I have a full life ahead of me. The family I always wanted. Redeeming my reputation is no longer important. Those I care about know I didn't hurt Devin. The rest will have forgotten I ever existed when the next sensational crime hits the news."

Fiona couldn't argue with her logic. She'd seen too many of today's headlines become tomorrow's bird cage liners.

Kara pulled a suitcase from the hall closet and began filling it with the cash. "I don't want anything to do with Vermont or that family or anyone else connected to Devin or Ian or Victor or whatever he was called. From what little I know about Devin's parents, if Sherry Lyn stayed around to take care of them, she earned anything she got. I'll keep my eyes open for a red-headed kid with crutches but if I don't make a claim for that farm I don't expect he'll bother me or my baby."

"What if the baby asks about his father?"

"I'll say when my husband died unexpectedly with complications from diabetes, I thought I'd lost my only chance to have a family so I went to a sperm bank. I don't know who his biological father is except some thoughtful and generous man."

"You'll have to launder the money."

Kara gave an almost smile. Possibly the first she'd ever seen from the woman. "I work in accounting. I know what to do."

"Good. But I was talking about in the washing machine. This stuff is covered in a fine white powder. Fang hit on it once. He'll do it again."

"Thanks. I'll take care of that tomorrow. I have the day off and Tyler has a class."

Fiona thought about Kara's plan. Could she live with that?

Why the hell not?

CHAPTER FORTY-NINE

Tom

Not even Thanksgiving, and Christmas decorations were popping up everywhere. A year ago, hell, a month ago, that would have irritated Tom.

Now it lifted his spirits.

He'd begun leaving the office once, sometimes twice a week for lunch, and it had definitely given him an attitude adjustment.

His secretary was still out when he got back and he caught himself whistling a carol as he strolled down the hall to his office.

Even the sight of Fiona reading one of his case files while draped over his sofa wasn't enough to dampen his mood. "Find anything interesting?"

"No. Nothing worth my while. Was there a reason you

asked me to drop by?"

"You missed the best one." Tom opened a cabinet and pulled out a file folder.

"Got this from the DA this morning." He tapped the folder against the corner of his desk before dropping it on the coffee table in front of her. "She dismissed the charges against Kara and attached Double Jeopardy, something they never do before trial starts because it means they can't file again later."

Fiona rolled her eyes. "I know what it means."

Of course she did. At this point, she knew as much about the law as he did.

"I tried to talk her into adding that the charges had been brought in bad faith but she resisted. I decided it would be prudent to take my win and leave."

"Have you told Kara?" Fiona dropped the folder onto the coffee table on top of the other papers.

"Not yet. I thought I'd let you do that. Y'all have become such good buddies." He might have overstepped there. Just because the two women were no longer enemies didn't mean they were friends. "I kept my promise and didn't mention that Lucian had come to the house, although I would have if necessary."

"They already had a handful of suspects. I doubt they needed another one."

"Ah, but you haven't heard the best part. Catherine has turned state's evidence and shoved all the bad things onto poor Evan who is dead and can't defend himself." He didn't plan to let anything spoil his good mood.

"Let's all cry a tear for poor mistreated Evan who did his best to murder me but failed. Although I hate to see Catherine get by with anything."

"She won't. None of them will. There are plenty of charges to go around. The only one to get off is our client. Wait till you see the papers tomorrow. I'll never have to pay for advertising again."

"Is that why you called me here? To brag?"

Okay. That did sound a little braggadocios, but this was a good day and he should be allowed to celebrate. "No. I have a job for you."

"Besides calling Kara?"

That woman seemed determined to bring him down. "I can call her if you don't want to. I thought you might enjoy spreading a bit of cheer."

"You're right. I'll do it. It might be nice to deliver good news for a change. So what do you have for me? I hope it's not one of those on your desk. They all look boring."

"This isn't on my desk. It's not anywhere yet. I've been doing a lot of thinking lately. Everything is a little boring since we got back from Louisiana. How would you like to try something new?"

She cocked her head to one side. He'd finally managed to intrigue her. "Go on."

"I'm tired of working myself to death. For what, more money? I'm handing over most of this stuff to the baby lawyers.

They'll never learn if I don't let them get their feet wet."

"You're retiring?" Fiona couldn't have looked more shocked if she'd stuck her finger in a light socket.

"Oh, hell no. I'll still work the big cases. I want to do more *pro bono* work. But only if it's interesting. That's where you come in. I want to hire you full time. With a regular salary and benefits. It'll be up to you to set your own hours. Just go out there and find me some cases no one else will touch. Something that will keep us on our toes. Do you think you can do it?"

"I'll work for you, but I'll still be my own boss?"

"Yes, but I'll expect you to use the front door. No more sneaking around. And one more thing. You'll need to become a licensed P.I. Don't worry about any scrape you got into as a kid. Anything short of murder won't keep you from getting a license. You didn't murder anyone, did you?"

He didn't like how long it took her to answer.

"I'll try it, but if you start telling me what to do, I'll quit."

"I wouldn't have it any other way. Shake?"

As they shook hands, he had a chilling thought.

Be careful what you wish for.

ACKNOWLEDGMENTS

How do you say thank you to the many people who pass through your life every day bringing joy and encouragement?

This has been a long, strange, year filled with worry, isolation, and uncertainty. I couldn't have made it without a little help from my friends. And that includes you, my readers. Thank you for your loyalty.

Ron and Karen, Angela and Jason, you have been my rock. Andrew, Sterling, Caroline, and Bode, you light up my life and make me smile. I love you all.

Jami, Carla, Stacey, Christie, Ruth, Mary, and Keith… backyard and driveway happy hours were a Godsend during this pandemic year as was Sunday morning breakfast on the patio with my son and Thursday crossword on the porch with Delma.

A great big special thank you to Maggie, who is always by my side, rain or shine (especially during thunderstorms!), keeping a sharp eye out—when she's awake—to protect me from marauding squirrels or possums or the FedEx guy.

As always, thanks to Christie and Steve for more than I can say in one line.

To my Beta readers—Kaylee, Altheia, Christie, and Bobby—your eagle eyes and spot on suggestions were greatly appreciated.

To my editor, Carla Rossi, you are a joy to work with. Thanks for all your help. Thanks to E.M. Tippetts Book Designs, and Najla Qamber Designs for making me look good.

Ron, thanks for catching all the legal errors in the story, even if I didn't always follow your advice. Any mistakes in the book are mine alone.

Last but certainly not least, Bobby Squire, your encouragement and companionship, laughter and inspiration, have made this pandemic year bearable. Thank you from the bottom of my heart.

BOOKS BY SUSAN C. MULLER

Occult Series

The House on Forest Bend

The Witch on Twisted Oak

Voodoo on Bayou Lafonte

Seasons Pass Series

Winter Song

Spring Shadow

Summer Storm

Autumn Secrets

'Tis the Season

There's Always Time for Murder Series

Time to Run

Time for Redemption

Other Must Read Books

Redeeming Santa

Circle of Redemption Anthology

Dear Readers,

I hope you enjoyed reading this book as much as I enjoyed writing it. If you did, please consider taking a moment to leave a review. Authors live and die by reviews. Reviews don't need to be long. A single paragraph works better than a long retelling of the story. Just say what you liked about the book. How it made you feel. Did it offer heart-racing excitement or heart-tugging emotions? Did the characters come to life? Were you invested in the outcome? Did the villain give you the creeps?

If you enjoyed meeting Lincoln Montgomery, the FBI agent with good hair and two last names, try reading *Time to Run,* the first book in the *There's Always Time for Murder Series.*

If you like Tom and Fiona, just wait. *Time for Justice* will be out next year. Continue reading for excerpts from *Time to Run* and *Winter Song.*

Thanks, and remember:
Life is a Mystery,
Reading is the clue.

Susan

TIME TO RUN

The April evening was mild for Sacramento, and the setting sun announced its departure by painting streaks of blood red through the darkening sky. Jax Duncan threaded her way carefully up the shadowy sidewalk to CoreySheppard's home. The sight of the popular California state senator's unlocked door sent a chill down her spine, but it was the voices that caused her heart to sink.

She shifted the stack of documents she carried to her other hand and knocked, allowing the door to swing open.

First one shot, then a second filled the foyer. The entire house vibrated from the sound. A whiff of gunpowder hung in the air. Her ears rang, and she grabbed a table for support.

As she started to back away, the senator fell half in, half out of the back room. His sightless eyes gazed at her as blood pooled around his head. When his body began to move, she felt a scream build in her throat. Slowly, in jerking motions, the senator's remains slid out of view.

WINTER SONG

Sleet beat against the roof of the car in a syncopated rhythm with the windshield wipers, creating a tune only winter could sing. Bitter night air seeped inside through the rusted floorboard. The driver shivered, yet never lowered his guard, watching from the darkened lot.

Waiting for his target to appear.

Cars zipped by his secluded spot, but not the one he expected. His heart rate kicked up with each minute that passed. Could she have slipped by him, unnoticed? Scooted around the corner when he wasn't paying attention?

Impossible. He'd hardly blinked for the last half-hour.

When her red BMW rounded the corner, she was speeding, but he'd been warned to expect that. His heart settled into a steady rhythm. *Tha-thump. Tha-thump.*

"Here she is," he called over his shoulder, the tremble in his voice betraying his excitement. "It's showtime." He switched on his lights and slipped into traffic, two car-lengths behind her.